Hidden Book Five

COLLEEN VANDERLINDEN

Nether: Hidden Book Five
Colleen Vanderlinden

For permission requests, email the author at
email@colleenvanderlinden.com.

Published in the United States
by Building Block Studios LLC

ISBN 0692339205
ISBN-13 978-0692339206

http://www.colleenvanderlinden.com/hidden
http://www.buildingblockstudios.com

DEDICATION

To Roger.
Love of my life,
partner in all things.
Thanks for believing in me.

CONTENTS

PROLOGUE

The Story of Aether and Nether
As told to the Fates by Nyx, Darkness Be Her Name

In the beginning there was Chaos, and out of Chaos was born Darkness, and from the Darkness came everything.
Darkness called Herself Nyx. And She brought order to Chaos.
The first thing She made was to become Her most beloved creation.
The first thing She created was Aether. Light. Her son.
After Aether, She created more.
Life.
And, because balance is essential, She created death as well.

She created Nether to balance Aether's light.

And She set to Aether and Nether the task of creating realms to house the beings She would one day bring into existence.

From the moment she saw Aether, Nether was entranced.
He was light in all the ways she was dark;
Good in all the ways she was evil.
And she felt unworthy.

And all of the things she saw in Aether, he saw in her as well:
Someone to shroud him in darkness when the light became too much to bear;
Dark to his light,
Cool to his warmth,
Passionate to his calm.
The other side of himself.

And so, they loved.
And it came to be that the differences that had enamored them so
Began to drive them apart.
Strife found her first breath in them,
As did Misery, Sadness, Rage, and Violence.

And so, they fought.
The heavens thundered with their power,
And the newly-formed realms were set ablaze.
And the stars came to be;
Eternal proof of their passion.

And of their downfall.

When it was over, Aether lay crumbled, broken.
Nether, weakened.

And Nether wept over her lover, begging unforgiving Nyx to save him.

But Nyx could not repair the damage that had been done to Her most beloved creation.

She could not let him go.
And yet, he was beginning to fade.
Death would have its first victim.

Instead, Nyx used her power to keep Her son alive the only way She could:
By turning him into the realm that would be home to Her next creations.
A place of light, beauty, and hope.
She would never hold him again, but She could feel his presence there, and it gave Her peace.

But Nyx is not a forgiving being.

She turned Her wrath on Nether,
And, as punishment for what she'd done to beloved Aether,
Nyx turned Nether into a realm as well;
A realm that would be home to monsters.
It would house evil,
And those who lived there would one day rule the dead.

There they would exist for eternity, alive, imprisoned, their strength powering what would, one day, be the homes of beings so great and cruel and powerful that odes would be written and people would pray their names.

They would watch life pass them by. Until the end of everything.

Because everything must come to an end. Balance demands that it be so.

When it was done, Nyx created the Fates and the Furies to provide guidance and punishment to those who would come after.

And, with Her work done,
With Her heart, Her soul, in mourning,
Nyx slept.

CHAPTER ONE

My name is Molly Brooks.

Not many know me by that name.

To them, I'm the Angel.

Superhero.

Goddess.

I can't even think either of those two words with a straight face.

And yet, here I am.

The people of my city are becoming accustomed to seeing me soaring in, wearing my customary black, and punching whoever needs to get punched.

They've seen me freeze troublemakers with a word.

And they believe the spin our government has put out about me.

It helps them sleep better at night.

What they don't know, in general, is that the villains don't listen to me out of fear or respect.

They listen because they can't *not* listen. Because I have control of their minds and actions, and unless they're mentally strong, they don't have a chance in hell of fighting back.

They don't know that I can steal the abilities of those around me, that I feed off of emotions and power. They don't know that, should I ever lose my mind, there's not a whole lot that can stop me.

Lucky for them, I have no goddamn intention of losing myself. Ever.

I have fought my way back from death. Torture. I have been at the edge of the abyss, and I'm still here.

I have been captive. I have had to fight for myself. I have been bonded to the immortals, possessed by an angry primordial being. And where she was, where Nether lived in my soul, I feel emptiness now.

And I welcome it.

For the first time in my entire life, I am learning exactly what I am. Who I am.

I was a lost girl.
I was a freak.
Widow.
Monster.
Goddess.
Prison.
Hero.

And now I'm figuring out what it means to be *me*, to

live by my own terms, to stop dancing to the tune set by those who came before me.

My life.
And I swear on everything I am that I am going to make it a good one.
That I'm going to be the hero I've always wanted to be.
The woman I want to be.
I am done playing games,
being afraid,
fighting what I am.

This is my life.
And there will be no help for those who try to take it from me.

Nain and I walked through the huge arched front door of Assumption Grotto just as the church's bells started ringing. I glanced over at him for about the millionth time since he'd come out of our room that evening.

"Stop gawking at me, woman," he muttered, even as a smile quirked at the corners of his mouth.

"You are wearing the hell out of that tux, babe," I said, and he laughed. "Damn." He pulled his hand out of mine and put it around my waist, pulled me close. The wedding party was already assembled in the foyer, minus the bride, of course. I glanced around and had to smile. Nain, Brennan, and one of Stone's best friends, a shifter from the Hamtramck pack, all stood there in their tuxes. The bridesmaids were three of Ada's best friends, fellow witches she'd known her entire life. We all greeted one another, and Eunomia walked in with Hephaestus and his girlfriend, Meaghan, who was an Earth-witch as well as the best assistant I'd ever had.

"A dress, Mollis? Will wonders never cease?" E asked, hugging me. I looked down at the pale purple long-sleeved dress I was wearing. Matching heels and everything, which had nearly killed me at least a dozen times. Screw Titans or insane immortals; it was the heels that would be the end of me.

"Ada picked this out. Can you believe she didn't trust my fashion sense?" I asked, and she laughed. We all chatted for a few minutes as guests filed in. A few minutes later, the priest came out of a little side room and smiled at all of us.

"Father Balester," I said respectfully when he came over and shook my hand.

"Angel. It is an absolute pleasure to see you under happier circumstances," he said, smiling.

"Definitely," I agreed.

Father Balester wasn't your average Catholic priest. His flock was not exactly normal, either. Father Balester was one of us.

Supernatural.

The man could turn into a tree. Not even kidding. He was an Earth guardian. His kind were rare, and their job was to try to keep the natural world in some kind of balance. He had his work cut out for him, working in an industrial city like Detroit. But he loved the city, and he'd gone into the priesthood because he could sense that there was a need for someone like him for our kind to turn to.

In the past three weeks, he'd had his hands full presiding over supernatural funerals. Levitt. Chief Jones. Three vampires from Queen Rayna's family. Five shifters from various packs. Two witches and a warlock who were allied with us. Things had been grim, and Ada and Stone had considered calling off the wedding they'd started planning before the world went insane.

As I stood there with my friends, I was even happier they'd decided to go ahead with it. Life was insane, and ours was even crazier. You had to grab happiness the second you had a chance at it, because it could be taken from you at any time. We knew that all too well.

"Shall we head in, then?" Father Balester asked, and the groomsmen all headed up the aisle toward the front of the church, where Stone was already waiting, looking more nervous than I'd ever seen him, his white handlebar mustache impeccably trimmed and combed. I smiled as I watched him pull yet again at the sleeves of his jacket. Nain kissed me before heading in, and Father Balester gave me another small smile. E took my hand, and we walked into the church together, heading for one of the front pews reserved for the bride's and groom's families. I spotted Shanti and Zero sitting with the rest of Rayna's family, and waved at both of them.

One of the pews on the right side of the church could easily have been dubbed the "immortal section." Heph, Athena, my aunt Meg, my mother, my father, Persephone (who had struck up a fast friendship with Ada over witchy stuff after the battle downtown), Asclepias, Apollo, and Artemis were all sitting there, and E and I joined them. I sat between E and Artemis, who had Sean on her lap.

I greeted everyone, then glanced at Sean, who looked pretty dapper in his tiny suit. He was almost a year old, and had just started walking. "Hey, kiddo," I said. My glowing eyes didn't impress him any more the way they had when he was an infant. Too many supernaturals around, all of us with varying colors of glowing, freaky eyes, and I was nothing special.

"This child is a nightmare," Artemis said, a small smile on her face. "I am starting to miss the playpen days."

I smiled. "He's keeping you in shape, old woman," I said, and she smacked my arm lightly, laughing. I glanced at her and her twin brother, Apollo, who was on the other side of her. They both wore their usual clothing; Artemis in her sleek white leather, Apollo in his impeccably-tailored gray suit. They shared the same golden hair, same perfect features, similar to most of the other Aether immortals. I'd gotten to know Apollo more, and while he was generally quiet, he adored his sister and seemed to be getting close to Brennan. Decent enough, for an immortal.

I looked down the row. The immortals weren't here because they were particularly close to the happy couple (though some of them were). They were here for security. Part of the reason we'd even considered holding off on the wedding was because things were still crazy among supernaturals, and a big gathering of our allies all in one place seemed like asking for trouble. Ada and her witch friends and Persephone had worked a whole lot of magic to shield and protect the church and its grounds, and it was unlikely anything that wasn't supposed to be there could get in.

But if they did, they'd have eleven immortals ready to kick their ass. Nothing was going to mess up Stone and Ada's day.

I glanced toward the front of the church to see Nain watching me. I gave him a tiny smile, then the organ music started, and the bridesmaids started making their way down the aisle. I turned with everyone else to watch them, and as I did, I surveyed the room. We were doing a good job working together. It was strange to see demons, immortals, shifters, werewolves, vampires, witches, and warlocks all in one place. It was even stranger to see them sitting, not solely in groups of their own kind, but all mixed up together. The battle for Detroit (as some in the media had started calling it) had brought us together, made us interact with one another in a way we never had.

I turned my attention back to the bridesmaids, and once the final one reached the altar, the music changed, the wedding march started, and everyone rose and turned toward the back of the church.

When Ada walked through, tears came to my eyes. She was radiant, her silver hair intricately braided around her head, her face glowing with happiness. She wore a long cream dress that trailed behind her, lace everywhere. I could see the silver pentacle she always wore, still around her throat. No veil, and I was glad. The look in her eyes, the happiness there, was absolutely breathtaking. She glanced toward me as she made her way up the aisle, and smiled. I smiled back and watched her continue up to the altar.

We all sat, and I dabbed at my eyes.

"I never would have taken you for the type to cry at weddings," E whispered, leaning toward me.

"Shut up," I said. "I'm not crying."

"Of course not," Artemis whispered on my other side, rolling her eyes.

I shushed them both and focused on the group at the front of the church. Father Balester started talking, and my attention went back to my husband.

Damn.

As crazy and sad as the last few weeks had been, between the continued fighting and all of the funerals we'd attended, it had been a happy time for the two of us. We were having that goofy, happy newlywed period we'd never had before. We were all over one another, and it still wasn't enough. Every day I learned something new about him that I loved. And every day, he did at least one thing that made me want to kick his ass.

He's a demon, after all.

I watched him, smiled to myself.

I can't wait to take that off later, I thought at him.

You are insatiable. Quiet, woman.

Though maybe you could keep the tie on.

I watched as he tried to keep a straight face.

You are gonna get it later.

Promise?

His eyes met mine, and I could see that he was trying not to laugh. And then I turned my attention back to Ada and Stone as they started saying their vows.

They were beautiful. That was all I could think as I watched them say their vows and exchange golden bands as if they were the only two people in existence. The way they focused on one another. The love between them was strong, warm. I wiped at my eyes again, and E passed me a tissue, right before she dabbed at her own eyes.

When it ended, everyone milled around taking photos, and then we all slowly but surely made our way back to the loft for the reception.

The loft was empty of most of our usual furniture, which was sitting in moving trucks down in the garage, waiting for us to move the rest of the stuff out. Nain had found us a quad over on the East Side. Between the four units, there would be enough room for everyone who currently lived at the loft.

I hated that we had to move.

But now that Nether was free, it was just a matter of time before she finished generating a body. And once that happened, she would come after me.

Which meant that she would come after everyone I loved. She'd told me as much, and I had no reason to doubt her. She hated me. And she knew everything I knew from sharing soulspace with me for so long, from sharing my mind and body. She knew who I loved. Where to find those people. Who my friends and allies were and where they lived.

Everyone was moving. Rayna had already relocated her people to a house in Indian Village. We would finish packing once Ada and Stone's reception was over, and then we'd be moving on from the loft, too. But it was the perfect place to host this little get-together, now that the main part was mostly empty. Long tables had been set up, each covered with a white tablecloth, with wooden folding chairs along all of them. The reception, like the wedding, would be fairly small, but we hadn't cut any corners. There was a towering white wedding cake on the kitchen island, where everyone could see it, and the former training floor was now a dance floor. Near that, one of the vampires was setting up his system. Yep, a vampire DJ, one of Rayna's people.

Rayna had brought us plenty of connections. She was a shrewd businesswoman, and it was becoming clear how she made her money. She had several small businesses, including a restaurant and a catering company. So we used them, and even got a discount because she likes us. The vampire servers were setting the food up on a long table along one wall, and I could smell it. I was starving.

Everyone milled around, talking and eating, congratulating the bride and groom. The cake was cut, and then the DJ started doing his thing and we watched Stone and Ada have their first dance. Nain stood beside me, huge hand on my hip, and I could feel his happiness for his two oldest friends.

"They look so happy," I said to him.

"They do."

I glanced up at him. "We should try to get them to retire. Move them to Florida or something," I said quietly.

He nodded. "We'll see. You know they won't take us up on that."

"We should still try."

He squeezed my waist, then took my hand and led me to the dance floor, where other couples were starting to sway to the music as well. I danced with him, loving the feel of being in his arms, his strong shoulder under my hand, his fingers twining with those of my other hand. I loved the way he leaned down and nuzzled the side of my neck.

"If you don't stop that I'm going to drag you into our room one last time," I whispered.

"We should have another go on the roof before we move out, too," he murmured, and I blushed. Our roof had seen more than a little action in the past couple of weeks. We'd broken the glider, and Nain had promised me he'd get it fixed.

I kissed his throat as the song ended, and then we both

started trying to be good hosts, mingling with our guests. Of course, any gathering of supernaturals is an opportunity for politics, and this was no different. Shifters and witches who were maybe not as high up in our hierarchy as Nain, Brennan, Rayna, Jamie, and I seemed, already, to always be trying to work their way up, as if leadership of Detroit's supernatural community was something to aspire to. I spent the next two hours listening to people complain. I promised meetings. I answered questions. When I finally freed myself from an especially irritating conversation with an older warlock, I looked for a quiet corner to hide in.

Ugh. Socializing. This so wasn't my thing.

I looked toward the living room, which was quieter than the dance floor and where the tables were set up. There were folding chairs there, too, arranged in small groups for conversation, as well as our sofa and the TV. Brennan sat in the corner, Sean on his lap. I glanced toward the dance floor, where Nain was dancing with Ada. I caught his eyes and glanced toward Brennan, and he nodded.

I walked over to Brennan and Sean and sat down in the chair next to his. I kicked the torturous heels off and tucked my feet under the chair, barely suppressing a sigh.

"It was a nice wedding, huh? I've never been to one before," I said. Sean dozed against Brennan's chest.

"It was nice. They looked happy," he said. I sensed for him. Nervousness. Sadness. Guilt.

"No date?" I asked him, and he shook his head.

"I'm taking a break. I think that's for the best," he said, and I didn't know how to respond to that.

We sat in awkward silence for a few minutes. "I'm surprised you're talking to me," he said finally. The past few weeks, since the revelation that he'd been working for the government, gathering information on me, had been pretty tense. He claimed it went both ways, that he was collecting just enough information on us to be able to keep his position there and feed us information about what the government knew. It made sense, but it was really, really hard for me to get over the sense of betrayal. For the first couple of weeks, I hadn't said a sentence to Brennan that didn't include the words "fuck," "you," or "asshole." Usually in that order. Then I stopped talking, and he knew me well enough to back off and leave it alone. I missed him, stupid though it was.

"Did you think I would give you the silent treatment forever?" I asked him.

"I wouldn't have blamed you if you did."

I sighed. "I have a hard time being mad at you. I mean, maybe someone saner than I am would look at everything that's happened and wonder why I haven't killed you yet."

"I've wondered that myself," he said, and I was happy to see a little bit of a smile on his lips.

"I can't hate you, Bren. Not for the witch, not for Sean. Not even for telling Ross and his guys about me." Agent Ross, who headed a special division of the Department of Homeland Security that was specifically tasked with watching supernaturals and responding to the chaos that had erupted because of Strife. Brennan's boss. "Like you said: I save the world my way, and you save it yours."

He was quiet for a minute. "So you get that none of what we had was a lie, right?"

I nodded. "I know."

He took a deep breath, and I felt relief roll off of him. "Good."

"Why did that relieve you so much?" I asked him.

"Because if you actually believed that I didn't really love you, that would only make you doubt yourself more, and that's the last thing you should do. And I am... was," he corrected himself with a grimace, "crazy in love with you and it matters that you know that."

"I do."

"Why the change of heart?" he asked me.

I shrugged. "Look how crazy everything has been. How many we've lost. Life is too short and too insane to stay mad at the people you care about. And no matter what else happened, you were there for me when no one else was. I mean, I'm not ready to start hanging out or anything like that, but I'm sick of losing people. And I'm sure the hell not going to lose someone who's still alive and well."

He just stared at me. "Who are you and what have you done with Molly?"

I laughed, and after a couple of seconds, he joined in.

I glanced around, saw that Nain was on his phone. He hung up and started walking toward me and Brennan. He leaned down.

"We have to take off," he said.

"What's going on?" I asked, standing up. Brennan stood up too, shifting his hold on Sean. Eunomia joined us, and we exchanged a glance.

"That was one of the Delray shifters. Apparently the whole fucking neighborhood just disappeared."

"What do you mean, disappeared?" I asked him.

"I mean it's gone. Nothing there, like the Earth just swallowed it up. That's what he says, anyway."

"Hopefully he's been hitting the bottle again," Brennan said, and Nain let out a grunt of agreement.

"That's what I'm hoping. With all the other weird shit going on, I doubt it, though," Nain said.

Brennan gestured to Artemis, and she walked over and took Sean. "I'm coming too. Can you watch him, Artemis?" he asked, and the immortal nodded and took Sean from him.

Within a few minutes, the four of us were heading out of the loft, still dressed in our wedding clothes, heading for a neighborhood that no longer existed.

In the truck on the way over, I brought up an enchantment so the Normals would see me the way they usually did: all black clothing, no wings. I had a feeling they'd probably had enough surprises for one night; if I could give them the small comfort of looking the way they expected me to, I would do it.

The first thing we saw when we arrived in the Delray neighborhood was all of the people milling around in the streets. We also saw that, despite the reports we'd received, not the entire neighborhood was gone. Most of the homes and businesses were still there.

But not all of them.

Delray was known for being one of the most polluted areas of the city, thanks to multiple factories and incinerators.

Someone or something had eliminated the polluters.

Where the factories and plants had stood, there was now what looked like ancient forests. Nain stared at it as he climbed out of the truck, took my hand and led me out the driver's side door.

It was one of the craziest things I've ever seen. And I have seen some crazy shit in my lifetime. As the people milling around recognized me, they started coming up to me, telling me in panicked tones what they'd seen.

"It was crazy," an older woman with snow-white hair was saying. "I was sitting in my living room, and I heard this rumbling sound. And I thought, really, we're having an earthquake? Stuff started falling out of the kitchen cabinets, and then the power went out." The others who were standing nearby were nodding.

"And then the shaking stopped, and I figured I'd step outside and see what was going on," a man picked up. "Everything was dark, so I made my way over in this direction because my mom lives over there." He pointed at a senior citizens' home. "Then I looked across the street and saw that."

At his words, all of us turned to look at the forest. The entire western side of the neighborhood was now woods. Whatever had caused the forest to grow had effectively snapped the energy and water lines where they were.

Power lines dangled, and water gushed from the street.

I blew out a breath and turned to Nain. "Call Heph. We're going to need him for this."

He nodded and turned away, raising the phone to his ear.

"Was anyone hurt?" I asked as a Detroit police officer walked up.

"It doesn't look like it, Angel," the officer said. He looked to be in his fifties, and gave me a respectful nod. "The factories were all quiet because it's a Sunday. They would have had a shift in there around four, but it was empty. Lucky."

I nodded, thinking it had a lot less to do with luck than it had to do with someone paying very close attention to things.

"What the hell did this?" the officer asked me. I was very aware of the people watching me, of their worry, fear, and a sense of wonder pressing on me.

I looked around at them. This was what I'd signed up for. Being out in the open, being a light in the dark. "We're going to find out," I said. "Right now, I'm just relieved no one was hurt. I have some people coming in to try to get the power and water and all of that fixed."

"It's going to take weeks," an older man said. "Look at this mess. We're going to have to move out, and it was clearly some super-powered freak like you who did this!"

I looked at him. Sensed Nain and Brennan's anger behind me. The group of Normals exploded in emotion just then, and I had to focus on dampening it, separating myself from what they were feeling. They were a mix of fear, but more than a few of them were enraged at the man for the insult he'd thrown at me.

I kind of loved those Normals just then.

"Clearly, whoever did this was a supernatural."

"Which means it's a good thing we have the Angel here to kick its ass, whatever it is," Brennan said, stepping effortlessly into his governmental role. He flashed his badge. I was amazed that this man, who'd shared my bed, who'd worshipped my body, had been keeping his own brand of secrets from me the entire time. And I wondered how I'd missed it, how I'd been so blind to something so obvious.

It was in everything he was. The way he carried himself, the authority in his tone. That cockiness that had annoyed me almost as much as it had attracted me.

He was made for this.

He glanced my way, caught me looking at him. He gave a small smile, a wink, as if he knew what I'd been thinking. "I'll conduct interviews and try to find out what they saw."

"We'll check the woods," I said, and he nodded. "When Heph shows up, just point him toward the broken things. He'll be in heaven."

Brennan laughed and turned back toward the Normals, who were all waiting to give him information about what they'd seen. I turned to Nain and gestured toward the newly formed, yet ancient-looking woods, and he nodded.

"This is insane," he muttered as we walked toward the woods.

As we did, I looked around. I could feel other power signatures around us, approaching us.

Demons, Nain thought at me, and I nodded.

Lots of them, I answered, sensing. They were everywhere. I could feel why. Whatever this was, whatever these woods were, they almost drew me to them.

You feel this, right? I asked Nain. *Are you feeling like you need to get there?*

Yeah. This is fucked up.

I nodded.

The closer we got, the stronger I felt it. And the closer we got, the more obvious it became that this wasn't a typical Earth forest. As I examined the trees in front of us, I kept expecting to see shades of green and brown, typical forest colors. Instead, it stayed black.

And I noticed more.

Plants I'd only ever seen in one other place. Through the branches, flashes of an amethyst sky.

I stopped a few feet away from the edge of the forest, reached out and put my hand on Nain's arm, pulled him back.

"It's the Nether," I said quietly.

CHAPTER TWO

He turned his head, looked at it again. I felt, through our bond, the second he realized it.

"Because of Nether?" he asked.

I stared at it. "I don't know. It doesn't make any sense."

That was the moment my family decided to make an appearance. Hades, Tisiphone, and Megaera appeared out of nowhere, and they stood beside us and stared. Eunomia also joined us, and she took my hand as she studied the scene before us.

"How the fuck did that happen?" Hades growled.

"Nether?" I asked.

"Why would she do that? She hated being imprisoned there," Tisiphone said. "And unless I'm completely wrong about what she can do, she can't do that," she added, gesturing toward the Nether woods thing. "She can't just create something that wasn't there."

Hades groaned. "Not that I don't miss home sweet home, because I do. But this makes no sense."

There was a loud crack beside us, and a tiny, yet

insanely powerful, woman stood there. Her skin was the color of rich, dark earth, her hair falling in silky shades of green down to her feet. Her sky blue eyes were glowing, and she was, at that moment, staring daggers at my father.

"It's because your kind corrupts everything you touch," she said, her voice reminding me of the lilting of a babbling stream, the calls of birds, even through her rage. "Every single thing. I was attempting to make something beautiful here, and look at what happened!"

"Gaia," my mom breathed. And then my mom did something she never does.

She got on her knees and bowed her head. My aunt Meg followed suit, as did Eunomia.

My father just crossed his arms. "This is my fault, huh? What possessed you to try to make woods here in the first place?"

"The Earth cried for me here. I was healing it. And then this…" she said, pointing angrily at the Netherwoods, "…happened. And it's all your fault. Too many of you in a place you shouldn't be. Leave it to the Olympians to ruin everything they come into contact with. It's your fault humankind destroyed this land in the first place," she finished, her voice approaching a shout.

"My fault? My fault? Seriously, woman?"

"Don't you 'woman' me, you overgrown imp," Gaia screeched. "You forget yourself, Mr. Lord of the Dead. You are not the most important…"

"You assholes lost, Gaia. Get over it," Hades said in a bored voice, and I winced. Nain pulled me behind him, sensing that the ridiculously powerful being standing before us was about to lose it.

"Yes. And humanity is so much better for your kind winning, Hades," Gaia said with what looked like an eye roll. It was hard to tell. "Where is your blustering buffoon of a brother, anyway?"

"His son killed him. So I'm guessing, trapped in the Aether acting as king to an empty realm, maybe?"

A look of surprise flitted across Gaia's features. "Really? Which son?"

"Hephaestus," Hades answered. In the meantime, my mother and aunt had stood up, and the level of anger seemed to have dissipated a bit.

"Hephaestus?" Gaia said thoughtfully. "Well, it's not as if the boy didn't earn the right to do that."

"Something we agree on," Hades said, nodding.

"He's mated to one of mine, I understand?" she asked, and Hades nodded again. "Good. Good. Maybe together they can work to balance your taint here."

And then it began again.

After a few minutes of traded insults (damn, immortals can get nasty when they're pissed...) I watched as several other beings started appearing, this time, it seemed, drawn by Gaia's presence. As they neared us, I started to make out shapes. Men and women, and one I knew quite well, since he'd just officiated the wedding of two of our friends and team members.

"Father Balester?" I asked as the priest neared us.

He smiled, and his eyes were alight with tears. "Angel," he said in greeting. Then he stared toward Gaia, reverence in his gaze. "She has returned. I can barely believe it," he finished in a whisper.

"Um..." I replied. Admittedly not my most eloquent moment.

"What do you know about Gaia?" Nain asked as we watched more beings approach the Titan and sink to their knees as my family started making their way toward the woods along with the rest of the Nether-creatures.

Father Balester sighed, a contented look on his face. "We are her servants, her followers. The Earth Guardians have always belonged to Mother Gaia."

"So you've been following her for thousands of years, then?" I asked, trying to gauge the priest's actual age.

He smiled kindly. "No, Angel. But my father and grandfather and many generations before me were. Same on my mother's side. It is a rare and proud lineage, to be one of Gaia's own." His face clouded, took on a hard look after a moment. "You know what she is, and I know, my immortal friend, what you and your family are. Your kind imprisoned her. Do not think for even a moment that we will allow that to happen again. Not when we've finally gotten her back."

"Not very priest-like with the threats there, padre," I murmured.

"I am unlike any priest you've ever known. We both know that. My devotion to Mother Gaia comes first, as it always has. I like you, but do not assume that will continue should you cross her."

Nain and I exchanged a glance.

I really don't want to have to take a priest out, he thought at me.

Getting religious in your old age, demon? I responded.

We both know there's only one goddess I worship. Let's get this finished up so we can go home and I'll show you.

I shook my head a little. "Care to explain, Father?" I said aloud to the priest, who was still standing, head bowed.

"Others will come. The Earth Guardians will heed her call. We will do her good work, as we always have."

"Where was she before?" I asked him.

He stared at me in disbelief. "Do you really know so little of your own history, Angel?"

"So enlighten me," I said, teeth clenched. I was getting a little tired of everyone pointing out how clueless I was about mythology. I was working on it. The problem was that most of my knowledge seemed to come when things were about to fall apart. As soon as I got a vacation, I figured I'd read up on it.

"Gaia was imprisoned in Tartarus with her fellow Titans. She helped the Titans, and when Zeus found out, he imprisoned Gaia along with them. He is a damned monster, and always has been," Father Balester snarled.

24

"It was war, right? War isn't pretty." I said. Then I groaned. "I didn't seriously just defend Zeus, did I?"

Father Balester was studying me closely. "Watch yourself, Angel. You're already finding yourself ensconced in questions of loyalty, believing the story fed to you by those you call a family. History is always written by the victors, have you noticed that? Don't believe everything you've heard."

"The Titans are dangerous," I said.

"Yes, indeed they are. Especially after an eternity of being imprisoned by your people." He paused. "I like you, Angel. I believe in you. But if you try to harm Gaia, I will help destroy you."

"She can't keep doing shit like this," Nain said, cutting in before things got heated. "This is a mess."

"She's doing what Gaia does," Father Balester explained with a shrug. "She arrives here and sees the Earth she loves filthy, littered, polluted. Of course she's going to try to fix it. Don't try to pretend the world was better with that facility here."

"She could have seriously hurt someone. People are without power and water…" I started, and Father Balester laughed.

"Do you seriously think she'd hurt any of them? Water and power can be restored. She'd never harm another living creature. Even those who deserve it. She will, however, get her revenge as only she can. Of course, this isn't exactly what she planned for this area, I suppose," he added.

"No, I got that," I said.

"She has returned," he repeated, as if he couldn't quite believe it.

Nain and I exchanged another glance. I detected movement to my right, then my left.

"My brothers and sisters are arriving. We will celebrate tonight," Balester said. "Remember what I said, Angel. I am on your side until you give me reason not to be."

As we watched, several more Earth Guardians arrived and greeted each other. Then, as one, the air shimmered around them, and their bodies transformed, from flesh to rich, dark tree bark, leaves and branches sprouting as they grew ever higher into the sky, creating a grove of oaks and maples just outside the black trees of the newly-formed Nether. Soon, it was just Nain and me again, and we stood in silence. It was easy for me to feel the joy emanating from the Earth Guardians, even stronger now that they were in their tree forms. Excitement, wonder flowed from them.

"I am not going in there," I said.

"Your family already went," Nain pointed out.

"That doesn't surprise me at all. They can get back to work, doing their judging and punishing thing."

"E didn't go, though," he added.

He was right. E was standing off to the side, arms crossed, looking at the Nether woods as if she was trying to make a decision.

"I think she wants to be alone right now," I murmured. Of all the Nether beings, E was the one whose life wasn't really changed by having a home to go back to. She was the last of her kind, and the crows had long since taken over her previous job of collecting the souls of the dead. Now, they'd be able to bring them to my father again. But E was still finding her place, and I knew all too well how hard that was. I pulled Nain toward the truck.

"At least our life is never boring," he said, following me.

"I could take a little boring, I think," I answered.

When we got back to where we had parked, we both stood and watched the chaos around us. Workers from the water and electric departments had arrived, and were mostly standing around watching Hephaestus do his thing. He'd already managed to make the water stop gushing, and he was currently intent on his work on one of the electrical poles. Even though I knew better, I still worried about him hurting himself. I couldn't even quite explain what he was doing. He was eliminating excess cable, somehow managing to cut off and reroute the power as he worked, and, slowly but surely, we started seeing the lights turn back on again.

"You have the most handy friends I've ever seen," one of the power company guys said as he walked past me, and I grinned. "This would have taken us weeks to repair. This is just crazy," he said and we both laughed.

We made our way back toward Brennan, and I saw that Jamie had also arrived.

"Hey," I said, and she greeted me with a hug. "I heard you joined up, too. Your dad would have been proud."

She smiled. "He would have. When Brennan asked me to join his little government team, I had about a second's worth of hesitation before saying yes."

I sensed for her. A bit of embarrassment, but, mostly, focus. She'd toned down her appearance a little since taking the job working with Brennan on the government's supernatural relations team. Gone was the bubblegum pink hair. She'd gone back to her natural dark brown, but with a streak of blue here and there. It worked on her. She was still dressed in her clothes from the wedding as well, a light blue strapless dress that accentuated her thin frame perfectly. She'd thrown her usual leather jacket over it to ward off the cool weather.

"So, did you find out anything?" Bren asked me.

I took a deep breath. "Titans," I said.

"Huh?"

I explained about Gaia and the Earth Guardians, about the Netherwoods and the fact that my family and any demons in the vicinity had already gone in. Brennan and Jamie both stood there and listened, surprise, then worry rolling off of them.

I asked Brennan, "What are the odds we can keep this whole Gaia development between us for now?"

"I'll tell them we're not sure."

"Good. I don't want anyone getting in the way of this. This is my mess to clean up, and I'll handle it."

"We'll handle it," Heph said, approaching the group. "The immortals are to blame for locking her up in the first place. We'll help clean up our fuckin' mess for once."

I smiled at him. "You are a very weird immortal, with your desire to take responsibility and shit like that."

"Thank you, Queenie. You always know just the right thing to say."

He put his arm around my shoulder and squeezed, and I leaned into him. The burly god had proven, over and over again, to be an absolute rock. Protective, encouraging, and just enough of a pain in the ass to keep me entertained. I didn't have any idea if that was really what it was like having an older brother around, but either way, I found I liked it. And he beat Nain at cards all the time, which pissed my husband off, and my husband is happiest when he's pissed, so it just worked all around.

"I don't know what will happen if the Normals try to enter the Netherwoods," I said.

"A few of them have gone toward it. They get within a few feet or so and end up deciding to turn around. It's almost like something is warning them off of it," Brennan told me.

"So, kind of how it was with the gateway," Nain said, thinking, and I nodded.

We all stuck around a little while longer, making sure things were as back to normal as possible. As the sky started getting brighter in the east, Nain and Brennan convinced me to get back in the truck and go home. "We still have boxes to pack," Nain reminded me.

"And I promised Ada and Stone I'd take them to the airport at seven," Brennan said, yawning.

"Yeah, okay," I said, stealing another glance toward the forest, the Nether, that hadn't been there a few hours ago. "I wonder how it's being powered. Before it was by

Nether. I mean, it was dying without Nether's energy. How can this even be?"

"We'll figure it out. Just not tonight," Nain said, opening the truck door for me. I got in, and it took every bit of energy I had to stay awake long enough to walk myself into the loft and fall into bed with Nain.

The next morning, I woke up the way I always wake up, the way I want to wake up every morning for the rest of my life: with Nain's hands on my body, his lips trailing over my skin.

"We should just stay in bed all day," Nain said as he trailed kisses over my shoulder.

"We should, but we can't," I said. I glanced at the alarm clock. "Fuck. And I'm already late for today's stupid press conference."

"So you're just gonna leave me suffering like this?" he asked with a smirk as I pulled myself out of his arms. I glanced down at the "this" he was referring to. How did he still manage to make me blush so easily, after all the time we'd spent together, all the things we'd done to one another? I leaned down and kissed him, and he immediately tangled his fingers in my hair and pulled me closer. I groaned and forced myself to pull away from him again.

"I'll make it up to you later," I murmured.

He ran his hands through my hair. "You will," he said. "It's enough for now knowing how bad you want it." There was that smirk again, the one that still made my heart pound.

"Pretty sure of yourself, huh, demon?" I asked, getting out of the bed.

He stood up, climbing out of our bed in all of his naked, muscled glory, and my mouth went dry while other parts of me did the exact opposite.

"I have every reason to be, baby," he said.

"Tonight," I promised him.

"Tonight," he said. He pulled on a pair of jeans, walked around the bed and pulled me into his arms. He kissed me tenderly, and I let myself melt against him.

"Thanks for trying to distract me, though," I murmured against him.

"Anytime. I know how much you hate this press bullshit." He rested his chin on the top of my head as he held me. "You want coffee before you go?"

"You know I do. Where will you be today?"

"I have a meeting with the shifter coalition and Rayna's people about what happened in Delray to bring them all up to speed. Then Heph and I are hunting down those shifters who were causing trouble near Hamtramck."

I nodded. "We need a vacation."

"On a deserted tropical island where no one else can find us," he agreed, and I laughed. "I love you, Molls," he said before he pulled away.

"I love you too," I said.

He released me and went out into the kitchen to make coffee while I finished getting ready. I could hear him talking to Artemis, who was there babysitting Sean. I got dressed and cleaned up as quickly as I could, and when I walked out into the kitchen, there was my favorite milk glass coffee cup full of coffee waiting for me on the counter. I greeted Artemis, listened to Sean babble for a minute about the toy truck he was holding at the time. I fed the dogs, patted them both and told them how awesome they were. I gulped the coffee down and put my cup in the sink.

"Okay. See you tonight," I said to Nain.

"Kick ass, baby," he said, leaning down to kiss me.

"Always," I said, and he smiled. He kissed me again, and I focused.

I rematerialized in the entryway of the Fisher Building, which seemed to be the place we were holding all of my press conferences. After what had happened in Delray, I'd been deluged with phone calls from just about everyone, from Ross with the feds to the new Detroit police chief. Even though he was a Normal, he actually seemed to be a decent guy and at least he wasn't terrified of me. I was lucky I had Meaghan to deal with most of the phone calls and emails, or I would have already been fed up with all of it.

I looked down at myself again. The usual. Black, black, black.

I pushed the door open, watching as the assembled media turned and stared at me.

I hated this. Every second of it. And I felt like slugging Brennan every time I had to do one of these. He was already there, standing in his dark suit near the podium where I'd be speaking.

It was the same every time. The reporters watched me walk toward them with a mix of fear and awe. Adoration, in some cases. When I'd first agreed to this, I'd pictured being skewered by the media, being called a menace or a monster. For the most part, what I had instead were more fans in my corner. Of course there were a few who despised and feared me. I was just surprised there weren't more.

"Hi, guys," I said as I walked toward the podium. Several of them answered back.

"Okay?" Brennan asked quietly.

I nodded.

"All right, Angel. We're on in thirty seconds," the field producer from the local ABC affiliate told me.

I nodded. Sarah, I thought to myself, remembering her name. She was a friendly, businesslike woman. She was also a witch, and one of the many supernaturals who were calling themselves "The Angel's Army," going around helping and re-building after the battles between the supers that we'd gone through in recent months. They kept themselves anonymous. For the most part, they worked with Heph, who was proving himself invaluable during this rebuilding phase.

I tried to settle my nerves.

"Ten," Sarah said, and I looked at the cameras, at the rows of reporters.

Never in a million years would I have ever considered this being part of my life.

Sarah gave the signal that we were on the air, and I looked toward the cameras.

"As you've undoubtedly heard, we had a situation in the Delray neighborhood of Detroit last night," I began, trying to keep my nerves under control. "Initial reports were that the entire neighborhood just vanished. What we found when we investigated was quite different." I paused. "The good news, first, is that we had no deaths or injuries. All residents of the neighborhood have been accounted for, and they've all come through it unscathed. Whatever happened, it appears that it ensured that living things, including people, pets, and wild animals, were spared."

I looked around, made note of a few of the faces in the crowd. "As for the damages... It was not the entire neighborhood. Whatever this was, it seems to have gone after two types of structures: facilities that cause pollution, namely, the large factory and incinerator there in Delray. What we found when we checked it all out was that those areas seem to have been turned back into wilderness in the blink of an eye. Where factories were yesterday, we now have what looks like a several hundred year old forest.

"We had damages to infrastructure, of course. Some roads, especially near areas that were destroyed, are gone, which means we have several roads that just kind of end in that neighborhood now. Power and phone and cable lines were destroyed in some cases, and providers are working right now to restore those services.

"And I know what it is that you really want to know: what did this? I don't have an answer for you yet. Obviously, we're dealing with a being with an insane amount of power. We're seeing something the world has never seen before. Right now, I'm just relieved that whatever it is, it is obviously making an effort not to harm people. But this needs to stop, and I'm hoping we can apprehend whoever it was before they do anything like this again. I'll take questions now," I said, dreading what came next.

"Was there any warning?" the reporter from the local NBC affiliate asked.

"No, Susan. We received a call around midnight that the neighborhood had disappeared, and when we got there, we found what I described. When I asked around, none of the residents had noticed anything strange that day, and there were no threats or anything like that made to any government agencies. Yes?" I said, pointing to the CBS reporter.

"Are there plans in place to prevent this from happening again?"

"Before we can come up with a plan, we need to figure out what exactly it is that we're dealing with," I said. "Until we know that, there is no way to plan. That's the frustrating thing. We're working on it, but until we know that, all we can do is keep our eyes open and hope it doesn't happen again."

I paused, looked at the camera. "I know that isn't very reassuring. I'm not good at this PR crap. I'm not going to stand up here and tell everyone it's going to be okay. We're working on it, but none of us is omniscient or all-powerful. All I'm asking is that you not panic now. From what we know, this thing doesn't want to hurt you. Please keep that in mind, as terrifying as it all seems."

I took a few more questions, and then Brennan told them we were done. I walked into one of the private offices with Brennan and Ross. After a few terse words, Ross left and it was just me and Bren, and I took a deep breath and closed my eyes. I could hear Brennan pouring coffee, and he pressed a cup into my hands. I laughed a little and opened my eyes.

"You did a good job. That's why they love you, you know," he said.

"What?"

"You empathize. That's what we keep hearing, anyway. They love you for that."

I shook my head. "They should be annoyed as hell with me. I lied to them. I'm clueless, and I promised them I'd protect them."

"You are protecting them. They know that."

I didn't know what to say to that.

"Someone's going to get beat up now, aren't they?" he asked, and I nodded.

"There's a spirit daemon that's been causing trouble along the riverfront the past few days."

"I heard about that. Which one is it?"

"From the reports we've gotten, Heph and my dad both figure it's Dolos, who's like a trickster spirit. He's mostly just messing with people, but he did toss that guy into the river yesterday, so it's getting out of hand now."

Brennan bit back a laugh, and then he failed and ended up laughing out loud. "God, our life is one giant freak show," he said, shaking his head.

"Seriously," I agreed. I dumped my untouched coffee in the sink and tossed the paper cup into the trash. "I'll see you later. Are you going back to the loft now?" I asked him, and he shook his head.

"I'm leaving early, but I have some reports and crap I have to finish first."

I nodded and focused, ready to rematerialize near Hart Plaza.

CHAPTER THREE

Finding and threatening Dolos wasn't all that hard. I found the fair-haired spirit daemon lounging on one of the benches in Hart Plaza. Spotting him was easy: ridiculously beautiful, a swirl of power. He reminded me a bit of how I'd always envisioned Peter Pan. Maybe it was the mischievous smirk. When he saw me coming across the plaza, he gave a deep sigh of resignation.

"Dolos," I said.

"Fury," he replied, looking down.

"No more throwing humans into the river."

"Yes, Fury," he said with another sigh, sounding even more like a bratty child.

"You really, really don't want to come to my attention again. Really," I said, leaving him with a few ideas of what I'd do to him if he caused any more trouble. He walked away with a muttered "this sucks," and I shook my head. There wasn't much point in actually killing the spirit daemon. He'd just appear again in a new form and continue doing what he did. He was trapped here, just like the rest of the immortals, and we'd all have to learn to deal with it. They'd also all have to learn that messing with the Normals was a definite no-no from now on.

I was getting ready to leave when I felt Nain somewhere nearby. I looked around, zeroing in on him as if some internal radar had picked him up. Which I guess it kind of had. There he was, striding toward me, that badass stalk that never failed to make me a little weak in the knees.

"Hey," I said, and he smiled as he approached. "What are you doing here?"

"Looking for you," he said. He pulled me into his arms and planted a kiss on me that just about had my head spinning. When we broke apart, I noticed someone pointing a phone at us. Nain noticed it, too, and started to head that way. I held him back.

"It's okay," I whispered. I focused, then watched in grim amusement as the guy deleted the video from his phone and walked away, with a little bit of psychic encouragement from me.

"This is fucking ridiculous," Nain muttered, still holding me tight.

"I know," I said. "Can we get out of here?"

Nain nodded, took my hand, and we walked toward the nearest street parking. He opened my door for me, and I climbed into his truck. It smelled like him inside, clean, masculine. I watched as he climbed in, loving the ripple of muscle. I knew every part of this man, every scar, every expression. The look in his eyes he only got for me. He turned to me, caught me staring. He gave me that smirk I love so much, leaned over and kissed me again. I wrapped my arms around his neck, and he pulled away only to draw my body closer to his. He held me, let me cling to him. He buried his face in the side of my neck, and I could hear him breathing me in.

"It's okay, baby," he murmured, and I held him tighter. He knew the things I never let anyone else see. He knew I slept like shit. He knew how stressed I was over Gaia, the media, the fact that everyone knew my face. And that some days I felt close to cracking. When I did, he was the one who held me together.

It wore on him, too. I am not an easy person to live with. He isn't, either. We make it work, because we've been apart, and we know life without "us" is not something we want to go through again.

"I'm starving," he said, and I laughed.

"And here I thought you were picking me up so you could take me somewhere secret and seduce me," I murmured as I released him. He started the truck and rested his big hand on my thigh.

"I did. But I think we should eat first. You're gonna need the energy later," he said, and I laughed as a little shiver went through me.

"Fine. As long as it involves macaroni and cheese," I said, stomach growling.

"Kinky, baby," he said, and I smacked his arm.

"I meant the restaurant, you ass," I said, and he laughed and squeezed my thigh. I ended up laughing, too.

"Sweet Lorraine's it is, then," he said, and he started driving toward the restaurant. I watched the scenery pass out the window, sensing for him as he drove. Ever-present demonic anger. Lots and lots of lust, which made my body temperature rise several degrees. Love.

We found the block where my favorite comfort food restaurant was, and the street parking was packed. We ended up parking on the next block, and walked down the street, my hand in his. We passed a bakery, and he stopped dead in front of the window.

"Do you see that?"

"What?" I asked, looking around and expecting to see some kind of purple monster or something, based on the disbelief in his tone.

"That," he said, gesturing at the window. "Five dollars? For a cupcake? Are they fucking kidding?"

I pulled him away. "They're probably really good cupcakes."

"It's flour, eggs, sugar, and shit like that. Five dollars? Back when it was French here, we had croissants, and they didn't come anywhere close to five dollars apiece. Do you have any idea how much work goes into a fucking croissant? And a cupcake is just mix, bake, and slap some frosting on it."

"I'm sure there's more to it than that," I said in amusement. "By the way, your crusty old French snob side is showing."

"Five dollar cupcakes," he muttered, shaking his head, and I laughed as we walked away.

We walked into the restaurant. The smell of fried chicken hit me, made my stomach rumble. We sat down in a booth near the back. After we ordered, we sat in silence, Nain watching, always watching, for signs of danger.

I gave his leg a gentle nudge with my foot. "How did your meetings go?" I asked him, and he shrugged.

"Okay. Everyone's up to speed now. Zero is going to fill Rayna and Ronan in on everything tonight."

"He's thinking about being turned," I said.

"He mentioned that."

"How is he about that whole thing?" I asked.

"The crazy fucker is excited."

I laughed and thanked the waitress as she began setting our food down.

"I think Shanti is worried he'll regret it," I said, digging into the macaroni and cheese.

"He'd regret it if he didn't do it," Nain said after swallowing a bite of his fried chicken. "Giving up the daylight is nothing to him. He wants to fight, and he feels like he's found his place with the vampires. His family isn't exactly close, so this is really the first good family experience he's had."

"That's messed up."

He snorted, nodded.

"He'd do anything for Shanti," I said quietly.

"It better stay that way or I'm going to kick his ass," Nain muttered, and I had to smile.

Just then, a trio of twenty-somethings approached our table, asking for my autograph. Nain and I exchanged a glance.

"I'm not a celebrity," I told them gently. "You don't want my autograph," I added, pushing power into my voice. They looked confused, walked away.

"These aren't the droids you're looking for," Nain said under his breath, and I shook my head.

"Can we take the rest of this home?" I asked. "We should probably get the packing and moving done." He nodded.

We got to-go containers and walked out, and I was more than aware of at least three people taking photos of us as we left. I gritted my teeth in irritation, held Nain's hand, and let myself be soothed by his hand on my thigh as we drove back to the loft.

When we got back, I was immediately called away to deal with some sprites that were causing trouble at an elementary school. Sprites were mischievous little assholes. Not harmful, really, just annoying. I dealt with them as quickly as I could and rematerialized back at the loft.

I was greeted by the sound of Marvin Gaye blasting through the stereo, along with Heph's booming laugh. A glance around showed that they'd gotten most of our remaining belongings packed in the few hours I'd spent in my press conference and lunch with Nain. Brennan was back, and he was currently trying to get Sean to eat something green, and Sean was having none of it, sitting in his high chair with his mouth clamped shut as Artemis looked on. Nain and Heph were disconnecting the television equipment in the living room, and they were both clearly on a trip down memory lane, talking about the first time they had watched a television. I caught Brennan's eye and shook my head.

"It must have been a big day the first time you talked on one of those new-fangled telephone machines," I said, and Heph flipped me the bird in a good-natured kind of way.

"I liked the phone," Nain said. "Email was something I could have done without."

Brennan grunted in agreement and managed to sneak a spoonful of peas into Sean's mouth. When Sean immediately opened his mouth and let the peas fall out onto his bib, all the while glaring at his father, I had to laugh.

"He wants a steak, I think," I said. Sean grinned at me in that cheeky way toddlers do and held his arms out.

"And now he knows you're going to rescue him," Brennan said, shaking his head and setting the spoon down in resignation.

"Of course I am." I picked Sean up out of the highchair and he wrapped his chubby little arms around my neck. Within moments, he was lazily messing with the feathers at the top of my wings. As long as he didn't start pulling, we would be just fine.

I carried Sean over to the huge pile of laundry Ada and Artemis had finished up before the wedding. It really was embarrassing how much clothing we went through in the course of a day, between Sean and his penchant for either knocking over or spitting up his food and the rest of us with our tendency to make people bleed. I started folding and packing the clothes into the duffel bag Artemis had left, and Sean went to work pulling things out just as quickly as I packed them.

"You have a unique way of helping," I informed him, and he gave me another grin and started shoving unfolded laundry into the bag. I watched him for a few seconds. "Also, you're totally brilliant." I glanced around to make sure no one was watching, then I helped him shove the rest of the pile of unfolded laundry into the bag. We finished, and I zipped it up.

I saw that, Nain thought at me.

I'm not very domestic.

I'm not complaining.

I caught his eye as he and Heph carried the couch to the elevator. It amazed me how, even now, after spending every spare moment together since we'd found our way back to one another, after countless hours spent making love to him, holding him, just the meeting of his eyes and mine still made my heart pound. Sometimes I looked at him and it was nearly impossible to breathe.

And he knew it. And I knew he felt the same way about me, and that knowledge never ceased to amaze me. Out of all of the crazy things that had happened to me over the past few years, Nain and me making our way back to one another, and crazy as it is, making it work together, was one of the most surprising.

As Nain and Heph walked out, Shanti walked in.

"There's still stuff to do, right?" she asked as she came in.

"Always. Want to help me pack up the rest of the office?" Shanti nodded, and I picked Sean up and carried him with us so he'd be out from under everyone's feet as they carried furniture and boxes out.

I opened the door to the office. It was definitely a mix of the two of us now; papers strewn here and there by me, evidence of Nain's attempts at organization in the neatly stacked piles of folders and mail. "If you want, you can finish putting those files in the box there," I said, gesturing toward a cardboard box sitting on the edge of the desk. Shanti nodded and started doing that while I gathered the bills and other mail from the desktop and put them in another folder for us to deal with when we had a chance. There was a mix of work-related stuff, thank you notes from people we'd helped, the current tax bill (addressed to me, since I was officially the owner of this place, thanks to

Nain). Seeing that huge "amount due" balance had nearly given me a heart attack. The idea of Nain's money being my money still didn't seem real. And then there were personal things. Congratulations cards from several supernaturals wishing us well on our marriage as word had spread that we were back together.

I packed, and when I focused, I could feel Shanti. She was tense. A bundle of nerves. Afraid. I looked up at her. Despite being eternally frozen in time to look like a sixteen-year-old thanks to the vampire who'd turned her against her will, Shanti was definitely pulling off the whole "self-assured, I have my shit together because I'm a grown-ass woman" look. Her dark hair was cut short, with long layers falling over her forehead. She was dressed in a pair of skinny jeans, black boots, and a tailored gray button-down that managed to be both feminine and badass at the same time. Very Shanti. Her outward appearance at that moment didn't match the emotions coming from her, though.

"What's wrong, kiddo?" I asked her.

She took a breath I knew she didn't actually need. "So, that stuff last night in Delray was one of the Titans, right?" she asked, dropping a folder into the box and flopping into one of the leather chairs near the desk.

"Yeah. Gaia."

"And there are two of them around?"

I nodded.

"Great." She paused, clasping her hands between her knees as she leaned forward in her chair. "I don't know how much you heard about the attacks Rayna keeps sustaining from other vampire factions. Even after relocating, we're getting sniped and attacked nearly every night by some asshole or another."

"I heard."

Ronan had filled me in at Ada and Stone's reception the night before. The vampire had been pure anger, talking about the attacks against his sister, the newly self-made vampire queen of Detroit. I'd promised him whatever assistance we could give, and he'd still turned it around and promised to help me when I needed it. I'm pretty sure my city's vampires are better than everyone else's. Rayna and Ronan took the safety of the Normals in our city seriously. They took the safety of their own family and the other supernaturals in the city seriously. As things had gotten more insane in my life, dealing with threats from the realm of the gods, Rayna's people had slowly but surely begun filling many of the roles Nain and I used to fill, policing the streets and even finding the occasional lost girl (at Shanti's insistence) along the way.

"It's a mess, from what Ronan says," I added.

"It is." Shanti was quiet for a moment. "Zero decided he wants to be turned now, so he's not the weak link in Rayna's family anymore. Ronan agreed." She looked down at her hands. Her entire posture was tense. I sensed for her. More than anything, she was worried. Zero was her boyfriend, whom she'd met during the time I'd been trapped in the Nether. He'd moved in with the vampires to learn about their way of life so he'd understand Shanti better, as well as to prepare for eventually being turned himself.

I sat in the chair near hers. "Ronan's turning him?"

She nodded.

"Why not Rayna?" I asked, knowing that she was the more powerful of the two, which was why she was queen. Ronan was up there, but Rayna was a little stronger.

"Because I don't want any other woman sucking on any part of my man's body," Shanti said, and I bit back a laugh. "I know that's stupid. I love Rayna. I trust her. I still don't want her mouth on him."

I did laugh then, and she shook her head and smiled. "Okay. Ronan's nearly as powerful as she is anyway. I don't think it'll matter."

"That's what I said," she said.

"What has you so terrified, then?" I asked.

"I *am* terrified. He's doing this for me. I mean... he says he's doing it for himself, too, that he wants to fight, that helping Rayna's family, battling and protecting people is what he does. And it is and he's really good at it. He's a warrior and we need those. But it still comes back to the fact that he's mostly being turned so he can be with me."

"Do you not want him anymore?" I asked.

She looked at me in shock. "Are you kidding? I want him more than I've ever wanted anything in my life. I love him. He's mine, and when I'm with him, wherever we are is home. You know what I mean?"

I nodded.

"But this life," she continued, shaking her head. "I keep trying to tell him how hard it is, how much he'll miss sunlight, how much everything just hurts in the beginning. And he's gonna go through all that. He's going to give up the sun and a normal life and he's going to totally change the way his business is run, because he met me and I happen to be a vampire and he wants to be with me." She shook her head again. "I just keep wondering if I'm the best thing for him. He might have been better off finding some pretty Normal to settle down with."

I smiled. "I don't think he'd agree with that. I'm pretty sure everything you said about loving and needing him is exactly what he'd say about you. And when it comes down to it, he's a big boy, Shanti. You've done everything you can to prepare him for what he's giving up, and I'd bet Rayna and Ronan have as well." She nodded, and I continued. "Zero doesn't strike me as impulsive, in the least."

She laughed a little, then. "No, he definitely is not. He's always about five steps ahead of everyone else."

"Okay. So he knows what he's getting into, as much as he can, anyway. And he still wants it. And you can't control the future."

"I know." She looked down again. "Um. I know it's stupid, and I know there are about a million things going on right now, but do you think you could come and sit with me on Saturday night when he's turned?" Then she shook her head. "Never mind. That sounded stupid even saying it."

I took her hand in mine. "It's not stupid, and yes, I'll be there."

"I just don't want to be alone while it's happening. I'm already a nervous wreck."

"I know. I'll be there, Shanti."

"If something else comes up—"

"Nain can handle it," I finished, and she laughed. At that moment, Sean abandoned the basket of toys we kept in the office for him when he was keeping us company and scrambled over to me. I picked him up, and he snuggled in to me. "Finally tired, eh? Your dad will be grateful."

Something deep inside of me ached, the same way it did every time I held Sean. Longing that came out of nowhere, blindsided me, for something I'd never have. Now that I'd made my way back to Nain, my mind had turned more and more often to the possibility of making a family with him, of having the kind of happy home I'd never had. Even with our insane life, even with the constant upheaval, I wanted it, stupid as it was. Nain and I had been going at it almost constantly since we'd been back together. And there was nothing. Creatures of the Nether. We don't create life, as a rule. For the first time in my life, I kind of hated that fact.

Seeming to catch my mood, Shanti put her hand on my arm.

"It's okay," I said. "Let me give him back to Brennan and then we'll finish packing."

She nodded, and I took Sean to Brennan, then Shanti and I finished packing up the office, talking and laughing as we worked. Within a few hours, we had most of the trucks unloaded at the new place, thanks to several Grosse Pointe shifters who helped get us moved in. We put beds together in each apartment, and then we all fell into them.

Really, I was just glad we'd gotten through moving without some kind of disaster happening.

CHAPTER FOUR

I wasn't asleep for long. Nain got a call that the vampires were being attacked again, and I got up to go help, glancing at the alarm clock to see that it was just before five in the morning. And then my phone went off. One of my Detroit Police Department contacts.

"Hey, Angel. Some... thing just attacked Wayne State," he said when I answered.

"Was anyone hurt?"

"Minor injuries. It was mostly empty, and the people who were injured were hit with debris from whatever it was."

I sighed. "Okay. I'll be there."

I told Nain what was going on, and headed out into the living room. Brennan was coming out of the connecting door that led into his unit.

"Wayne State?" he asked me, and I nodded. I kissed Nain and told him I'd be in touch when I knew anything.

"Be careful," he said.

"You too." I gave him one more look, then took Brennan's hand and focused on rematerializing on Wayne State University's campus. And it was chaos.

There were police cars everywhere, lights flashing. Students who apparently lived on campus and other bystanders standing around. I looked around. I'd worked in one of the offices on campus for years, and I knew it well. This part of campus, between the Student Center and State Hall, was a popular place to sit. During nice weather, bands sometimes played. There was an ugly-ass fountain there, and lots of benches.

In the middle of it all, the concrete was cracked and caved in, and one of the sides of State Hall was bashed in. It reminded me of one of those old cartoons where a character would run through a wall, leaving the shape of their body behind. Except that, in this case, whatever had gone through was freaking humongous.

"Uh. So did anyone see anything?" I asked, shaking my head. One of the DPD officers on the scene introduced himself.

"All we got is that it looked kind of metallic, that it crashed and then it bashed into the building and then it was gone."

I blew out a breath in exasperation. "So it just disappeared?"

"We think so, yes. Um. We can't seem to rally anyone to actually go into State Hall and see if it's still there or not."

I looked at him, and he squirmed uncomfortably.

"I'll do it," I said. I looked around to see Brennan interviewing witnesses. "Bren," I called. "Call Heph."

He nodded, took his phone out. Poor Heph. He was getting even less rest than the rest of us lately.

We were trying, really, really hard not to leave things a mess. We figured that if the city was constantly getting destroyed, the least we could do was try to fix it as soon as possible. Since Heph was our main fixer-of-things, he was usually in charge of that. And as guilty as I felt over how busy we kept him, he kept insisting he enjoyed the work.

I did wonder how Meaghan felt about us constantly

calling him out in the middle of the night. That had to be annoying if you were new to this life. I looked toward State Hall, and that gaping hole in the side of the building. It seemed like they'd maybe already cut power to the building, though I could see several wires hanging in the damaged wall, and there was water gushing from some of the broken pipes.

State Hall was one of the buildings where a lot of the general undergrad classes were held. Three floors of classrooms. Really, it looked a lot like my former high school inside, just bigger. Whatever it was that had attacked or crashed had bashed into one of the classrooms, and through several walls. I walked through the hole it had created, staying clear of the wires just in case. I'd survive an electrocution, but I wasn't in a hurry to try it out.

Where the thing had crashed through, it had splintered desks and walls. Windows were shattered, and the entire classroom was in disarray. It went through the next wall, into the classroom next to it. I made my way in there, only to see more destruction.

And that was it. I pulled a small flashlight out of my pocket and swung it around. No more holes, and definitely no big, scary things. The building was empty, and there were no power signatures nearby.

What the hell was the point of this?

I looked around, trying to find some sign or clue about what it could have been. This didn't look like Gaia's work. There were no trees growing where they shouldn't.

I moved broken desks out of the way, sifted through some of the rubble from the walls. Mostly, I listened and tried to keep my mind open so I'd be able to sense anything. I was about to give up when I saw a dull glint of metal nearby.

It was so small, I nearly missed it in the mess. A dagger, in the corner near some broken furniture. I picked it up, hefted it in my hand.

I'd only seen one type of being ever carry a dagger like that. Imps.

Did this mean Nether had done this? And if she had, why?

I inspected the dagger more closely, bringing it right in front of my eyes and shining my flashlight on it.

There. There was a thin shaving of what looked like gold, or some gold-colored metal, on the lower part of the blade, as if it had been drawn across something gold and scraped some of it off.

Did Nether have them robbing shit or something?

And even if she did, what the hell were they doing there? Was Nether metallic? Was she what the witnesses had seen? Or were the imps fighting the metallic thing the bystanders had seen?

I looked around some more, trying to see if I could get any more answers, but there was nothing. I headed back out to where Brennan was and filled him in on what little I'd put together. He told me that everyone said they had seen something gold-colored smash into the courtyard like it had fallen out of the sky, and then it had run roaring toward State Hall and crashed into it.

"What the ever-loving hell?" I asked.

"And what do your imps have to do with it?"

Neither of us was pleased when we saw a black SUV pull up.

"Son of a bitch," Brennan growled. "What the hell is he doing here?"

I watched as Ross and one of his underlings got out of the SUV, and looked back at Brennan. One look at him told me all I needed to know, even if I couldn't sense emotions: the man was pissed. That slight tic in his cheek, the way his eyes blazed when he looked at Ross as he approached.

Either Ross was a really good actor, extremely confident, or extremely clueless, because he didn't seem to realize that he was in bodily danger.

Personally, I voted for clueless.

I moved away from the Normals and Brennan and Ross followed. This probably wasn't a conversation they needed to hear. I took it as a sign of respect that they didn't insist on coming with me, trying to hear what we were saying. They were taking me at my word that it would be handled, and there aren't even words to express how crazy that still is to me. And when Heph arrived and they all flocked to him, I had to smile. The man was probably even more popular than I was. He was, after all, the one who got the lights back on and life back to normal. He gave me a wink before I turned back toward Ross and his guys.

"Angel," Ross said.

"Agent Ross," I said, with just as much warmth in my tone as he'd had in his. I had to wonder how he ever got his job. The man had the personality of a damp rag. His men always looked either bored or confused, and usually both.

I glanced at Brennan, who was still shooting Ross looks that would have made me cower, had I been on the receiving end of them.

"As you can see, there is absolutely nothing for you to do here, unless you count getting in the way as being productive," Brennan said. The other agent, who I wasn't familiar with, chuffed out a breath in a sound that might have been a laugh. "I know you need to feel important here, Ross, but you're useless unless you want to help Heph shovel some of that mess out of the way so he can fix the building."

"No one asked you, Matthews," Ross snarled. "So this is another immortal doing this?" he barked at me, and I raised my eyebrow.

"Yes."

"And what are you doing about it? Because from what I see, you have your pals fixing the messes, yet I don't see you out there doing what you're supposed to do."

"And what is it you think I'm supposed to do?" I asked him.

"You're supposed to be out chasing it down, not standing around here basking in the glow of your fame."

"Basking? Really?"

"You love it. The adoration. And for what? As long as you've been with us, you haven't done shit beyond give press conferences."

Before I could react, Brennan had Ross by the front of his shirt, his face inches from the shorter, thinner man's.

"You have no clue. You have no idea what she does every single day to keep everyone, including your smarmy ass, safe. And considering that you came to her, begging for her help," he continued as Ross struggled to get out of his grip, "I'd suggest showing her a little fucking respect before you really piss me off." He released Ross with a look of disgust.

I watched in amusement as Ross took a few steps away from Brennan, shooting him looks as he straightened his tie. It was rare for Brennan to actually show that he was pissed. Usually, by the time he was angry enough to act, it was too late for whoever had pissed him off to save themselves.

"Any other agent would have been written up for insubordination for shit like that, Matthews," Ross said, pointing a trembling finger at Brennan, which did absolutely nothing to help regain the appearance of control. The other agent was standing next to Brennan, arms crossed over his chest, looking more than pleased with the turn of events. Honestly, he looked like a kid at an ice cream parlor.

I liked him. I sensed for him, and felt his good mood over seeing his boss shown his true place. Respect for me and Brennan, and an undertone of concern for the circumstances. He was a Normal, but unlike Ross, he didn't seem perpetually freaked out by all of this.

"Yeah, well. I'm not just any agent, am I, Ross? And we

all know you're on your way out. I wonder who'll replace you when your demotion kicks in," Bren said with a smirk.

"Seriously?" I said.

He grinned at me. "It's all but a done deal. The higher-ups think he's made more than a few missteps, the main of which is that he doesn't understand a damn thing about how the supernatural community works because he's lazily relied on my reports all these years."

I smiled. "So why not put the man who actually knows shit in charge, right? Finally."

"And they're not happy with the way he's treated you. You wouldn't know it from the interactions you've had, mostly with him," he said, gesturing toward Ross, who was standing there seething, "but you have a ton of fans in the agency and in higher levels as well. Pissing you off is not something anyone wants to do."

"Well, congratulations. It'll be a major improvement."

"Yeah, it will," Bren said, nodding. I had to laugh. There was that cockiness, that self-assuredness I hadn't seen since before Nain had died. His gaze met mine, and he nodded once before looking away.

"It's not a done deal, Matthews," Ross said.

"So I can only assume this is our other Titan," I said to Bren. We started walking toward where Heph was, Ross trailing behind us like a cranky toddler, the other agent at Bren's side. "Golden thing comes from the sky and just starts breaking shit."

"Why, though?"

I shook my head. "Maybe it's looking for a fight. Maybe more. I can't even pretend to understand these immortal assholes."

Brennan grimaced, and I continued. "Heph is making the repairs now to limit any chaos. Restoring the building here will be child's play to him. I'm guessing it'll be done by the end of the day."

"An hour, tops, Queenie," Heph shouted. "Give me some fuckin' credit." The assembled Normals cheered and laughed, watching in amazement as Heph moved the steel structure, using some of his crazy fire ability to weld the broken parts back together. A Normal held his phone up, taking photos, and the assembled crowd applauded when Heph stepped back and the steel support was back together.

"He's loving this, isn't he?" Bren asked quietly as we kept walking.

"Every single moment," I answered, and he laughed.

"I'll keep looking for Gaia," I continued. "And try to figure out which one this is. I'm guessing my parents will know. The hard part will be trying to figure out where either of them will strike next. I'm guessing we can monitor other polluted areas of the city to try to head off Gaia, if that's what's bothering her. This thing? I have no clue."

"I can put some men on the polluted areas, too, so we can cover more of the possibilities."

"I'd appreciate it, thanks," I said. "I really miss the imps at times like this. They were masters at surveillance."

Brennan reached over and took my hand, gave it a squeeze. "You'll get them back."

I heard another car approaching and turned to watch. It was another black SUV, and Jamie and another government guy climbed out. Brennan nudged me with his arm.

"Listen," he said. I nodded.

This is Director Petersen. He's in charge of homeland security now. Ross's boss. Also a huge fan of yours.

"Thanks," I said softly, and he nodded.

"Agent Matthews," Petersen said, walking up to Brennan, hand extended.

He was a good-looking man. Early to mid forties, maybe. Tall and broad, muscular. Blond hair, blue eyes. He could have been related to Brennan, from looking at the two of them.

And he was a warlock.

"Director Petersen," Bren replied, shaking the man's hand. It didn't go unnoticed that Petersen had addressed Brennan, and not Ross. "I'd like to introduce you to the Angel," he said, nodding toward me.

Petersen turned to me with a smile. "Finally! I've been looking forward to meeting you and thanking you in person for all of the help you've given us."

"Thank you," I said, shaking his hand. I sensed for him. Respect. I watched him take in the scene around us, noting Heph working on the building, the Normals standing around. "I admit I wasn't excited to join up, but other than a bit of unpleasantness, it hasn't been as hellish as I'd imagined."

Petersen nodded, and his gaze landed on Ross. "Yes. As far as the unpleasantness... I'm sorry about that."

I nodded.

"You will meet with me at nine tomorrow, Ross," Petersen said, and Ross gave a terse nod.

"What was that?" Petersen asked in a mild voice

"Yes, sir," Ross grated.

"Good." Then Petersen turned back to me. "I can't believe how fast you and your friends get things back to normal. This would be a giant pain in the ass otherwise."

"Instead, it's just mildly terrifying," I said, and Petersen smiled.

"I'm just sorry there's nothing I can do about Delray. From what we've seen, no one's able to even get close enough to the woods there now to do anything. One of my people got close and tried cutting a tree down," I paused, grimaced.

"And what happened?" Petersen asked.

"The tree tried to impale him with its branches." Poor Heph, I added to myself.

Petersen's eyebrows shot up. "Wow."

"Yeah."

"Well, if none of the Normals or most of the supernaturals can get close to it, I'm guessing it's lost officially now. The company that owns that site is just going to have to move on, probably encouraged by a good bit of recompense from my department." He paused. "You know who's doing this, I assume? Agent Matthews has been typically tight-lipped about anything related to you."

I shot a glance at Brennan. "And I appreciate that. As you've undoubtedly heard, I like as little interference as possible when I'm working."

"Absolutely. All I need to know is that you know what's going on and you're working on it."

"And I am," I assured him. "This isn't something any of your agents could deal with. It has to be me."

Petersen surveyed the area. "I can see that. It's mind-blowing."

"I'm working on tracking the being responsible down. Hopefully we can stop this from happening again. It's my top priority right now, in addition to tracking down the being who did the Delray thing the other day."

"Two separate beings, then? I was hoping it was all the work of one insane, powerful being," Petersen said.

"Nah. That would be too easy, director," I said, and he smiled again. "I know what they are. It's something my friends and I are uniquely suited to handle, and we will."

"You have my eternal gratitude, Angel," Petersen said. "If there's anything at all I can do for you, please don't hesitate to contact me." He reached into the inner pocket of his blazer and pulled out a business card.

"I will. Thank you," I said.

I was getting antsy. Too much talking, not enough smashing. And every second I stood around, Nether or Gaia or whichever crazy Titan had done this was undoubtedly preparing to do something else insane. I looked at my watch, shocked that I'd already spent over four hours on the scene. I had to find out if everything had gone okay with the vampires.

"I need to get going," I said to Bren.

He nodded. "Thanks again. I'll stick around in case there are any questions and hitch a ride home with Jamie."

I was about to leave when another DPD car pulled up. I waited, figuring I'd either have to answer questions or deal with yet another mess. As I watched, a female officer got out of the cruiser. She recognized Ross, it looked like, and from her emotions, she wasn't especially fond of him. She walked over to him anyway, greeted him.

"Officer Malone," Ross said in return. The woman looked toward me, and I sensed surprise, nervousness coming from her.

"Director Ross," Officer Malone said. "I was in the area and I knew I'd find you here. We've had a crew out at Grand Circus Park for about an hour. There are people freaking out and no one knows why. They're fighting and acting terrified and every time we get one calmed down, another starts acting up. It's like they're possessed or something."

Dread settled into the pit of my stomach. I knew what this sounded like. I'd seen it first-hand, back when I'd first started with Nain's team.

Imps.

What the fuck else could go wrong in one day?

"I can take care of it," I said. "I'm going that way anyway." Without waiting for a response, I rose into the air.

Really, I was almost hoping my imps would be gone by the time I got there. The last thing I wanted was to see them, not just because it meant Nether had finished generating a body, but even more because I didn't want to see them forced into their old ways, reduced to terrorizing people for the benefit of their master. That thought, more than the fact that they were forced to follow Nether because she was stronger than me, bothered me more than anything else. I wasn't pleased that it was so obvious that

57

Nether was stronger than me, but it wasn't something that bothered me much (other than the obvious *oh, hey, she can probably kill me* thing). What did bother me was that I'd let my imps live a more honorable existence, and they'd enjoyed it, and now that had been taken from them.

Please don't be there, I wished, fruitlessly. As I got closer, I could hear the chaos.

I heard screams from the streets below, and I focused, making sure the glamour that hid my wings was still in place. It took some concentration to hold it, but I still did it because I figured my wings would only freak the Normals out more than they already were about me. To them, it looked like I was just soaring in like Superman or something.

I kicked, then put myself into a nosedive, able to see the Normals fighting, or, in some cases, just screaming and crying, terror rolling off of them. And it was all caused by beings they couldn't see, because imps can only be seen by supernaturals. I recognized several of my imps, whispering into the ears of the Normals, inciting terror. Really, I wondered if Nether actually felt the effects of what they were doing or if she was just doing this to mess with me. Knowing Nether, I kind of suspected it was the second. She knew damn well how much I liked and respected my imps.

As I looked around, I could see Dahael standing, arms crossed, as if she was in pain. Refusing to do what she'd been ordered to do, and watching her mate give in to Nether's demand and terrorize the Normals. I tore my gaze away from her and flew into the center of the chaos, causing the imps to scatter.

And then, as if they'd never been there at all, they disappeared.

When I landed, the gathering crowd erupted into applause. There were phones raised into the air, and I knew there would be more YouTube videos, more pictures of me and my glowing eyes plastered all over Twitter and

Facebook. Tumblr gifs.

Shanti thought it was funny. I wasn't amused.

I glanced around, looking for any signs of the imps, but they were long gone. Several of the women walked up to me and thanked me. One took a selfie with me and it took everything in me not to grab her expensive little phone and set it on fire.

I was in the process of disentangling myself from the crowd that had formed when I heard a shrill laugh from overhead.

I looked up, took a deep breath.

"Nether," I said, focusing on keeping my voice calm. It wasn't easy. I'd felt, when I was her prison, how strong Nether really is. And, as powerful as I am, the level of power coming from Nether just then made my stomach turn, even more than it already had been.

She landed with a smirk. The crowd watched us, and I had to marvel at the instincts of some of the Normals. They didn't know what they were facing, but they knew that this new arrival was trouble. Some of them ran for cover. Most at least backed away.

Filming and snapping pictures, of course.

I readied my power, let it grow within me as I observed Nether. She stood there, hip thrust out, arms crossed across her body, that smirk still on her face.

And if the power coming from her didn't have me ready to run screaming, looking at her did. It wasn't that she was frightening, because she wasn't.

It was like looking at a mirror image of myself, or one of those camera effects that changes the colors of things.

Where my hair is almost black, hers is pure white.

Where my wings are jet black, hers are covered in pure white feathers.

And where my eyes glow white, hers are black as the depths of hell.

"Mollis," she said. I knew she was holding her power at the ready, just as I did I sensed for her, and she was almost impossible to read, her emotions an absolute mess. Chaos, with a good mix of rage.

"We don't need to do this now," I said.

"Oh, sure we do," she said softly. Then she glanced around and smiled. "I don't doubt that your first concern is to protect them," she said, nodding her head toward the crowd. "Let's see how much of a hero you really are."

Then she surprised me. I'd expected her to lunge for me, to shoot flames or energy or whatever the hell other freakish powers she had at me. Instead, she flashed to the side of two young men who'd been stupid enough to stick around, and grabbed them each by the back of their shirts. She took to the air, cackling.

"Fuck," I muttered, kicking off the ground and going after her, keeping my eyes on her, on the men she'd captured, the entire time.

"This one's not a keeper," she shouted as she chucked one of the men toward the side of a nearby skyscraper. I changed direction, dove, willing my wings to flap faster, trying to predict how far he'd fall before I got there.

I snagged him about eight feet off the ground, then set him down as the gathered crowd clapped.

"Go inside, you assholes," I shouted, knowing damn well they wouldn't listen to me. I took back my appreciation of the Normals' instincts.

"Oh, Little Fury! Forget something?" Nether called as she dangled the other man by his collar. She hovered near the top of one of the nearby office buildings, and the man was kicking wildly, screaming.

"Nether! Come on. You want me. Let's go. Leave them out of it, though."

"Very well."

And she dropped him, just as she released a stream of flames at me. I was already airborne, and I had to dodge the flames. I still felt the fabric of my shirt burning, but my focus was entirely on the man, who was screaming, praying, as he plummeted to the ground.

Nether laughed and shot something else at me, a push of pure white energy much like what she'd tried to use against Brennan.

The same power that had nearly killed my mother.

"Ooh, fly faster, Fury. Faster!" she cackled, applauding and turning in midair like some kind of deranged fairy.

I watched him fall.

I'm not going to make it, I told myself as I tried for another burst of speed. My left wing was burning, which must have looked pretty fucking bizarre to the onlookers.

As if that was the weirdest thing about this entire encounter.

I focused, dove, barely snagged the man around his waist before he splattered on the ground. He was a big guy, and I felt my shoulder snap under the impact of trying to stop his descent.

"Shit!" I screamed.

I set him on the ground and pushed back into the air, my arm dangling limply at my side. I aimed for Nether, used a force of pure energy to push her back, and she slammed into the limestone facade of the building behind her.

She stopped laughing, and her smirk turned into a snarl. "That was rude, Mollis," she hissed.

"You have a bone to pick with me? Let's go," I said. "Why you're pissed off at me is beyond me. I'm the one you fucking possessed. You used my powers to nearly kill my mother."

Just remembering it made me want to kill Nether.

"I was aiming for the shifter. It's hardly my fault your mother was stupid enough to get in the way," she said, shooting more flames at me.

My flames, by the way. One of the powers she'd absorbed from me as she took up residence in my body.

I snarled, dove out of the way, then redirected, heading for her. All I wanted was for my fist to connect with her face, just once, the memory of my mother's ruined body, the surety that I would not be enough to save her, still raw in my memory.

The knowledge that, for eight days after I nearly died saving my mother and then getting beheaded by Strife, I was... somewhere else, and I still don't understand what happened to me.

I reached her and she ducked away, throwing enough energy at me to send me spiraling through the air. Every twist and turn as I tried to right myself threw my still-damaged shoulder into agony. It was healing, but not nearly fast enough. Never fast enough, and I had to make sure she didn't hurt anyone else.

I dove toward her again, thought I had her, and realized at the last second that I'd miscalculated badly. She grabbed my throat and rocketed forward. The next thing I knew, the back of my head was slamming into the side of a brick building. I heard the crowd below let out a collective "Oh!" of commiseration as the bricks exploded around me.

"You forget, my Prison. I am evil personified. You don't stand a chance," she whispered.

I tried to shake some of the fuzziness from my mind, tried to fight the blackout that I could feel coming thanks to the impact of my head hitting the side of the building. I could feel blood trickling down the back of my scalp. My wings were crunched at a crazy angle, and I realized that when she released me, I'd fall.

"Aw, is the widdle princess hurt?" she said, her voice turning into some sick parody of baby talk. Nausea rose in me as she yanked me back into midair.

"You had some handy powers, princess," Nether said, looking into my eyes as she held me aloft by my throat. "I think I'd like more."

I willed my body to heal faster so I could get away from her. I had no desire to splat to the ground. Then I'd be useless to everyone if she decided to go after the dumbass Normals again.

I felt a presence poking into my mind, and I struggled against the dizziness and pain to try to fight it back, but Nether kept hammering at my mental shields. Tired as I was, I could feel myself weakening against her onslaught.

"No," I whispered when I realized what she was doing.

"Yes," she said simply, and I fought. I fought to keep my mind strong, doing everything I could to prevent Nether from using my own mindflaying powers against me.

I felt her struggling, pushing more power into what she was doing. I could feel her in my mind. I felt her trying to siphon off my power and take it as her own.

It was like living a nightmare. I struggled, useless with my broken body. I put all of my focus into keeping her out of my mind, keeping her from taking my powers.

It wasn't working the way she'd hoped, it seemed. Frustration, rage, coursed from her through the connection she'd forged with me.

Then she screeched in fury and hurled me across the sky. I turned and twisted like a rag doll.

I slammed into the side of the Broderick Tower.

Then I fell at least twenty stories or so to the concrete below. The second I hit, everything went black.

CHAPTER FIVE

I knew I wasn't dead. Everything hurt too much for me to be dead. And I could hear chaos around me. Weeping. Shouting. A random scream.

A cackle.

Bile rose in my throat. I'd hoped that once she'd hurled me that way, Nether would just take off. I should have known I wasn't that lucky.

"Are you serious, you ridiculous mortals?" I heard her saying in her high-pitched, sing-song voice. "What do you think you're going to do, exactly, against a being like me?"

I forced my eyes open.

My eyelids hurt. That was a new one. Who knew?

My vision swam. I blinked, and slowly but surely the shadows, the light and dark I saw when I looked up came into focus.

There was a ring of Normals around me. Fear, absolute terror flowed from them, washing over me, making my stomach twist.

Yet, there they stood, looking at a point somewhere to my right.

Dumbass Normals, I thought, even as tears leaked from my eyes.

"She's a monster, just like me. Look at her," Nether drawled. "I've seen what that one can do. She's vicious. Do you really want someone like that among you?"

"We do when she's protecting us," a man said, and several people called out their agreement.

"And if she decides to use all of that power against you?" Nether asked. Through the legs of the people standing around me I could see her walking, her feet clad in white boots. It was quiet, other than the sirens in the distance and the occasional sob from the people around me.

"She wouldn't," a young woman said. "She's been saving us for years."

Nether laughed. "Are you stupid? How can you blindly trust someone like that?"

"We know her," another woman said.

I hated myself a little just then for feeding off of their emotions. I'd make it up to them by protecting them from Nether, just as soon as my bones knitted themselves back together.

Damn, it hurts to heal.

"You know her? You fool yourself with the belief that you know what she is."

Oh, Nether, shut the fuck up, I thought.

I was almost healed enough to get up. Now, what I'd actually do against her once I stood up was another matter entirely. It wasn't like I had a ton of energy or strength to do anything. But hopefully I could distract her from the Normals for a bit.

Then I felt power signatures I knew.

Powerful ones. I breathed a sigh of relief.

"Time to stop this shit, Nether," Heph's voice called through the silence.

More. I could feel Nain, Brennan, Athena, my parents, Eunomia.

"Oh, look. It's the god squad. How quaint," Nether sang.

"Stand down, Nether," Athena ordered. "Back away from the mortals."

Screams.

Fuck.

I grimaced, tried to pull myself up. It felt like a few of my ribs were still not quite where they should have been, though I was able to move my head now, which was a definite improvement.

Stay down, baby. You can't do anything now. Heal.

They need me. I'm okay.

Please, Molls. Just do this.

"Oh, cute. And her mate is here, too," Nether said with a laugh. "Do you know what he is? He's a demon. A murdering, thieving, torturing demon'"

Her words were cut short by the sound of fist meeting face.

"You will pay for that, Fury. Have you already forgotten the last time you crossed me?"

"You will leave my daughter alone, Nether," I heard my mom say.

"Oh? And what do you plan to do about it?"

Okay. That was that. She wasn't going to kill my mom, or almost kill my mom, again. I forced myself up, knowing full well that I'd hear about it from Nain later.

"Okay, Nether," I said, pulling myself up and trying not to let on how much it hurt. The crowd erupted into a wave of shock and a chorus of applause and shouts of "Hell, yeah" and "Now you're gonna get it." I gently pushed past them. "Enough."

She laughed. "Gods, you're pathetic. Another day, Mollis. I'm bored, and there is too much interference now. You will be punished, and I will enjoy it."

And with that, she took a bow and disappeared. The Normals around us gasped, and my parents strode over to me. My mom wrapped me in her arms and I grimaced at the pressure against my still-broken body.

"Sorry," she whispered.

"It's okay," I said. I looked up at my dad, who was watching the crowd around us, ready to hurt someone.

"I wanted to hurt her so bad. I wanted to see her bleed," he was muttering.

"That makes two of us," Nain rumbled from behind me.

"Next time. And I don't care who's around to see it happen. I know you wanted the humans protected, Mollis, so we agreed not to fight her if we didn't have to. Next time, there is no way in this world or any other that I'm going to let her walk away like that," my father seethed.

"Relax, Hades," my mom said quietly.

I pulled myself out of my mom's arms and took a step forward. The Normals were still watching us.

"Thank you," I told them. "Do you have any idea how stupid that was? She could have killed you with a thought."

"Yeah. And if we'd let her kill you, then all of us, everyone, would have been in deep shit," a teenage boy told me, and several other Normals nodded in agreement.

"It confused her," said one of the office workers, a middle-aged woman dressed in what had previously been a crisp cream suit. Now it was smudged with dirt and it looked like someone had spilled coffee all down her front. "You could tell. She was confused by us protecting you like that."

I nodded, slowly. "I think you're right."

"Because she hates you?" one of the men in the crowd asked.

"I think, maybe, more because she doesn't know what it's like to have anyone who'd give their life for hers," I said quietly. "She's had an insane existence. That doesn't forgive a damn thing she's done, and I am absolutely going to kick her ass next time we meet. But I think she doesn't understand loyalty or sacrifice, not the way we do." I took a breath, aware now of news cameras pointed at me, police on the scene. "Please do something for me. If she appears again, if she shows up and even if she kicks my a— butt, again, please run. Run as far and as fast as you can. Take cover. Save yourselves. Save one another. Because if even one of you died because you got between her and me, I'd never forgive myself. She can't kill me," I said, knowing it was a lie. This little face-off with Nether had proven to me that she most definitely was powerful enough to kill me. But they didn't need to know that. "She can shove me around. But she can't kill me. Okay?"

I turned around, met Nain's eyes.

"How did you get here?" I asked him softly.

"Rematerialized with your dad," he said. "You don't have enough to get us back."

I shook my head, irritated.

"Not a problem," Heph said from Nain's other side. "I'll take Queenie home. Hades will escort you back," he said to Nain, and Nain nodded.

I took Heph's hand, and he gave my hand a gentle squeeze in return. Within moments, we were standing in the kitchen of the quad we were renting. Brennan, Jamie, Artemis, and Sean were already there, and instants later, the other immortals had all rematerialized in our kitchen as well.

As soon as they were all there, the talking started. Because they're immortals and they each believe they're the most important being in the room, they all started talking at once, talking over each other, louder and louder.

"Shut up a minute," I shouted, and they all stopped. Everyone from the scene downtown was there, but now we had Demeter and Persephone, Asclepias, Hestia, Apollo, my aunt Meg, and Heph's girlfriend Meaghan as well. "Thanks," I muttered.

"We can't allow that to happen again," my dad said. "That was ridiculous. She tossed you around like you were nothing. Were you even trying to fight back?"

"Wow. Thanks for the support, Dad," I said, glaring at him.

"I'm not kidding, Mollis. That was pathetic. You are more powerful than that."

"No, I'm not," I shouted, pissed now. "If it looked like she was playing around, like she had me so overpowered it was almost comical, it's because she fucking did. The only time I managed to hurt her was when I caught her by surprise. And I'll tell you right now that none of you is a fucking match for her either. You think she kicked my ass? She'd wipe the floor with any of you in about five seconds. So don't give me any shit about how I could have tried harder."

"You could have," my mother said. "You know that."

I stared at her incredulously. "Did you not see the part where she tossed me through the sky like it was nothing? Was I the only one who caught that part?"

"Your speech there to the mortals belied your feelings about Nether. You pity her," my mother said, and I could swear, just for a moment, that I felt disappointment from her. "There is no room for pity in the life of a Fury."

Yeah. I was definitely a disappointment.

"You held back," my Aunt Megaera said in agreement. My stomach turned, a combination of my ever-present nausea and the nausea that comes with healing.

"Look. Maybe you're all fucking delusional, but I know what I felt. She's powerful. A lot more powerful than I am…"

"For fuck's sake, kid, you're the daughter of the Lord of the Dead and a Fury. Woman up and stop making excuses," Hades said, raising his voice. I just stared at him in shock. At that moment, the dogs came shuffling into the kitchen and sat on either side of my feet. I felt a torrent of shock from my dad, who was glaring at my mom, who was looking anywhere but at him.

"Where did you get the Netherhounds?" he asked in a slow, deliberate voice.

I shook my head, then looked at my dogs. Kurt and Courtney. Big-ass German Shepherds. "They're German Shepherds, Dad."

He was still looking at my mom.

"Do you know, Tisiphone, how it is that our daughter happened to end up with not one, but two Netherhounds?"

She glared at him. "Shut up, Hades," she snapped, and I felt guilt from her.

"Guys. Holy shit. They're freaking German Shepherds. They wandered up to me one day and just kind of never left. They were starving and all full of fleas and they stunk so bad my eyes watered. Get a grip."

Then I looked at Nain, who just shrugged.

"Those are not German Shepherds. And now maybe we know how it is that our enemies were able to find her, huh, Tis?" Hades said, his voice a low growl. "Not everyone would have a pair of Netherhounds protecting them."

"Protecting me?" I asked with a laugh. "These two are practically worthless. They did nothing when the Puppeteer broke into my house."

"Was the Puppeteer truly that much of a danger?" my father asked.

"Uh, yeah. She broke into my— never mind. I'm not talking about that right now." Too many memories. The sight of Brennan's hate-filled face when she had control of him.

"Tis?" Hades pressed.

"Did you really expect me to leave her here alone, Hades?" she exploded.

I looked between the two of them, both of them tense, angry. I caught Nain's gaze, and he looked as confused as I felt.

"Guys. These dogs are—"

"Lift the enchantment, Tisiphone," Hades said, crossing his arms.

She glared at him. "I couldn't leave her here alone," she repeated, voice softer, sad.

My dad's face softened as well. He dropped his arms to his sides. "I know. But we both know that's likely how Hermes and your sister recognized her, right?"

"Wait. You guys have been around my house. You've seen these dogs before."

"They always take off when I'm around. Have you noticed that?" Hades asked. "Because they know I'd recognize them for what they are." He transferred his gaze to my mom again. "Lift it, Tis."

My mother sighed, closed her eyes, and focused. I could feel her power swirling around us, and, before my eyes, my two German Shepherds, the dogs I'd had since I was nineteen years old, who had lived in my car with me, who had slept in abandoned houses and empty garages with me, who had been my only company for years, transformed.

Their brown and black fur changed, became sleek, almost metallic-looking black.

They grew to about three times their already-huge size..

Their snouts shortened, their teeth sharpened, and their eyes glowed a deep blood-red. Obsidian claws clicked against the kitchen linoleum, and they looked at me with much too much knowledge in their eyes.

"Netherhounds," my dad said, gesturing at them. "I did wonder where they went. I assumed these two had managed to get themselves killed by something in the forest."

My mom just looked away.

I started to talk, stopped. Opened my mouth again. Tried to cap the rage that was fighting to come up. So many fucking lies. So many things hidden from me, over and over and over again.

"So these things were supposed to be protecting me?" I asked, and Nain tensed. He knows my "Oh, someone's about to get hurt" voice better than anyone else.

"Calm down, Mollis," my dad said.

"No. They were supposed to be protecting me, huh? Where were they when I was getting my ass kicked after school every week when I was a kid? Where were they when that sick bastard had me locked in his basement? Where were they when I spent night after night alone on the streets, hoping no one would mess with me?" By the time I was finished, I was shouting and didn't care. "Where were they when that vampire nearly drained me, when the Puppeteer nearly had Brennan kill me, when I got fucking exploded into nothingness? You are so full of shit…"

"Enough," my father thundered, and my mom smothered a sob. I looked at her and immediately felt guilty. Still angry as hell. Still confused. But now I had guilt to add to it. Nain was enraged, and got more so the longer I ranted, and now his eyes were glowing red.

"They couldn't find you until your powers manifested," my mother said softly. "I had hoped it would never get to that point, but it did. And all of the things afterward... Netherhounds are mysterious creatures. They may not have saved you from all of that. Maybe they didn't believe you needed to be saved. Did you never wonder how it was that you slept soundly so many nights when you had so many enemies? Did you seriously think that no one knew where you lived, or that you lived alone? All of that empty land around your old house is likely full of the graves of those who tried to take you by surprise."

"I would have known," I said.

One of the dogs made a low sound, and I looked at it. The larger of the two, the one I had always called Kurt. It made me want to laugh and cry now. My two stray German Shepherds, whom I'd jokingly named after a couple of grunge rock stars. The dog looked up at me, opened its mind, and my psyche was bombarded with scene after scene of the two Netherhounds hunting and ripping the throats from werewolves, vampires, shifters, and witches, dragging the bodies into empty lots. There were no graves, though. From what the Netherhound showed me, the dog I'd known as Courtney, at least, could breathe fire, and the bodies had been incinerated.

"I don't want to talk about this anymore," I said to Hades. "Not now. Take them back to the Netherwoods with you when you go."

The dogs each let out a low growl, sat, obviously offended and stubbornly insisting on staying.

"I am not taking them. They're yours," Hades replied. "But let's get back to more important matters, shall we? Like Nether."

"Okay. That's it. Get the fuck out, now," Nain told him.

"Go, now," Heph said, his voice a low growl as he stood beside Nain. Brennan readied himself to shift.

"If a fight breaks out here, I'm going to kill every single one of you and then we'll see just how much I need to 'woman up.' Get lost," I said, and after a moment of hesitation all of the immortals except for Artemis, Heph, E, and Asclepias disappeared. Meaghan came over toward me, started looking me over.

"I'm okay," I told her. I sat in one of the kitchen chairs and as soon as I was settled, Sean toddled over to me and climbed up in my lap.

"Not now, man," Brennan said, preparing to lift him off of me.

"It's okay. I won't feed from him," I said.

Brennan stared at me. "Do you seriously think that's what I'm worried about? I know you won't. You're tired and hurting and I don't want him to add to it if he starts jumping around on you."

"It's okay," I said. "And thanks."

"You know damn well I've never believed you're a monster, Molly," he told me, passing the issue.

"I know."

I found hurt and anger in his eyes. Fear still, after what

I'd been through with Nether. "Nether told them all I'm a monster. And I was feeding off of those Normals so I could heal. I feel guilty about that."

"You shouldn't, and I know you'd never feed off of Sean," he said in irritation.

"Okay," I said. "So, back to Nether. Do you agree with my parents that I was holding back?"

The room settled into uncomfortable silence.

"You do," I said under my breath. "Are you all insane?"

"Queenie, I've seen you throw gods like Ares and Dionysus around a room and it didn't take any more effort than it would have taken you to swat a fly. I've seen you destroy a Fury with little more than a flick of your finger. It didn't even look like you were fuckin' trying, from what we saw on TV before we rushed outta here."

"When I did that, I was sharing soulspace with Nether," I said. "I had her power in addition to mine. I don't have that anymore. And while she seems to have absorbed plenty of my powers, the only things I got from her were a bunch of nightmares and memories that aren't my own."

Nain was watching me, rage and worry coming from him. He knew about the nightmares, of course. About things that suddenly seemed to trigger anxiety in me in a way they never had before. "Drop it," he growled. "Or I'm kicking all of your asses out, too."

The subject was dropped. E put on a pot of coffee, and we all sat around the kitchen table while I filled them in on what had happened with Nether, what I'd felt from her, what she'd said.

"So I need you all to help me understand something," I said as I finished filling them in. "So one of you can't kill another immortal. They'll resurrect in the Aether or Nether or whatever, even if you destroy the body. What about the Titans?"

Artemis sighed. "We can't kill them, but they can kill

us. We lost several in the war with them."

"If we could have killed them, we never would have bothered imprisoning them," Heph said. "Zeus would have had every one of them executed."

"Okay. So what about beings like Nyx?"

"What do you mean?" Heph asked, furrowing his brow.

"I mean, can she kill Titans? Could she kill Nether?"

"Nyx is powerful enough, but she can't kill. She's the Creator. She's not going to snuff out her own creations."

"But she'll let you guys do it to each other?" I asked, and he shrugged. "All right. Well what about Nether? I mean, she nearly killed Aether, right?"

"I think it's kind of like a pyramid, my friend," E said, and I turned to her. "The closer you are to the beginning of creation, to the top, the stronger you are, and the more likely you can kill those that came after you. So Nyx could kill whatever she wanted, but she doesn't kill. Nether and Aether, being her next creations, can kill just about anything that came after them, one would assume. The Titans can kill us, but we can't kill them. And we can kill mortals, but the mortals can't kill us."

"And where do I fit in that?" I asked.

"Well," Heph said, "You're Tisiphone's. And Tisiphone was one of the few beings created directly by Nyx herself. So I think you likely break the rule of not being able to kill those that technically came before you."

"But then my mom should be able to as well," I argued.

"Ah, but you're not factoring Hades' blood into the mix. The daughter of a Fury, a direct descendent of Nyx herself, *and* the daughter of the Lord of the Dead, a being who has spent his entire existence in the Nether. It's a strange brew, but I'm not surprised it grants you abilities no one else has. This was foreseen, Queenie," he reminded me.

"I know. I just don't think I'm powerful enough to kill

Nether. But it sure the hell felt like she was powerful enough to kill me." I paused. "And despite what you all seem to think, I hit her as hard as I could. It just didn't seem to make much of a difference."

CHAPTER SIX

Nain didn't waste much time in getting everyone else out of the house after that. He tried to get me to eat something, and I shook my head, glancing at the no-longer-enchanted Netherhounds before I headed into the bathroom.

I started a bath and stripped off my destroyed clothing, tossed it onto the floor. I'd throw it out later. I climbed into the searing water, giving my wings a disgusted glare as I maneuvered them into the tub. I dipped my head back into the water and got my hair wet, watching as the water turned a pinkish hue from all of the blood in my hair.

Man, scalps bleed a lot, I thought numbly. I rinsed off as much as I could, drained the tub, then filled it with fresh water. I was just about to start shampooing my hair when I heard Nain walk up to the door.

"Are you decent?" he rumbled.

"Nope," I answered.

"Perfect." He pushed the bathroom door open, and his gaze lingered on me. Hunger, always. Every single time the man looked at me, and I felt the same for him. He had that way of making me feel desirable. Wanted. Treasured. And that isn't something you'd expect from a demon, maybe. Brennan had been good at making me feel that way, too, when we were together. But from Nain, it was so much more. I was his mate. His one and only, and we'd fought our way back from death to be together.

I swallowed, tearing my eyes away from him as he started rolling up his shirt sleeves.

"Did you wash your hair yet?" he asked, and I shook my head. "Good." He knelt next to the tub and took the lavender-scented shampoo that I liked off of the corner of the tub. "I've always wanted to do this for you."

"You're a strange man," I murmured, and he smiled a little. I watched as he squeezed a dollop of the fragrant shampoo into his palm.

"You're so tense, baby," he said.

"It's really irritating that you can do that," I grumbled.

"Payback is a bitch, isn't it?"

It was one of the things we'd discovered upon doing the marriage bond again (and again, because the feeling of bonding that way, our blood mingling, our powers marrying, was completely addictive) Nain could now sense my emotions. Not just my physical state, which had always been part of the demon marriage bond. Now, he could feel when I was angry or scared or happy. For someone like me, who'd spent my entire life trying to pretend to be an absolute badass, it was an adjustment. It made me vulnerable to him in a way that would have terrified me with anyone else.

There were other side-effects of our enthusiasm for the mating ritual. He was starting to show signs that some of my self-healing abilities had transferred to him as well. We were keeping that to ourselves, mostly. I'd confided it to my mother, and she'd said she hadn't heard of anything like that, but that we'd done the bond much more often than was necessary and what the hell was wrong with us anyway?

I'd ignored her.

He put his hands in my hair, and the feel of his fingers gently, yet firmly, massaging my scalp made me sigh in contentment. I closed my eyes and he worked for a while in silence.

"That feels so nice," I said.

Nain finished washing my hair, then he turned on the handheld sprayer and gently rinsed the shampoo from my hair. Absolute focus, as if this was the most important job in the world.

"I love you," I whispered.

He turned the water off and picked up the sponge, soaped it up, and started washing my shoulders and upper back.

"I love you too, Molly," he said. He was tense, worried. Turned on (we always seemed to be, when we were together).

I took a deep breath. "I can't beat her."

He let his gaze wander over my shoulders, down my back. He rinsed my back, then started running his fingertips through my wing feathers, straightening the mess they'd become. Silence stretched between us. I knew this side of him well. This was his "I'm going to withdraw so I can figure this shit out" side. We didn't talk for quite a while, comforted by one another's presence, both lost in our own thoughts as his fingers worked at my wings. Finally, he picked up the sponge again, ran it over my shoulders and down my arms.

"You think she's that much more powerful than you?" he asked.

I nodded. "I mean, I might get lucky if she was distracted and I had the jump on her. It would have to work that way, I think." He nodded, still lost in thought. "And thanks for not acting like I don't want to beat her or something."

"It all comes down to the same thing in the end, doesn't it? If you can't, then you can't." He ran the sponge down my chest, between my breasts, to my stomach. "I think they're all discounting the fact that you lived with her for a long time. Maybe you have a better sense of her than any of us can imagine."

"I'm so tired of this. All of it," I whispered, hating the weakness in my voice. "I'm tired of the lies. The secrets. I just want to end it, once and for all."

He stayed quiet, ran the sponge over my thighs. "Do you think Nether is the end?"

I nodded again. "I mean, really, who's left now? The immortals I know I can deal with if I need to. The spirit daemons mostly just hide from me, and the ones that do step out of line aren't exactly a challenge. God, I sound full of myself."

"No," he said. "You sound like someone who's made it clear that she's the top of the fucking food chain."

"Until now," I corrected him.

"I think everyone's missing something," he said.

"Yeah?"

He nodded, took my hand and helped me stand. He handed me one of the big bath towels, and I wrapped myself in it. We went into the bedroom, and he watched hungrily as I dried off and lay down in bed. He grabbed the bottle of vanilla-scented lotion I'd been using lately, squeezed a dollop into his hand, and started smearing the thick lotion over my legs, long, slow, firm movements that had me trying to remember to breathe.

"Before you totally scramble my brain here," I said, and he let out a low laugh, "what is everyone missing?"

His hands smoothed up my hips, across my abdomen, and I bit my lip, on the edge of losing my mind.

"If she could have killed you, she would have. Something stopped her, or you wouldn't be here."

I stared up at him. "Maybe she's just fucking nuts," I said.

"I'm sure she is. But she had you at her mercy and stopped. Why?"

I shook my head. His hands were on my arms now, and

he was straddling my body. He rubbed up my arms, pulling them above my head, holding my wrists in his hands. His eyes were glowing, his entire body tense.

"Make me forget, Bael," I whispered.

It was all the encouragement he needed.

The next morning, I was up early, mostly due to Artemis pounding on our bedroom door like a loon.

"Up and at 'em, princess," she shouted. "We've got Titans to find. Let's go."

Nain pulled his pillow over his head and I ducked further under the covers with a groan.

"Separate houses. I should have done separate houses for all of us," he muttered. I leaned over and pulled his pillow aside, then gave him a long, lingering kiss that had him reaching for me and trying to pull me closer.

"Not now," I said gently. "There's a drill sergeant standing outside our door."

"I heard that. Let's go. You can screw later."

Nain pulled the pillow back over his face and I laughed, then patted his thigh and got out of bed.

"All right, I'm coming," I called to Artemis.

"I don't need to know that. Just hurry up so we can go," she said, and I laughed, heard Nain do the same under his pillow.

A few minutes later, I was dressed and ready to go. I met Artemis in the living room. "Belle Isle, maybe? I'm thinking maybe Gaia would stick to the more natural areas of the city," she said in greeting.

I nodded. "The greenhouse and gardens first." A moment later, I focused, and found myself standing in the perennial garden outside of the Whitcomb Conservatory on Belle Isle. The conservatory was open year round, full of plants from around the world, including a huge orchid collection. Artemis appeared next to me, and we looked around the gardens outside first.

"Inside?" she asked, and I nodded. A quick tour of the conservatory netted us nothing, though a few Normals did end up with photos of me in the cactus room. Artemis sniggered, and I shot her a glare.

"We'll check the woods next," I said.

There was a lot of area to cover, and neither of us had any clue where she might be, or if she was even there at all. So we started near the Nature Center, and strolled the woods, working farther and farther into the forest, listening and watching for any sign of the Earth mother.

"She's not a bad type, really," Artemis explained. "Actually, I like her a lot. And if she wanted you guys to hurt, she would have hurt you the other night."

"I know," I said. "I just don't want her to pull that shit again. Someone might get hurt next time. And how are we supposed to explain forests popping up all over the city?"

"My grandson would figure something out if it came to that," she said with a shrug. "By the way – thank you for not being such a bitch to him anymore. It's much appreciated."

I raised an eyebrow. "That's kind of between us, not you. And if I'm a bitch, I have every reason to be."

"Or so you think," she muttered.

"No. I know. He lied. He cheated. He sold me out to his little government friends. I like Brennan, and I'm not going to kill him, which you should be thanking me for, but I definitely don't trust him."

"Yes, he only gave you the will to live when the demon tricked you into murdering him. But please, do go on about what a bastard he is," she said, and I could feel her temper rising.

"He lied. And he used me. And that's it."

Artemis shoved me, hard, and I crashed into a tree. I leapt up and sprung back up at her. "What the fuck is your problem?" I demanded, shoving her, but not as hard as she'd shoved me.

She shoved me back. "I am so sick of everyone

dumping on my grandson. Take your high and mighty bullshit and shove it up your ass, little girl."

I stopped. Held my hands up. "Stop. Settle down."

"No. Screw you. You have your happily ever after. You have your bond, you have your husband. And do you know what Brennan is left with? Nothing. He's alone, and he gets to spend every day of his life watching you with the demon. So fuck off, princess. I like you, but if you badmouth my grandson again, I will break something."

"He won't be alone forever," I said quietly, hating the stab of guilt that her words brought.

She gave a derisive laugh. "For someone as powerful as you are, you really know nothing."

I crossed my arms. "What the hell is that supposed to mean? He'll fall in love again. He'll get married someday and be happy."

"No, Mollis. He'll never have what he should have had. His future relationships will all be missing something. Something he should have. Something our kind craves more than anything else."

"What the hell are you talking about?"

"The bond, you thoughtless bitch. He'll never bond with anyone else. He'll never have that again. We can do that precisely once, and it is instinctive." She stopped, shook her head. "Think, Fury. I don't disagree with you that he messed up. I don't even disagree with the fact that maybe the two of you were wrong together, somehow, though I do think you could have worked at it a bit harder, had there not been someone else in the picture. He bonded to you, fell in love with you. He couldn't have prevented it even if he wanted to. Breaking that bond, losing something he knew he'd never have again... that takes a tremendous amount of love. He set you free, sacrificed the one thing he's ever really wanted, because you asked him to. And he didn't have to do it. So think about that the next time you want to run him down. Think about what loving you has cost him. I'm done here."

With that, she winked out of sight, and I was left alone.

"Fucking shifters," I muttered. I kept walking, mulling over what she'd said. I swiped at my eyes in irritation. Why hadn't he told me that? How could I not know he could only do it once? I mean, not that it would have changed anything, but at least I would have known what I was asking of him.

Still. He'd lied. And he'd told the government god-knows-what about me. And the cheating. Let's not forget the cheating.

I trudged through the woods for a few more hours, mostly just so I could be alone for a while, and eventually, I had to admit that the chances of finding Gaia that way were pretty much zero.

When I got home, the house was empty.

Or, it should have been. But when I opened my apartment door, Gaia was suddenly standing in my kitchen.

I shook my head. Oh, someone out there had a sense of humor, didn't they?

"You are aware that two of us came through the gateway," she said in greeting.

"That's what my grandmother said, yes," I replied.

"Your grandmother," she echoed. "I don't suppose that as the granddaughter of Nyx, you have any insight into what's powering the Nether?"

I shook my head. "I assumed Nether was powering it."

"God, you Olympians are utter morons."

"Well, Maybe you could enlighten us," I said, determined not to hurt the Earth goddess.

She glared at me. "Nether and Aether powered the realms of the gods. But they weren't all that powered them. Had that been true, the Nether would have died the instant you freed Nether," she said.

I sat down in one of the kitchen chairs. "So what else is powering them?"

"The realms are sentient. They were alive. Most of their

power came from Aether and Nether, and from what I understand, the Aether still stands, for now, even if it is overrun with creatures from Tartarus. The Nether, however, seems to have finally died." She paused. "Except that it hasn't, really. Life will find a way to continue, and my guess is that there is enough of the sentient power in you Nether beings, Furies and Hades, as well as Nether herself, that when I tried to heal the Earth, my power ended up being exactly what it needed to fully live again."

"God, this is crazy," I muttered.

"I can't do my work. I can't do any of the things I planned to do when I returned to find my creation so defiled," she complained.

"Life's tough all around," I said before I could think, and she gave me an icy glare. "I don't suppose you know who else came through with you."

"Oh, I do. I came here specifically to tell you."

"Not just to bitch about my family corrupting everything? Wonderful," I sniped.

"You have quite a mouth on you, Fury."

"Thank you."

She clamped her mouth shut.

"Are you going to tell me who? With all due respect, I have shit to do today."

"Gods, you are clearly Hades' daughter," she muttered, looking away in irritation.

I wasn't sure how happy I was to hear that. My dad *was* kind of an asshole. But whatever.

"Who came through, Gaia?" I asked. I could sense that she at least didn't hate me. There was no malice from her, no hatred. I'd felt plenty of that one to recognize it easily by now.

"His name is Hyperion."

"What's his deal?" I asked. I supposed it would be too much to hope after his little fit at Wayne State (at least, I still assumed that was him) that he just wanted to visit Disneyland or something like that.

"He wants to eradicate the Olympians and all of their offspring. Completely erase their existence."

I stared at her. "Uh..."

"You'll want to ask your father about that. In the meantime, watch out for those you care for, Fury."

I let my head sink into my hands. Leave it to an immortal to drop a bomb like that and act as if it was nothing. "You aren't going to destroy any more neighborhoods, are you?" I asked.

"I would hardly call that destruction," she said, offended.

"You can't keep doing that. You messed up all kinds of shit that we had to fix later. You scared the hell out of people who were pretty sure the world was ending."

She sat in ornery silence for a while. "And what am I supposed to do with my time, then, Fury? Am I supposed to stand by and watch my creation wither?"

I thought.

"You said Hephaestus' mate was one of yours, right?"

She nodded. "An Earth-witch, yes."

"She and Hephaestus have a small farm in the city. And Demeter and Persephone spend a lot of time there as well. I think they'd appreciate your guidance, Mother Gaia."

She was watching me suspiciously.

"And, maybe, you could keep an eye on Hephaestus and try to not let Hyperion murder him if he appears," I added.

She still sat in silence.

"Meaghan is all about protecting the earth as well. And making sure the people who live on it are taken care of. This sounds like something you'd be into," I pressed.

She seemed to decide something. "Very well. I will visit Hephaestus and his mate."

I started talking and she waved me off.

"Yes, yes, and I'll keep an eye on Hephaestus. It's the least I can do considering the boy did what we've all been wanting to do and got rid of Zeus."

I took a breath of relief. "Thank you. Ready to head over there?"

She nodded, and I took her small hand in mine and focused on rematerializing at Heph and Meaghan's place.

I almost felt guilty for saddling them with more, considering they were already busy with figuring out how to live together and the day-to-day insanity that comes with being friends with me.

I dispatched Gaia as quickly as I could and could have kissed Heph and Meaghan for how graciously they accepted the new intrusion into their household. Honestly, Meaghan seemed like she was about to have some kind of crying fit, as overwhelmed with joy as she was when she met the Earth mother. Heph gave me a small wink and a smile and sent me on my way.

How someone like me, someone as crabby and introverted and prickly as I am, ended up with such great friends, is an absolute mystery.

CHAPTER SEVEN

The next couple of days passed much more calmly than I could have hoped for. Other than continued attacks on Rayna's household, things were pretty quiet. Gaia was settling into life at Heph and Meaghan's, and at least I had one Titan mostly figured out. That gave me some time to work on a few of the lost girl cases that were giving Shanti trouble. We'd found one, but the other one continued to stump us, and I was determined to find her.

The sky was overcast, and the fall leaves, in all of their glory, had finally fallen, leaving everything with a kind of sad, lonely look. The neighborhood I was searching was one I'd slowly but surely zeroed in on in trying to find my lost girl, Dayna Addams, a shifter from the Hamtramck pack. Over the past day or so, I'd questioned and read the minds of just about anyone who knew Dayna's habits and where she hung out, and this neighborhood, this squalid, depressing neighborhood, kept coming up. Everyone seemed sure of one thing: she had been seeing someone from the area until recently. And her scent was here; her pack members had verified that, but they'd lost it, almost as if her trail had been deliberately hidden once she got here. They'd gone through houses, businesses, and I'd been with them. Sensing their fear and frustration, and then their growing surety that she was a lost cause had worn on me just as much as the frustration over not finding her.

"Today, I'm gonna find her today," I muttered to myself.

As I walked, I kept my mind open, my senses open so I could pick up any emotions. From a few houses, faces peeked at me from behind curtains and blinds. I scanned them all, found that they were either terrified to see me or happy that I was there.

So, par for the course, really.

I snaked between houses, walked through back yards and garages. Honestly, it was a relief to be alone to work for a while. At first, Nain had been a pain in the ass about wanting to come with me everywhere, until I finally made him understand that his being around just messed up my focus, and that, no, I didn't want Heph or anyone else with me, either. This was my thing. This was still personal to me in a way I just couldn't shake, and my only regret was that I didn't do this kind of work as often as I should.

I kept walking, kept rematerializing inside empty houses, searching basements, attics, for some sign of my lost girl. She'd been nine months pregnant at the time of her disappearance, and that only added to the necessity to find her quickly. I'd asked her pack members if maybe she'd just run off with her lover, whoever he was, and, to a one, they'd argued that she wasn't the type, that she was a good girl who was mostly level-headed. I'd kept to myself that even the most level-headed among us do really stupid things in the name of love.

I searched through early afternoon, into late afternoon, widening the area of my search, questioning anyone I came into contact with. November meant that my daylight was limited, and when the sun started setting, I just kept going.

I wasn't afraid of the dark.

I approached a rickety-looking bungalow, its formerly-white clapboard siding flaking, falling off the house. The front porch had collapsed long ago, and the windows on the upper floor were crooked, as if the house was beginning to lean. I was walking around to the back, heading to the garage first, when I picked up an emotion.

Fear. Hunger. Fear. Fear. Fear.

I spun and headed into the house instead. There was something different about the way the emotions felt, something I didn't really have time to think about as I crept in the back door, letting myself into the dark house.

I kept my mind open, called forth my fire. I let it dance over my palm, my fingers, as I lifted it so I could get a better sense of the room. A kitchen, long since stripped of anything useful. Empty, other than trash in the corners. I continued through a doorway into what must have been the living room. I did a quick scan of the room, nearly dismissed something lying there as another pile of trash.

But it wasn't. It was blankets. And a creamy white hand.

Fucking hell.

As I got closer, it became obvious that I'd found Dayna, and that she was very much not with the living anymore. There was blood all over the floor around her, not from any wounds I could see, though.

And then I saw it. The source of the emotions I'd felt, and now I understood why they felt weird. I'd felt them from Sean, too, the frenzied, unformed, chaotic emotions of a baby. Primal.

She was probably a few hours old at the most, or she'd be dead already, I realized. Someone –Dayna, I supposed– had had the foresight to cut the umbilical cord and knot it. It was partially wrapped in a blanket, but not very well.

I threw my hands up into the air in helplessness.

"So what the hell am I supposed to do now?" I asked, and the baby opened her eyes and looked up at me. So quiet, so still.

"Well, I'm not going to lose two girls today," I said in a softer tone, determined not to freak the baby out any more than I probably already had. I looked at the scene. "I wonder why she had you here," I said. I let my fire go out.

"Okay. I guess you have to eat, or I'm gonna lose you, kiddo," I said. There was a coat Dayna had apparently worn, and after searching the pockets and finding nothing, I shrugged and set it down on the floor. I picked the baby up, more than a little awkwardly, and set her into the coat, then wrapped it around her. She was a mess; dried blood and fluids, really gross baby poo. I wrinkled my nose. "You stink, kid," I murmured, even as I felt something inside me melt at the feel of her tiny form in my arms.

"Okay. Food," I said. I went out into the yard, flew into the air, not wanting to rematerialize with her, not knowing how it would affect a baby. I knew it hurt, and that was enough. I landed at a grocery store, begged a hapless stock person to help me gather diapers and wipes and formula and bottles and other shit I knew nothing about, then checked out and flew away, feeding her the bottle one of the older cashier ladies had mixed for me at the store.

"I can just see the headlines about this tomorrow," I said to the baby, who was drinking greedily, not even seeming to care that she was about a hundred feet up in the air, in the arms of a winged, glowy-eyed freak.

I landed in Hamtramck, and carried the baby up to the front door of the pack's home, which used to be a rooming house. I knocked, and the pack leader and his mate opened the door.

"I'm sorry. I was too late to save Dayna," I said, telling them where her body was. They were both staring at the baby, disgust and fear rolling off of them. "But this is her daughter. I figured you'd want her."

The pack leader glared at me. "Would have been better if you'd left that thing to die. I don't want it nowhere near my pack," he finished, then he slammed the door in my face and turned off the porch light, as if that would stop me if I really wanted to get in and press the issue.

"Well, you're welcome. Asshole," I muttered, walking down the front walk again. "Fuck."

I looked down at the tiny, sleeping bundle of warmth in my arms. "Well. You won't be the first kid we've taken in for a while, I suppose," I said, then I rose into the air again, heading toward home.

When I walked in, awkwardly carrying the baby, Nain, Eunomia, and Brennan were in the kitchen. They stopped talking immediately, their gazes landing on the wriggling bundle in my arms.

"What the fuck is that?" Nain asked.

"I'm pretty sure they call them babies," I said. "And this one lost her mother."

"We're not taking it in. Turn it over to one of the shifter packs or something."

I stared at him. "Are you serious? I'm not turning her over to anyone. I tried, and they slammed the fucking door in my face. You've taken kids in before." I was surprised by how badly I wanted this already, by how annoyed I was at his automatic rejection.

"I've never taken in a baby," Nain said. "And that one is bad news."

"It's a baby, not a nuclear bomb," I said.

"Sense for her. What is she?" he said, that stubborn look on his face that told me he'd already made up his mind like the cranky old man he is. Brennan and E just watched, both of them tense.

"I already know what she is. Her mom was a shifter and her father was a demon."

Brennan nodded then. "Yeah. Demon shifter." The feelings coming off of both Brennan and Nain were anything but good. Discomfort, dislike. E just seemed confused.

"And you seriously want us to take her in?" Nain asked irritably. "Do you even know what you're asking?"

"Why don't one of you explain it to me, since all I see is a baby and you're acting like she's a monster?" I said. My eyes were on the baby. She was tiny, delicate. Perfect creamy skin, big emerald-green eyes that seemed to take in everything. A shock of nearly black, soft curls formed a dark halo at the top of her head. She was awake again, and her gaze rested on me, and she stopped kicking, stopped fidgeting in my arms.

She was mine already. I couldn't explain it, knew it was insane. No matter how many times I'd told myself that it was a good thing nothing would likely ever grow in my womb, I couldn't lie to myself. I wanted a family. I wanted to watch someone grow. I wanted to treasure someone and give him or her the kind of childhood I'd never had.

"Molly," Nain warned, some of my emotions apparently spilling through our connection.

"Tell me," I said softly, tearing my eyes away from her.

He came up to me and gave my hip a squeeze. "Remember what I said about how demon kids are nuts? Full of energy, rage that seems to come out of nowhere? They're impossible. Really it's no surprise that their parents end up killing them," he said. I raised my eyebrows. "I'm not saying it's right. I'm just saying it's not surprising."

"And you've been around Sean enough to know what shifter kids are like," Brennan said, picking up where Nain had left off. "It's freaking exhausting, trying to keep up with a shifter kid. And it only gets more insane once they start learning how to shift. Hyper as hell," he muttered. "So imagine having all of that hyperactivity in one kid."

"Except that that's not the worst of it," Nain said. "A demon baby wouldn't naturally look like that kid," he said, nodding toward the baby again, studying her. "Demons don't know how to bring up a glamour until they're old enough to start controlling their powers."

"Yeah. The shifter side of her blocks her from having a demon form. At least, that's my understanding of it," Brennan said.

Nain nodded. "Yeah. So think about that. This kid is half demon, half shifter. And its shifter side is keeping the demon side kind of repressed, so it's got all of these demonic urges and no way to get them out. Except that, oh, right, it can turn into an animal. What was Dayna again?"

I sighed. "Dayna shifted into a tiger," I said, repressing a grimace as Nain swore.

"Great. So it has these demonic urges, and then it gets to turn into a tiger, and I can tell you right now that she'll be a huge fucking tiger when she shifts, because demon, right? And she's powerful."

I started talking, and he shook his head a little.

"What?"

"Demon and shifter were never, ever meant to mix. They usually don't. The cost of having its demonic side constantly repressed by its shifter side will drive that kid nuts eventually, and then we'll have a raging demon tiger on the loose."

"We've seen this shit before, Molly. It's not good," Brennan said gently.

Nain nodded in agreement. "Luckily that one only shifted into a fox. It was easy enough to overpower it. A tiger, though?" He shook his head in disgust. "Everyone would have been better off if you'd been too late to save her."

I stared at him in shock, then started to leave the room with the baby. He put his hand around my biceps, pulling me close to him.

"This baby is going to have a miserable life. Death would have been merciful," he said softly. "Okay?"

I glared at him, but stopped trying to fight my way out of his embrace.

"I'm guessing none of the shifters will take her in

anyway, if they know all of that," I said.

"They know better," Brennan said.

"You mean you agree with Nain about this?" I asked him.

He shook his head again. "I don't know. All I do know is that we've seen what happens. And you have more than enough to worry about already, right?"

"I'll decide how much I can take, thanks," I said icily.

Brennan rolled his eyes and looked away from me.

"And what do you think of this, E?" I asked.

She gave a small smile. "I think you've made up your mind already, my friend."

I turned my gaze to Nain, and I knew, because Nain knew me, that he could guess exactly what I wanted.

He groaned. "Don't look at me like that, baby."

I tilted my head, just a little, and he groaned again.

"You have no idea what you'd be getting into," he said.

"I want to think about it, at least," I said softly. "We can't just turn away from her, Nain."

He didn't answer, but he didn't argue either.

Brennan crossed his arms over his chest, irritation rolling off of him in hot waves. "Don't you have enough to do, between insane Titans destroying shit and crazy-ass immortals everywhere? You really need this now?"

I took a breath. This was a big reason why Bren and I never would have lasted. His version of taking care of me would have driven me up the wall eventually. "Well, if anyone can handle it, I can," I said, trying very hard to keep my voice calm.

I looked back at the baby. She was starting to doze off, and I felt a little tug at my heart.

"I'll talk to you tomorrow, Brennan," Nain said. "Later, E," he added, and I was very aware of his eyes on me. Brennan got up without another word and walked out behind Eunomia, irritation still rolling off of him. I heard her say something to him as they walked away, but I didn't catch the words.

Nain sat back down, and I took the baby into our room and settled her in the center of the bed. I watched her for a moment, then went back to the kitchen. Once she woke up and ate again, I'd attempt to clean her up.

I went over to Nain and sat, straddling his lap, pressing myself against him. I smiled a little. He responded to me immediately.

"You're all stressed out again," he said, voice low, eyes already starting to glow.

"I am," I said, tracing my hands down his stomach, toward his waistband. I felt the tremor run through him, as it did so often when I touched him. "Want to help take the edge off?"

He picked me up and carried me over to the living room couch.

"Don't start thinking you're gonna win me over with sex, woman," he grunted. Then he lowered me to the cushions, and there was no need for words.

Afterward, we sprawled on the living room floor, letting our breathing come back to normal, our heart rates slow. Sweat gleamed on his body. I was lying on his chest, listening to his heartbeat, loving the feel of his skin against mine. I raised my head so I could look at him.

"We could do that all day, every day of our lives, and it still wouldn't be enough," he said, a satisfied smile on his face.

I grinned, nipped at his shoulder, and he grunted. I rested my chin on my hands so I could look at him.

"Are you in a better mood now?" I asked him.

"I'm not in that good of a mood," he said. "We can't do that, Molly. I know what you want, but..."

"But, what?"

He sat up and I sat on his lap, straddling his thighs. He wrapped his arms around me. "Did you not hear what I said about demon shifters? She's going to lose her mind. Her life is going to be one long struggle to relieve the rage inside of her. And anyone who loves her is in for heartbreak, because they'll have to watch it happen." He paused. "Brennan is worried about your ability to deal with hyperactivity. I know you can do that. You know what I can't handle, though? Seeing you heartbroken. And I can't think of any situation in which this won't end up breaking your heart, Molls." He paused. "If you want a baby, we'll start looking into adopting. There are plenty of supernatural kids out there who aren't wanted. We can adopt a whole football team of kids if you want them."

"I want this one," I said softly.

He rested his forehead against mine.

"She's going to be crazy. You get that, right?"

"Who's better equipped to handle crazy than us?" He grunted in response, and I started running my hands over his shoulders, loving the way they felt under my hands. "Think about it, Nain. She has nobody. No one will even take a chance on her. She's creeping people out, and she hasn't even done anything yet. Sound familiar?"

He sighed, and I knew I had him. He knew my past, my childhood. In our time together, I'd shown him scenes from my lonely, loveless childhood, and he'd shared his own memories with me.

"You are a stubborn pain in the ass, you know that?" he asked, his voice rumbling in the darkening room, the sound of it warming me, just as it always did.

"Takes one to know one," I murmured.

"I want you to think about something else," he said.

"Okay." I rubbed slow circles over his shoulders, and he practically purred in response.

"Stop trying to distract me," he said.

"Sorry, dear."

"Liar."

I laughed, and got a grin in response. "One: everyone will realize that this isn't just another random freak we're bringing in. You're terrible at hiding your feelings, baby. Everyone will know you love her. Think of all the enemies we have. This kid is going to be a target for every sick fuck we've ever crossed."

"Then we'll just have to be scarier," I said.

"You know it makes me hot when you say shit like that."

"I know," I said, leaning forward and nibbling the side of his neck. He growled. "But continue. What were you saying?"

"And two: who's gonna watch her while we're off saving the world?" he asked, then groaned as I bit him harder. "I can't see you retiring to stay home and bake cookies."

"I'll bake cookies and kick ass. My parents will help. So will E."

"I can't see Hades babysitting, somehow," he grumbled. It was an act at this point, and we both knew it. He didn't bend often, but when it mattered, I knew I could count on him to meet me halfway. It was why we worked. I took his earlobe between my teeth and gently nipped it.

"We'll work it out," I said softly.

He held me tighter. He was silent for several long moments, and I could feel the emotions flowing through him. Irritation, worry, that ever-present anger. Love. Then, finally, he muttered, "You want it this bad, we'll do what it takes to make it work."

"I love you, Bael," I whispered, endlessly grateful that I had him in my life.

He kissed the side of my neck, held me tighter. "I love you too. If you ever doubt how completely fucking out of my mind I am for you, remember this day."

"I will."

And, just then, the baby started crying from our bedroom, and I disentangled myself from Nain's arms. He muttered something about how we better get used to having quickies and I flipped him the bird as I pulled my shirt over my head and walked toward the room. He laughed, and as I bent over the baby to change her diaper (really grateful now that I'd changed a few of Sean's diapers so I wasn't totally clueless) I heard him in the kitchen, going through the bags I'd brought home. When I brought the baby out to the kitchen, he was shaking a bottle of formula. He handed it to me wordlessly.

"There you go, mama," he said, and I smiled. We went back into the living room and he sat on the end of the couch, pulled me down onto his lap, and I held the baby, watching her as she took her bottle.

"Isn't she beautiful?" I murmured.

"Babies are weird," Nain said, and I rolled my eyes. His hand was rubbing up and down my back, and his other hand was cradling the baby's tiny feet. "And formula smells gross."

"Shut up, you crabby old man," I said, laughing. Just then, my dad let himself in (because of all the immortals, he had refused to learn the importance of boundaries and privacy) and his gaze landed on the three of us.

"What's that?" he asked, sitting on the other end of the couch.

"Baby. She's gonna call you Grandpa," I said.

He looked at her again. "Demon shifter?"

I nodded, waiting for the onslaught of, "That's nuts. You can't keep her."

"She'll be vicious someday," he said in approval. "What's her name?"

I shrugged. "I have no idea. Any suggestions?"

"Hades," Hades said, and I rolled my eyes.

"I am not naming our daughter Hades," I said.

"Fine. Her loss. If I had had my way, I would have named you Zoe," he said.

"Oh, yeah? Why?" I asked.

"Zoe means 'alive.' And there's nothing more alive, nothing with more potential for greatness, than a newborn baby. A whole life of possibility before her. Your mother overruled me, though," he said, shrugging.

I exchanged a glance with Nain, and he gave a small nod.

I looked down at the baby. "Zoe... Brooks, I guess? You have no last name," I said to Nain.

"Neither do you, really, unless 'Eth-Hades' counts. Brooks will work," he said.

"Welcome to the family, Zoe Brooks," I said softly to the dozing baby in my arms.

"Welcome to the nuthouse," Nain said. "You'll be a fine addition."

I elbowed him, and he laughed and put his arms around us. I sat there in our rented living room with my husband, my father, and this child who was now my daughter, and tried not to dwell on hoping that I was enough to keep us all safe.

It was a long night. It was going to be an adjustment getting used to a newborn's feeding schedule. It felt like I had just fallen asleep after her four o'clock feeding when I was awakened again.

It wasn't Zoe's crying that woke me up, for once.

It wasn't Nain's hands on me, ready for his morning lay.

No. It was Gaia and Hephaestus standing beside our bed, Gaia shaking my arm wildly.

"Gah!" I said, pulling the sheet up to my chin. Nain sat up, shooting a glare at Hephaestus. Our room was still dim, and a glance at the digital clock on my nightstand showed that it was just after six. My first thought, right after "what are they doing in our bedroom?" was "if they wake Zoe, I'm going to kill them."

Nain pulled another blanket up over me, glaring at Hephaestus and Gaia as he did. "If I don't get a good explanation for why you two are standing in our fucking bedroom, someone's gonna be bleeding," he growled.

"Apollo is dead," Hephaestus said, voice low. I sensed for him, and caught not just sadness, but, more, rage and worry.

I stared at him, then at Gaia, who only nodded sadly.

"Nether?" I asked.

Heph shook his head. "It was Hyperion. Gaia told us she knew who it was and told you. He got him when Apollo was leaving our house this morning." He shook his head. "He stayed late last night and he put away so much whiskey he could barely move. He ended up passing out on the couch. Gaia and Meaghan were up early like they always are, and he got up and headed out. Hyperion got him just as he was leaving."

Hephaestus's rage level had shot up, and I cringed.

"I'm sorry, Heph. I should have moved faster trying to find him. I—"

"I'm not pissed at you, Queenie," he said. "This all happened fast and it's not like you don't have shit going on."

I studied him. His entire body was tense, and his barely-restrained rage surprised me.

"I didn't know you and Apollo were that close," I said.

"We're not," he said, letting out a frustrated breath. "Not really. He's all right to play cards with once in a while, which is why he was over last night." He shook his head. "I can't have this shit around my home. Not now."

"Is Meaghan okay?" I asked, and he gave a short nod. "She's with Demeter and Persephone. Neither of them are leaving her side, and I'm grateful."

I watched him. His anger was very un-Heph-like. "I swear we won't let anything happen to her."

"I know, Queenie," he said. He raked his fingers through his unruly hair. "She's pregnant," he said, voice low. "And I will do whatever it takes to protect her and our child."

Nain and I exchanged a look.

He recovered faster than I did.

"Congratulations, man," he said, sticking his hand out. Heph shook it, a happy, somewhat sheepish look on his face.

"Thanks," he said.

"Congrats," I said, still holding the sheet up over my body. "I'll take care of this. All right?"

He nodded, and I felt him relax, just a little. He always had more faith in me than I did.

"There's one other thing," he said.

"What?" Nain asked.

"Who's going to break it to Artemis?" Heph asked, and we all looked in the direction of Brennan, Artemis, and Sean's apartment.

"It won't be me. I'm going back to watch over Meaghan," Gaia said, and without another word, she was gone.

"You know her better than I do," I said to Heph.

"Debatable, Queenie," he said. "She likes you more than she likes me."

I closed my eyes. This would break her. I knew that. Apollo was her twin brother. And while they didn't always see completely eye-to-eye, they were very close. Apollo had been a regular fixture at the loft and now here, spending time with his sister and her descendants.

"Brennan's not gonna be happy, either," Nain said.

"Brennan's on the list," I said quietly.

Silence.

"What?" Nain finally said.

"Gaia said that Hyperion wants to destroy the Olympians and their offspring. All of them. That includes Brennan and Sean."

The already-dark mood in the room darkened considerably.

"I'll tell them," I said. They were awake. I could hear Sean's energetic babbles and laughs, Brennan's low voice responding. I looked up at Heph. "Uh. Can you go in the other room?"

He nodded and left, and when he went into the living room, I heard him mutter, "What the hell is this, now?" I supposed the "this" he was talking about was Zoe, whose bassinet was in the corner of the living room. Nain and I got up and got dressed. About midway through, when I was about to start pulling my jeans on, Nain pulled me into his arms and held me tight.

"It'll be okay," I told him, putting my arms around his waist.

"Too much crazy shit. Nether and now this? It's taking everything in me not to steal you away and keep you hidden."

I forced myself to smile up at him. "My parents tried that once already, remember? Didn't work out all that well."

He leaned down and kissed me, rested his forehead against mine.

"It'll be okay," I said. After a moment, he released me, and I could tell he didn't want to. I finished getting dressed, and Nain and I walked out into the living room, where Heph was pacing. He gestured to the bassinet.

"Zoe. We adopted her," Nain said, and Heph gave a thoughtful nod.

"Well, watching you parent a girl should be interesting, if nothing else," Heph said, and Nain flipped him off.

I was watching the door to Brennan's apartment. I wished I could put it off. "I'll be right back."

I walked across the kitchen, knocked on the door that led into their apartment. Brennan answered, dressed in the dark pants he wore to work. His shirt was partially buttoned, as if I'd interrupted him in the middle of getting dressed.

"Hey," he said.

I tried to smile. "Hey."

"What's wrong?" he asked.

"Is Artemis awake?"

He nodded, and gestured for me to come inside.

Artemis was sitting on the living room sofa, Sean in her lap. It hit me, then, how much Brennan and Sean both took after Artemis. They both had her blond hair, though Brennan's was darker than Artemis and Sean's. It was the eyes. All three of them had those slate-blue eyes fringed with thick black lashes. And when they smiled, as Artemis and Sean were just then, the family resemblance was even more pronounced. They were reading a pop-up book, and Sean was laughing. I felt happiness from Artemis, a huge amount of love for the toddler in her lap.

I felt like even more of a shithead for having to ruin that.

She turned her head, noticed that I was there. "Good morning, Mollis," she said, and Sean held the book up for her to read more. Artemis was studying me. "You look like someone just died."

I was speechless. This wasn't my thing. How are you even supposed to handle telling someone that one of their loved ones has died? I wanted to turn and run, save her, for just a few minutes, from the pain that would come.

"Molly?" Brennan asked, putting his hand on my lower back. Such a familiar feeling, and I let it comfort me, even though I knew better.

"Artemis, Heph and Gaia were just here," I began. "Apollo spent the night at their house, I guess, because he and Heph were having some epic card playing drinking night or something."

"Yes. Idiots," Artemis said with a small smile.

I looked at Brennan. "He was leaving this morning, and on his way out, he was attacked by the other Titan that escaped through the gateway. Hyperion," I added.

Artemis gently set Sean on the couch, and stood up.

"And?" she asked softly. Her shoulders were already slumped. Her hand shook when she brought it to her face.

"I'm sorry," I whispered.

She stared at me. It was as if time had stopped, as if the air had all gone out of the room.

"Um. Gaia told me he was the other Titan. I didn't think he'd move so fast," I said.

"And what else did she say?" Brennan asked.

"She said that he wants to destroy the Olympians. Wipe them from existence as revenge for locking him up in Tartarus. That means you, too," I said to him.

"I'm not Olympian," he said.

"You're my offspring. It is enough," Artemis said, voice shaking. Her gaze met mine, and I was struck by how hard the news had truly hit her. Artemis had always been larger-than-life. Tough. She'd helped me survive my first confused days when I was trapped in the Nether.

She'd wanted me to be part of her family. And that is something I'll never forget.

She seemed shrunken. Pale. Her eyes had a wild gleam to them, as if she was just on the edge of madness. And the feelings coming from her, the pain... it was heartbreaking.

The one constant in her long existence, her best friend and only true confidant, her brother, was gone.

"I need to go," she said.

"What? Where?" Brennan asked, moving away from me and toward his grandmother. She shook her head.

"I need time. Time," she repeated. Her face crumpled, and she made a visible effort to get herself under control. My heart ached for her. I would have hugged her (awkward though I was at the hugging thing) but Artemis is not really affectionate that way. Instead, I stood there dumbly and let her pain wash over me. My hands hung awkwardly at my sides. Brennan looked just as helpless as I felt, watching his grandmother with concern on his face.

"You don't have to go," he said softly. "Stay with us. We're not him, but we're still family."

She shook her head. "I need to mourn him alone. I need..." She trailed off.

"She needs to mourn where no one will see how ruined she is," I said, filling in the blanks. "She needs to control her own mourning, since it's the only thing she can control right now."

Artemis nodded, patted Brennan absentmindedly on the shoulder. Then she fixed me with a steely gaze.

"Avenge my brother, Fury," she said, her voice full of rage and unshed tears. "If you ever valued our friendship, avenge him."

"Grandma," Brennan intoned.

I took Artemis's hand, and I bowed my head just a little, keeping my eyes on hers.

"I swear it. He will be avenged." It was the only thing I could give her now.

Once she had my promise, Artemis turned, gave Sean a quick kiss on the top of his head, and disappeared. Which left me and Brennan standing awkwardly in their living room.

He ran his hands over his face.

"He's a Titan," he said, and I nodded. I told him what little Gaia had told me about Hyperion, feeling guilty the entire time for not having told him before it had affected his family. He listened, arms crossed over his chest.

"I'm sorry I didn't say anything before. I just found out that day with Gaia, and things have been nuts ever since. I'm sorry," I repeated.

He waved it off. "You don't have anything to be sorry about." He glanced toward Sean, who was now pulling wooden blocks out of a plastic bin in the corner of the living room. "My grandmother is in mourning, my great-uncle or whatever he is is dead, and you're telling me that this thing wants to destroy my son?"

"And you," I said.

"I don't care about me," he said.

"I'll take care of it."

"You can't do everything."

"I can do this much. I promised her."

"Is this the thing that attacked at Wayne State?" he asked.

"I think so. I heard Heph saying something to Nain about gold armor when I was heading over here. It fits."

He nodded, lost in thought. "I'm an asshole, but I just realized I have no one to watch Sean. I depended on her for everything."

"It's not selfish. It's life," I said.

He looked away. "I was not ready for any of this."

I honestly didn't want to hear what his "any of this" was. Partially because I knew it would somehow come back to the two of us, because that's a conversation we needed to have and I kept avoiding it. Kept putting bandaids on it, hoping it would just go away. When it came down to it, I'd mostly forgiven him for my own sanity, but I didn't trust him. And I hated that, because I wanted to. For a million reasons, some that made sense and some that didn't, I really wanted to trust him again.

Bandaids would do, for now. Because despite what everyone seems to want to believe, I have no problem admitting that sometimes, I'm a coward.

"Um. We can help watch Sean while you work. Since we have Zoe around, I mean. I'm hoping my parents and E will help. They can watch Sean too, maybe, until Artemis comes back."

He didn't answer.

"Unless you maybe don't want him to be around Nether types all the time," I added, remembering the previous night's conversation about Zoe. "Or around Zoe all the time."

"Why the hell would that bother me?" he asked irritably.

"I don't know. Because you're sure Zoe's going to be a menace. Or, the whole 'shifter and demon never mix' thing from last night. We should have thought of that before we started up, huh? Maybe there's a reason, or... I don't know," I said. "I am so fucking lost right now."

He shook his head. "Why are you determined to believe that I don't still worship the ground you walk on?"

I backed away, toward the door that led into my and Nain's apartment.

"You never should have worshipped anything about me," I said. "And you didn't. Not really."

He gave a bitter-looking smile. "Right. Because if I had, I wouldn't have messed around."

"Bingo. Or lied to me, but in the end it's all the same, so..." I paused, shook my head. He always managed to push my buttons lately. "And we don't need to do this now. Like I said, we can work it out with having people watch Sean. And maybe sometimes you can help us with Zoe."

He looked away from me. "Yeah. We can do that. Thanks."

I left his apartment without another word. By then, our apartment was full of immortals out for blood and feeling impotent because they couldn't end Hyperion.

I held my hands up, and they all settled down. Heph stood there with his arm around Meaghan's waist. Gaia stood beside the window as if aching to be out of the building. My family was all there. E, Asclepias, Hestia, and Athena were there as well. Nain stood to the side, watching me, and as I got ready to speak, Brennan and Sean walked in.

"Okay," I said. "So Hyperion is the other Titan who escaped before Nyx destroyed the gateway. He wants your blood. He wants to end the Olympians. That means all of you," I noted, meeting my dad's eyes. "Every immortal in this room, as well as Brennan and his son, because why not, right?" I went on, then shook my head, trying, and mostly failing, to keep my anger in check. "I knew. Gaia warned me, and I thought we had time. I didn't believe he'd strike so quickly. That was stupid, and Apollo's death is on my hands. If you'd known, you would have all been more careful. I should have fucking warned you he was out there."

"It wouldn't have made a bit of difference if you had.

He struck out of nowhere," Heph said, and Meghan nodded, her eyes still red from crying. "Before we could even react, he was dead."

"Still. Maybe he would have been more careful," I said. "Artemis asked me to avenge her brother, and I promised her I would." I transferred my gaze to Gaia. "I don't suppose you can give us any more insight into Hyperion?"

She silent for a moment, then said, "All I know of Hyperion is that he's full of rage and hatred and desires vengeance above all else. He was one of the leaders of the Titans during the war against the Olympians. He believed, as we all did," she said, meeting the eyes of the increasingly angry Olympians, "that the Olympians, should they come to power, would cause nothing but hardship for the fledgling human race. We were focused on helping the humans thrive. The Olympians were about ensuring that the humans gave the proper sacrifices when they prayed. They punished, and we did not."

"Yeah, you were all so benevolent. How many human women did Hyperion attack again?" Hades asked. "And don't try to pretend it didn't happen. Him and the other…"

"Yes, and none of you Olympian men ever took what wasn't yours," Gaia sneered. "We could come up with a sizable list of Zeus's sickening acts alone. And you stole Persephone…"

"He didn't steal me. Why does everyone keep saying that?" Persephone asked in irritation as her mother glared at Hades.

"My point was," Hades said, raising his voice, "that you weren't all peace and light either, so get off your fucking high horse."

"Okay," I said. "Let's not get into ancient history now, all right?" The last thing I wanted was to piss Gaia off and have another vengeful Titan to deal with. "Go on, Gaia," I added.

She gave my father one last pointed glare. "So it came

to war. And the Olympians were no match for the Titans. I stayed out of it, because I believe in peace. But in time, it became clear that the Olympians were using trickery to trap the Titans, since they couldn't defeat them in actual combat. And I started gathering information for the Titans. I believed, as the rest of them did, that the Olympians were the worst thing to happen to humankind. I still do," she added. "Once Zeus discovered my role, he had several of the Olympians capture me. Many of them are in this very room, actually," she said, looking around. I sensed a bit of guilt from Athena, my mother, my aunt, and Hestia. "I was tossed into Tartarus, and without my information, soon the other Titans followed. Hyperion remained free the longest, and when they finally captured him, the Olympians did much more than just throw him in Tartarus. They mocked him, tortured him, let the other prisoners throw things at him. Feces," she clarified. "And he swore he would get his revenge. By then, it was no longer about saving humankind from the Olympians. It was about regaining his pride and getting vengeance on his captors."

We stood around in silence. My hand was clasped with Nain's.

God, they are all such fuckheads, I thought at him.

It is really, really hard to like your family, Molls, he agreed.

"Yeah? And I don't suppose he told you what he'd done that made us treat him that way?" Hades asked, his voice purposely mild. That was always a bad sign.

Gaia frowned at him. "He was our leader. That is enough."

"We're not monsters, Gaia," Hades said. "The treatment he received was the least of what I, at least, wanted to do."

"What did he do?" I asked.

The Olympians all went silent, and Gaia watched in confusion.

As I looked around at the Olympians, I met my mom's eyes. "Tell them. I can't," she said to the Olympians, and my father took her hand.

"We sent Tis in, trying to lure him out of hiding. He'd always liked and respected her. And she wasn't afraid to do it. She's ever been the warrior," Athena began. "So brave. Determined to do what is right. Megaera, Artemis, and I stood watch near the cave where he was hiding, and waited for the signal from Tisiphone that he'd taken the sleeping potion Demeter had concocted. She was going to feed him. We knew he was starving, and he'd possibly trust Tisiphone enough to eat the food. When he fell into a stupor, we'd capture him."

My aunt Meg picked up the story then. "The signal never came, and after a day had passed, we rallied the other Olympians to go into the cave. We feared we'd find Tis dead," she finished, her voice trembling.

"At the time, I wished I was," my mom put in, and rage rolled over me, coming from my father. "We were stupid to count on any respect he'd had for me."

"He'd captured Tisiphone," Athena went on. "And you can probably guess what he did with her," she finished quietly. I closed my eyes, fought the bile rising in my throat. Oh, the bastard was going to pay, I promised myself.

"We were determined to hurt him after that. We were like animals, hacking and stabbing at him," Hades said. "For a while, we were glad it wasn't possible for us to actually kill him. Death would have been too kind, and I wouldn't have been able to punish him in the afterlife," he finished.

I nodded, remembering that he'd told me that none of us had any life after death. We could resurrect, usually, because we were mostly just this weird energy stuff. And while it's true that energy is never actually destroyed, there is nothing left of us — of the things that make us, us — once we truly die. While our bodies can die and we can resurrect, certain beings can end us for good. No one really understands why, except to assume that Nyx, in all her wisdom, set it up that way for a reason. While mortal souls exist in certain areas of the Nether, depending on how good or evil they were in life, gods, when they die, just cease to be. Gods and demons. There is some kind of irony there.

"Eventually we stopped punishing him. He was weak, and we took him to Tartarus. If we let the prisoners throw shit at him, it was the least he deserved," he finished, addressing this last to Gaia. "I'm not claiming we were always right. I know we're selfish assholes a lot of the time. But he had that coming, and so much more."

Gaia nodded slowly. "He did neglect that part of the story," she finally said. "And while I wouldn't believe a word that came from most of you, I believe Tisiphone's word."

"Thank you," my mom said.

I looked around. "Okay," I said. "Well, now I have two reasons to destroy him." I took a breath. Then I looked back at Heph. I couldn't do this now. Couldn't think of my mom at the mercy of the Titan. She would be pissed if she saw pity in my eyes, so I pushed it aside. "So no one recognized a power signature?" I asked Heph.

"We can't feel them that way," Heph said. "That was how he caught Apollo so easily."

"Um. I can feel Gaia just fine. Can't you?" I asked the Olympians, and they shook their heads.

"Nyx's line," my mother said. "We can sense the Titans, but they can hide themselves from the rest of you."

"Well, that's just great," Brennan said. "So what are we supposed to do? How am I going to keep my son safe if I can't even see Hyperion coming? And don't tell me to trust you, Molly. You can't be everywhere."

I clamped my mouth shut. He was right. I was about to say those exact words. "I'll just have to get to him first," I said. "I'll find him."

"Yeah, well, Nether wants to kill me too, so, hey: maybe I should be bait," Brennan said, and at first I thought he was just being an asshole. Maybe he was, but a thoughtful look replaced the angry expression on his face. "Draw them out, and you can do your thing," he said, looking at me.

I shook my head. "No way."

"Why not?"

"Because I don't know if I can actually kill either of them and I'm not putting you in harm's way while I try to figure it out."

"He's already in harm's way," my father said. "At least this would be of his choosing."

"No. And fuck you for even suggesting it," I said. "I have a psycho to find. Stick together," I muttered, then focused on rematerializing elsewhere before anyone could stop me.

CHAPTER EIGHT

I ended up in the neighborhood where Heph and Meaghan lived, hoping to find some sign of Hyperion. I knew the possibility of him being there was unlikely, but it was all I could think of.

Man. My imps would have been so helpful. I could do it myself; I always had, but I had been spoiled by how quickly the imps could find things out. Now, I was left to listening in on conversations and thoughts and trying to detect power signatures. I was walking through open fields around Heph and Meaghan's house when my phone rang. I glanced at the screen. Nain's number.

"Hey," I said when I answered.

"Hey," he said.

"I'm sorry I took off like that. They were making me nuts," I said.

"I'm glad you did. I know you do better when you're out actually doing shit instead of standing around. We just got a report that Nether's on I-94 near Wayne State. Apparently there's a huge pileup and she's there acting nuts."

I didn't say anything for a second. I have never in my

life backed down from a fight, but facing Nether again, being so totally and completely overpowered, was not something I had even the smallest desire to do. I shook my head.

"Okay. I'm on my way. Don't come," I added, and then I hung up and focused on the freeway. There was an overpass that would give me a pretty good idea of the surrounding area, so I focused on making it there.

The first thing I noticed was the mass of cars in both directions on the freeway. Backed up.

The second thing I noticed was the silence. Usually, at times like this, people would be honking their horns or shouting profanities. Right then, it looked like everyone trapped in a car was just hoping the insane being on the freeway wouldn't notice them.

Nether was flying, hovering just a couple feet above the concrete, back and forth across the freeway. She was talking, but even in the quiet I couldn't pick up what she was saying. I focused, and rematerialized closer, on the embankment at the side of the freeway.

I listened harder, and it really did sound like she was speaking gibberish, more noise than words. I studied her, glad she hadn't noticed me yet.

Nether looked like hell.

Her long white hair was in snarls, bits of leaves caught in the strands. The white outfit she'd been wearing the day she kicked my ass still sported blood (likely mine) and was gray with filth. Her wings were filthy as well, the pristine white now smudged, the feathers in disarray.

She looked at the pylons for the overpass nearby, and then, in the next second, she flew toward it, faster than I've ever seen anyone fly, and she ran head-first into the concrete pillar. The bridge shook with the impact. It was still morning rush hour, and there were people everywhere, including on the bridge. She backed up and did it again. I flew toward her before I could talk myself out of it, and just as she was rearing up to fly into it again, I lunged toward her and pulled her back.

"Stop it. What the hell are you doing?" I said, and she struggled against me.

"It won't stop. In Nyx's name, it just won't stop!" she screeched, and she clawed at my arms, trying to get away to do it again.

I had to get her out of there, away from the crowds of morning commuters. I held on to her tight, and focused, and we ended up in the empty lot where my house had once stood. My old neighborhood, which had long since been deserted by everyone but me. When we got there, she was struggling, screaming against me, but I held on.

"Stop," I said, trying to get through to her, past whatever insanity was going on in her head. "Just stop."

Soon her screams died down, and she stopped struggling, instead resting her head on my shoulder. Sobs shuddered through her thin body, and she just kept repeating, "It won't stop, it won't stop, it won't stop."

"Nether," I said softly. I patted her shoulder awkwardly. I didn't even want to think about how stupid I was being. My parents were right. I was soft. I should have been trying to kill her while she was off-balance and distracted. It really would have been my best chance at destroying her, when she was like this. "What won't stop?"

"All the noise. The noise. The noise never ends and it hurts, my Prison. It hurts," she whispered, as if even her own voice was too loud for her to bear.

I lowered my voice to a whisper as well. "Nether. It's quiet here," I said, "listen. No one lives around here. No traffic. That's why I liked living here so much." She covered her ears and shook her head manically. She slumped down to the ground.

"Too much. Too much," she said, and I looked around. I sensed for her, and the biggest thing I felt was fear. Confusion. "I should be killing you now," she whispered, rocking back and forth, holding her knees. "You so deserve to be punished, my Prison," she said.

"Yes, well," I said. "Tomorrow's another day, right?"

"It's too much. Tomorrow is a nightmare," she answered, still rocking back and forth. I focused on her emotions. In addition to the fear and confusion, she seemed to be in genuine pain.

"Nether, what's hurting you?" I asked, focusing on keeping my voice low and calm.

"Everything," she answered.

We sat in silence for a long time, and she rocked back and forth in that manic way the entire time, eyes nearly glassed over. The whole time, I was debating whether I should be trying to kill her or not.

"Aren't we supposed to be fighting?" I finally said.

She didn't answer.

I couldn't take it anymore. I knew damn well there was not a chance in hell I was going to try to attack her when she was down, and that irritated me. My parents would have a field day with this. And I knew that the choice not to try to kill her would come back to bite me in the ass eventually.

I stood up and unfolded my wings.

"Freedom is a nightmare," she murmured, so low I barely heard her.

"It can be," I agreed.

"I was not created for this." Then she looked up at me, finally focusing. "If you're not going to fight me, then leave. I have no desire to spend quality time with Nyx's little tool."

"Nyx's tool, huh?" I asked. Maybe I'd get a fight out of this yet.

"Traveling the path set for you by Nyx like a good little soldier," she said, voice still low.

"I was on this path long before I ever knew about Nyx," I said. "The only path I'm on is the one I chose for myself."

She smiled then. "Believe what you must, then. But know that I have dwelled in your soul, and I have seen you as no one else has. You try to be light. You try to be a savior. Inside, you are just as dark and damaged as I am. You surround yourself with beings who have betrayed you over and over again. Your parents. Your mate. Your former mate," she sneered. "You hold them so close, yet every single one has proven themselves unworthy."

I didn't answer.

"You are weak, Fury," she said. "And one day, you will learn to be strong."

I snorted then. Honestly, I can only be expected to take so much bullshit. "Yeah. Strong like you. You forget that just as you think you know me, I shared soulspace with you as well. All I felt from you, ever, was hatred and fear, Nether."

I rose into the air. She made no move to get up, and had gone back to her hypnotic rocking.

I started to fly toward home, and I heard her parting words to me: "Hatred makes me strong."

CHAPTER NINE

On Saturday, I spent the day trying to figure out how to put together Zoe's new crib and trying to soothe both her and Sean at the same time, since Brennan and Nain were out patrolling with Heph and my father, trying to get a read on where Hyperion might be. By late afternoon, both of the kids were exhausted, and I passed out on the living room couch, which was where Nain found me when he walked in that evening.

He pointed me toward my bed and told me he'd wake me up at nightfall so I could go sit with Shanti, and I was happy to take him up on that.

Kids are completely exhausting. Tiring in a way I never would have imagined. It seemed like Sean was always on the verge of hurting himself somehow, and when Zoe wasn't eating or crying, she was pooping or just generally fussing.

I fell asleep again for what felt like seconds, and then Nain was gently shaking my hip, his lips at the back of my neck.

"I cannot do this," I muttered into my pillow.

"Can't do what?" he asked, pulling me into his arms.

"This kid thing. I am so clueless. Fighting is so much simpler. See the bad guy, smash the bad guy. I have no idea what to do for her, other than keep trying things until she stops crying."

Nain nuzzled my neck. "You're doing a good job with her, baby. She's calmer for you than she is for the rest of us. But if you want, we can find somewhere else for her to stay."

I shook my head. The thought hadn't even crossed my mind. "She's ours. I'm just feeling whiny and inadequate."

"Those are two words I'd never associate with you," he said. I closed my eyes and let myself be comforted by my mate. He was so good that way. There weren't a lot of sweet, flowery speeches from Nain. He never tried to butter me up or stroke my ego. Straightforward words and physical contact. He knew how it comforted me when he touched me. I was thankful, for about the fiftieth time that day, that I had him back.

"You're a pretty good husband," I said, patting his arm so I could get up.

He gave me one more squeeze and kissed the side of my neck before releasing me. "I try. Later, I'll try *harder*," he added, and I laughed.

"Horny demon."

He gave me a grin before heading out of the room so I could get myself cleaned up and ready to go to Rayna's.

A few minutes later, I kissed both Nain and Zoe and headed out to the vampires' house. I flew, hoping to clear the last of the grogginess from my brain.

It wasn't hard to spot the sprawling French Tudor with its wrought-iron fence and gate. The grounds were lit by even more floodlights than they'd had at the old house, a testament to how often they'd been attacked in recent weeks. I landed just inside the gate and raised my hands in a placating gesture to the two armed vampire guards who came rushing off of the porch.

"I'm the Angel. Rayna and Ronan are expecting me," I said.

At that moment, the front door opened and one of the vampires I recognized from before, Sam, came walking out. I didn't really understand the intricacies of the family but from what Shanti had said, Sam was in charge of helping rehabilitate vampires after they'd been turned. He helped them deal with their new lives, their new senses. Their new cravings.

I guessed he'd be spending quite a bit of time with Zero after this.

He strolled down the front stairs and held his hand out to me after he had waved the guards away. I smiled at him in greeting.

If my vampires weren't so loyal, I'd kind of hate them. Every single member of Rayna's family, including Shanti and, soon, Zero, was so damn gorgeous it was almost impossible not to stare. And they only seemed to become more beautiful after being turned. Sam, with his dark wavy hair and smoldering smoke-gray eyes, could have been on the cover of any romance novel on the planet.

"How are things?" I asked Sam as he gestured toward the porch.

He shrugged as we started walking. "We're managing. We're grateful to you and Brennan for sending the shifters to guard things during the day. It has helped."

I nodded. I could hardly take credit for that at all. That was mostly Bren's doing. It was weird to me, watching how quickly he'd established himself as not just the guy who coordinated the packs, but as kind of the ultimate alpha. When the alphas of other packs listened to him, when they did as he ordered... that said something about the kind of shifter Bren was. So when he'd told them to send some of their best to guard Rayna's home during the day, they'd done it, and gladly, all wanting to be on his good side.

I scrunched my face, thinking. Why hadn't I seen any

of this when we'd been together? Had I really been so blind that I'd been unable to recognize what everyone else seemed to see in him?

Well. I'd been blind to other things, too, right? I pushed it out of my head as I followed Sam into the house. I took careful note of the hallways and rooms we passed through, so that, if I had to, if they needed me, I could rematerialize here someday. I can't do that unless I have a good sense of a place. Heph can do it from a photo or a video, and, sometimes, even from a verbal description if it's good enough. I'm not there yet.

Sam led me into what looked to be a family room or den. There was a large stone fireplace at one end of the room, and on the two sofas near it, Rayna, Ronan, Shanti, and Zero sat. When they noted my presence, they rose, and, to my discomfort, gave me the salute my imps so often did: hand thumped to the chest, head bowed.

"Hey," I said. Shanti came up to me and gave me a hug, and I squeezed her tight, sensing her overwhelming nervousness. Ronan shook my hand warmly, and Rayna leaned in for a quick hug. Then I looked at Zero.

Shanti had excellent taste. Good lord, the man was drool-worthy. Skin like light caramel, eyes that looked gold in the right light. He stood protectively near Shanti, and regarded me with a serious gaze.

"Zero," I said to him. "Nice to see you again."

"Likewise, Angel," he said.

"We're kind of family or whatever this is. You can call me Molly," I said, and he gave a small smile and nodded.

Ronan spoke up. "Thanks for your help with the day guards, Molly. We would have perished eventually if not for that."

I looked up at the huge vampire. Serious, straight-laced. He and Brennan had seemed to become friends over the past weeks, and I could understand why. They were opposites in many ways, similar in others. "That was mostly Brennan's doing," I said.

"He had to get your approval to do it," he said, and, after a moment, I nodded. It was true. He ran just about everything by me, even when I told him he didn't have to.

"I'm glad it's helping," I said. "We'll deal with the vampires and their people."

"I know there's a lot going on for you. The help you've given us already is more than enough," Rayna said. "Is there anything we can do to help you?"

That's just like my vampires. Getting attacked left and right, and asking what they can do for me. To think I used to hate vampires.

I shook my head. "It's all stuff I have to deal with."

Ronan transferred his gaze to Zero. "Ready, man?" he asked.

Zero took a deep breath. "I am. But, can we have a minute before we do this?"

"Sure. Head in. When Shanti comes back out, we'll begin," Ronan said.

Zero nodded his thanks and held his hand out for Shanti. Her nervousness for her lover was making my stomach twist. She put her hand in his, and they headed up the stairs, which is where I guessed Zero would be turned. I watched them go, hoping all would go well.

My girl was a wreck. It kind of pissed me off that there was no one to hit.

I hated that.

I turned back to Rayna. "So, how does it work?" I asked her.

She gestured for me to take a seat, and I did. Ronan sat next to me on the sofa, and Rayna took a chair nearby. "He chose Ronan to turn him, so Ronan will be in there with him, along with Sam," Rayna began. "Ronan will begin by draining most of his blood. Not all. If it goes that far, then he's dead."

"Drained," I said, and she nodded.

"So he'll drink most of Zero's blood. Just before Zero's heart stops, Ronan will slice his own wrist, and feed his blood to Zero. It won't take much. A few sips, and soon, Zero will begin regenerating his own blood. Except that, then, it will be imbued with our powers."

"How long does that take?" I asked, trying not to be squicked out by the whole thing.

"The actual feeding takes mere minutes," Ronan said. "The metastasis takes several hours. And there is always the chance that his body will reject the feeding."

"And if that happens?" I asked, not really wanting to hear what I knew he'd say.

"Then he dies."

"Is that common?"

He shook his head. "Especially not when the new vampire is young and healthy. And Zero is a strong son of a bitch. I'm sure he'll be fine."

I let out a breath. "Okay. So what is Sam in there for?"

"When he wakes," Rayna said, "he'll be starving. The remotest scent of mortal flesh will drive him insane with hunger. Sam will be there to help Ronan hold him back and to provide him with some of the blood we keep on hand for new vampires." She transferred her gaze to her brother. "We will have to air the house out well. If he smells her," she said, glancing at me, "It will drive him nuts."

"She smells good," Ronan agreed with a nod.

"Ugh, vampires," I muttered, and they both laughed.

Shanti walked into the room, and we all sobered. Her eyes were tinged in pink, her hands were shaking, and she looked more like the lost teenager I'd first met than I could bear. I stood up and folded her into my arms. She held me tight.

"It's gonna be fine," I said, glaring at Ronan over her head. It better fucking be fine, I thought, sure he got the message by the look in my eyes.

"He'll be fine, Shanti," Ronan said, looking coolly back at me. "He's strong. He's motivated to do this, and he's not afraid."

"He's an idiot," Shanti said, her voice muffled against my shoulder, and I had to smile. I patted her on the back.

"A few hours, then?" I asked Ronan, and he nodded.

He reached out and gave Shanti's hand a squeeze. "I'll take care of him. I swear it," he told her, and I liked the vampire even more in that moment.

Shanti nodded, and he left, going up the stairs Shanti and Zero had taken earlier. Rayna excused herself to deal with one of the vampires who'd been caught attacking the previous night. That left me and Shanti standing awkwardly in the den.

"Well, we may as well take a load off or something. Ronan said it'll be a while," I said.

Shanti clasped her hands in front of her. "Um. Can we fight instead? I can't just sit here and wait to find out if he's dead or not."

"He's not gonna die. If he does, I'll kill Ronan myself," I said. "But, yeah, we can fight."

Shanti nodded and led me through the house. I wondered if Rayna had a decorator somewhere on staff as well. The house was freaking perfect, and they'd barely had time to get settled. Meanwhile, I had the feeling our apartment would be sporting the cardboard box look for quite some time.

Shanti led me down some stairs.

"I know how much you hate basements. Sorry," Shanti said.

"It's fine," I said. "Do you guys sleep down here, too?"

She nodded. "At the other house, all of the rooms were reinforced so we could sleep in them. Here, we haven't had time to do that yet."

We reached the bottom step, and I took a look around. The main part of the basement was open, and there was a punching bag in one corner. Along both ends of the basement, there were doors, which I guessed led to the private sleeping quarters for each vampire.

"Must be dinky rooms," I said, and she nodded.

"It's like sleeping in a closet. But it's not like we notice that, once day breaks, so..." She shrugged. "Once things settle down, Rayna said she can work on having the upstairs rooms reinforced like the old ones."

"Hopefully it won't come to that, and you guys can move back soon."

"Hey," Shanti said. "Knock it off, Molly."

"Knock what off?"

"Blaming yourself for everything. We'll move back, or we won't. It doesn't matter."

I looked away. "Pretty much everyone thinks I went easy on her when I faced her downtown," I said.

"Did you?"

I threw my hands up in exasperation and started to pace. "Have you ever known me to go easy in a fight?"

"When you feel kinda sorry for the person, yeah."

I glared at her. "Now you sound like my mother. 'There's no room for pity in the life of a Fury,' I intoned in a terrible imitation of Tisiphone.

"You didn't answer the question."

"No. I wasn't going easy on her. She was throwing me around, bashing my head against the side of the building, and I could barely even muster the strength to try to shove her away. She's ridiculously fucking strong, Shanti."

"Is she stronger than you?" she asked quietly.

I looked down, irritated, mostly with myself. After a moment, I nodded. I hated admitting it to her. I knew Shanti would worry about me.

She was silent for a moment. "Can you use your mindflaying stuff on her?" she finally asked.

"I'm not sure," I answered. "I didn't try." I kept to myself that I felt filthy every time I used that ability. Wrong. I also didn't tell her about how broken Nether was, and that I had probably had the chance to take her out and blew it. I waved it off. "I'm supposed to be distracting you by kicking your ass, not giving you more to worry about."

She let out an irritated breath. "Oh my god, Molly," she muttered.

"What?"

"Give me shit to worry about, okay? Don't shut people out thinking you're protecting them, because that's absolute bull crap. Any of us; me, Brennan, Nain, any of us would give our last breath fighting by your side. And we'd be proud to do it. All right? So don't do this whole lone hero thing, because that's stupid. It's what you had to do once upon a time. It's not the way it is anymore."

I shook my head, touched by her words, hating the idea that any of them would ever die by my side. "It's not that. It's just that I know I'm way more badass than the rest of you, so..." I shrugged.

She rolled her eyes. "All right. Let's go then, badass."

I laughed, and we started circling one another. When Shanti struck out, I barely ducked in time.

"Getting slow and soft, chica," Shanti said, and I took the opportunity to kick out at her. Which she dodged.

It went on like that for who knows how long, the two of us circling, jabbing, kicking. Every once in a while, we'd each land a hit, and I was impressed by how strong she'd gotten, how disciplined she was as a fighter. I was still all smash. She actually strategized.

I'd have to try that some time.

All I knew was that however long it took, I was eventually sweating and panting. Bruises had bloomed on my thighs, stomach, and arms, and had since healed. She didn't look tired at all. Brat.

We kept sparring, the only sound in the basement my breath, and the occasional "oof" as one of us landed a punch or kick. After a while, Shanti called time out, and I nodded and backed up, wiping sweat from my face. She went to a small refrigerator nearby, took out a bottle of water and tossed it to me.

"Thanks."

"Sure," she said. She rooted around for a moment

more, and brought out a small bottle of blood for herself. Synthetic. Rayna owned a company that made that, too.

I looked away as she drank. Yes, one of the people I love most in the world is a vampire. Yes, some of my closest friends and allies are vampires. Doesn't mean the whole blood-drinking thing isn't totally disgusting.

"So what's this stuff E's telling me about you adopting a baby?" she asked after a moment, as she tossed her empty bottle in the trash.

"We did. Well. Her pack wouldn't take her in. Her mother are dead. So I brought her home."

"Why do I feel like there's more to the story than that?"

I sat on the basement floor, leaning my back against one of the concrete block walls. She settled in next to me. "Because there is, I guess," I said.

I filled her in on everything. How I'd found Zoe, her pack's reaction, Nain and Bren's reaction when I brought her home.

Her brow furrowed as she listened. "So, this demon shifter thing, then?" she finally asked.

I nodded. "Yeah. Nain isn't happy about that. He's making this work, because I want it so badly."

"I can see where he's coming from, though," Shanti said. "And before you get pissed at me, I think you did the right thing, okay?"

I nodded.

"But I see his side of it, too. She loses her mind someday, and she goes nuts and starts hurting people. Who's gonna have to take her down if that happens?"

She left the question hanging. There was no need for an answer, because we both knew whose job it would be.

"You think you can destroy someone you love?" she asked, more gently.

"I know," I said, rubbing the back of my neck. "And I get it. But that doesn't change the fact that she needs us and I already love her."

"I know. It's how you are." We sat in silence for a bit. "Maybe it won't happen the way they think," she added.

"Maybe," I said. "I'll figure something out."

"Can you take her out if it happens? Could you let Nain do it, and still love him afterward?"

"That's not something we'll have to worry about for a while," I said, not wanting to think about it. "I'll figure something out."

She didn't respond, and we let the matter drop. We went upstairs again and sat in the den, watching the flames in the fireplace, sitting mostly in silence. I called once to check in with Nain, and he filled me in on the meeting he'd just had with some of the shifters at our house.

"How's she doing?" he asked.

"Okay. This is stressful. I can't believe how well she's handling it," I said, knowing Shanti would hear me.

"I'd be out of my mind if it was you," he said, voice low.

I closed my eyes. Remembering what it had been like, losing him. The fear of that ever happening again was almost more than I could take. "Same here," I finally said.

"Zoe's asleep," he said, changing the subject, both of us clearly not wanting to take that particular trip down memory lane. "She woke up right after you left, and she wasn't happy. She was fussing a lot for E, and even Brennan was kind of lost. He took over for E after a while while I was talking to the shifters."

"So what finally worked?" I asked.

"I picked her up and started walking her back and forth. She likes walking," he said.

I smiled. "I think she likes you. That whole demon thing."

"Maybe."

"I like you too," I said.

"Just like, huh?"

"Eh. Maybe more."

He laughed, and the sound of it had my heart skipping.

129

"How much longer?"

"Shouldn't be much longer," I said. "Really, we're waiting for him to wake up now. As soon as he does, they told me I have to leave because of the whole delicious immortal blood thing."

"Make sure you do, then. I don't want to have to kick Zero's ass for freaking you out."

The man knew me. That's all there was to it. I could pretend to be okay with vampires. I could pretend I didn't still have nightmares about being nearly drained. I could love Shanti as much as I'd loved just about anyone, and he still knew that, at heart, I was freaked the hell out by vampires.

"I will," I said. "I don't want to add to the stress."

We talked a bit more, and then I hung up. Shanti stood up and started pacing. "What the hell is taking so long?" she finally asked. "I should go up there..."

"No, you shouldn't," I said. "Ronan said to stay put."

She gave a growl of irritation, then kept pacing.

When we heard steps on the staircase a few minutes later, we both stood up. Shanti clasped her hands. Ronan entered the room and took her hand.

"It's done. He's feeding now. Come on," he said to Shanti. Then he looked at me. "Time for you to go. He can smell you already."

I nodded, hugged Shanti.

"Thanks, Molly. I'll call you as soon as I can," she said, hugging me hard.

"Anytime."

I walked myself out, then focused and rose into the sky, toward our rental house.

I checked on Zoe, and walked into our room to find Nain already stretched out on the bed, chest bared, and, I could just imagine, bare elsewhere under the white sheet. I stripped, knowing he was watching me. By the time I crawled into bed beside him, the hunger coming from him had my heart pounding, my stomach clenching.

As soon I was beside him, he pulled me on top of him, holding me tight.

"Eager, huh demon?" I said as I lay kisses across his chest and collarbone. He pressed his hips up, just a little, making it even more obvious than it already was what I was doing to him. I laughed and kept kissing him.

"Molls," he said, his voice hoarse.

I sat up so I was straddling his waist. "What?"

"Considering this is me, I've been really patient about this shit. You need to tell me, though: what happened with Nether? What haven't you told me?"

I just looked at him. I'd really hoped he had put the whole Nether thing behind him. We'd gone days without talking about her, and I was more than happy to keep it that way.

"I don't want to do this now," I said, waving him off.

"You're keeping shit from me. We said we weren't gonna do that," he said, voice low. Being reasonable. I hate that. "There's something keeping you from trying to go after her. Maybe you feel sorry for her, and I'm not going to argue about that with you. You decide how you want to handle her. But I've been sitting here tonight thinking, and I realized something. You're afraid of her. I've never seen you afraid of anyone. Not like this. And it's more than just the beating she gave you, because you've been beat up before and it usually just makes you pissed off. I didn't realize that until I stopped to think about it."

I closed my eyes. Remembering. It wasn't the beating. He was right about that. The thing that really scared me about Nether was what she'd tried, what she'd come so close to doing.

I took a deep breath. "She tried to take my powers. Don't freak out," I added, feeling his anxiety level rise immediately.

He made an effort to calm down.

"Thanks," I murmured. "She started to try to use the mindflaying powers she absorbed from me. I never knew what it felt like to be on the other end of them." I swallowed as I felt my stomach turning at the memory. A shiver went through my body.

"What does it feel like?" Nain asked, holding me tighter.

"Like you're drowning, and no matter how hard you try to surface, you can't. You're at the mercy of everything around you. Powerless."

"She stopped."

"Yeah."

"Why?"

I lifted my shoulder in a shrug. "I don't even think she knows why she stopped. She was almost there."

"Maybe it's for the same reason you don't seem all that keen on hurting her."

"Maybe. I didn't know it felt like that," I said, still thinking about my mindflaying ability. So many times, I'd been on the other side, I'd been the one with the power, and I'd never bothered to wonder what it felt like. "I don't want to use that any more," I said, closing my eyes, as if doing such a simple thing would shake free the memory of what it felt like.

"But you will if you have to."

"If I have to. I don't have to, though. It was a lazy fallback."

"What about when you face Nether again? When it comes down to a fight, because you know damn well it's going to come to that?" he asked, and I shoved his body away from mine.

"No. No. Never again. I didn't know'"

He stood up, raked his hands through his hair. "Baby, what did you expect? That when you mess someone up, when you drain them, when you burn them to a crisp, that it fucking feels good?"

"Don't take that tone with me," I said. I stood up and walked toward the bathroom that was connected to our room.

"What tone? The tone where I remind you that your enemies aren't fucking around and you can't either?"

"Do you think I'm stupid? I know that," I said, completely irritated by that point. "She's broken, Nain. You should have seen her this morning'"

"What happened after you got her off the freeway?"

"I took her to my old neighborhood to get her away. She's a mess. She was out of it, and it was probably the perfect chance for me to kill her, and I couldn't. I couldn't goddamn do it," I said, irritated with myself, and with him for making me think about it.

"This isn't the time to become a pacifist, Molls."

"My god, you are such an asshole sometimes," I muttered.

"Sometimes? Sometimes? You know me better than anyone else. You know damn well I'm an asshole all the time."

I bit back a laugh.

"You are an asshole," I said, watching him as he walked around the bed toward me. It was enough to make my knees weak, all of that naked maleness closing in on me, his muscles bunching with each movement, his eyes on me, always on me. He pulled me into his arms, bent his head and claimed my lips.

"I know I am," he said, kissing me again. "And I love you. Everything else can end right now, but losing you is not an option. You promised me forever, remember?"

"Christ. What in the hell ever made me do something like that?" I asked, though my sarcasm was somewhat tempered by the gasp I let out when his teeth grazed the sensitive skin at the side of my neck.

"I wonder," he murmured. He leaned his head down, rested his forehead against mine. "If it's them or you, you always make sure you're the one walking away alive.

Always. You can feel guilty later if you really need to."

"You old men are very bossy," I said.

He picked me up, pressing my back against the wall. He hooked his forearms under my knees and held me there, helpless.

"Very bossy," he said. "And we tend to know exactly what we want."

He entered me, slowly, stretching me, filling me, and, just like every time we were together, I was amazed I could take all of him. I knew what was coming. He had that look in his eye. I'd scared him with that news about Nether and the mindflaying thing, made him face the prospect of losing me again. Because if she ever did manage to strip me of my powers, I was a goner. She wasn't the only danger out there, and there were more than a few beings who would love to see me powerless.

He needed to reassure himself that I was here, I was his, and we were together. I needed it, too.

"What are you waiting for, demon?" I asked, my voice already hoarse with need. "You know what I need."

He thrust into me again, hard, deep, and I cried out.

"Now who's the bossy one?" he growled. Oh, hell, yeah. His eyes were glowing, his muscles bunching as he tried to hold on to control. He'd lose it soon.

I ran my fingertips over his shoulders, gently scraping his flesh with my fingernails. Then I leaned forward and started kissing his neck.

I sucked his earlobe between my lips, sucked and nibbled it, gently, and his hips started moving faster. Harder. He pushed my thighs open as wide as they could go, trying, always trying to be as deep in me as he possibly could.

"Good thing you're so flexible," he growled.

I couldn't answer. He was seated all the way inside me, pressing me hard up against the wall, and every grind of his hips sent waves of pleasure through me. I knew, too, that he was making damn sure to stay in close contact with me, trying to give me as much strength as he could. He was protecting me in his own way as he loved me. I was feeding from him, taking strength, but when he was like this, when his power was swirling around us and his eyes were glowing and his heart was pounding, he had more than enough for both of us.

He was doing it again, claiming ownership, taking what he needed from me, and damn if it wasn't everything I needed.

"I need to be under you," I whispered. He carried me to the bed, lay me down and settled himself between my thighs again.

Gods. Having his cool, heavy weight pressing me into the mattress was one of the best sensations in existence.

When he entered me, slowly, agonizingly so, after the way he'd already brought me to the edge of ecstasy, I was reminded of what one of the other best sensations is.

Nain held me, his body crushing me. He's not a polite lover, and he knows that's what I want. I want him crushing me, making me feel every single bit of him.

I want him out of control for me.

I smiled to myself as he leaned down for another kiss, his hips still pistoning hard, the pressure inside me rising so fast, so hard I was nearly dizzy with it.

But I wanted more. He'd never just do it, but I knew my husband needed to let off more than a bit of steam. He was on edge. Holding on to control, barely. The closer he got to losing control, the harder he took me, and the more excited it made me.

More, I thought.

I kissed and licked his chest, his throat, nibbling my way to the side of his neck, to that place I love where his neck meets the hard muscles of his shoulders.

I bit, hard, and I felt his desire go through the roof.

"Fuck," he growled. The next thing I knew, I was face-down on the bed and he was behind me, the coarse hair on his legs tickling the backs of my thighs as he spread me.

"This what you wanted, Molly?" he asked as he entered me again, hard, deep.

"Yes," I cried, nearly breathless with the sensations running through my body. He held my hips in his big hands. That was all he needed, my permission to lose control, and he did. He started hammering into me from behind, filling me, and every thrust had me smothering screams of pleasure into my pillow. He pulled the pillow away, threw it aside.

"I want to hear you moan my name," he growled. And I did, crying out as I went over the edge. Soon, I was pressed flat to the bed again, trapped between his huge, hard body and the mattress, and he was out of his mind, thrusting into me, growling, his hands on my breasts, squeezing, pinching as he took me.

I cried out, muffling my screams against the mattress as I came, hard, and he kept going. I grabbed, desperately finding something to hold onto. I gripped the edge of our mattress as another wave of pleasure tore through me, everything in me clenching, everything I was belonging to him. His thoughts had taken on that tone, that more animalistic feel that he has when he's full demon. I could see from his hands (which were now gripping my upper arms, holding me right where he wanted me) that he'd let his demon loose completely. I knew it the second he flipped me over. He was bulkier, his body temperature even colder than usual, his thoughts full of animalistic lust.

Nain pressed into me, and I cried out, losing control again, and he ground against me and I felt his release. He shook with it, grinding himself harder and harder into my body, until, finally, he came back down.

He slumped, laying the full weight of his body on top of mine, still joined with me, my legs and wings spread wide to accommodate him as he pressed me into the mattress. I was still on my stomach, and I turned my face to the side. He rested his face against the side of my neck, and I nuzzled him, and he rubbed his face against mine.

I started dozing off, exhausted and aching from his attentions. Also, feeling more peaceful than I'd felt in a long time. Yeah, all of my problems were still out there, waiting for me. But this... what I had with Nain was hard to explain to anyone other than us. The way he loved me exactly the way I needed him to, the way I fed from him, his energy sustaining and strengthening me, his lust and rage giving me that little extra lift.

He was exhausting. And I wouldn't have it any other way.

"Do you want me to let you up?" he asked drowsily, his voice hoarse.

I practically purred beneath him. "No, don't go anywhere. I love this."

He nuzzled the side of my neck again, kissed a trail down to my shoulder. "I didn't intend to lose it like that," he said accusingly.

"I know," I said, gasping when he nipped the sensitive flesh at the side of my neck, almost exactly where I'd bitten him earlier. "But you needed it, and so did I."

He ran his hand up my body, trailing his fingertips from my shoulders, down my arms, and, finally, to my hands, where I still gripped the edge of our mattress. He twined his fingers with mine, and I looked at the matching bands on our left hands, shining just a little in the dark bedroom.

"I love you," he said, that low rumble.

I smiled sleepily. "I love you more."

"Not even possible, woman." He paused. "Don't keep shit from me anymore, baby. You need to know that I'm here, forever, no matter what. I'm not going anywhere unless you kick my ass out. I'm yours. We can fight. We can disagree. We can get pissed off at each other. You'll probably get pissed off a lot more at me than I do at you," he amended, and I smiled. "It doesn't matter. There isn't a thing in this world or any other that will make me love you less. I love you more every second. Whatever's going on with Nether, I trust your judgment. You know her better than anyone else. Just don't let her kill you. If it comes to that, promise me you'll end her first."

"I promise," I said.

I brought his hand to my mouth, kissed his knuckles, and dozed off, comforted in the way that only my mate knows how to comfort me. When Zoe started crying a while later, I started to get up. Nain kissed my shoulder and told me to go back to sleep. When he came back to bed, he loved me again, slowly, tenderly, whispering his love for me, kisses and caresses branding it across my flesh. We went over the edge together, and I knew, as much as I know anything, that I would never, ever have enough of him.

CHAPTER TEN

I waited outside the Netherwoods for my father. We were supposed to be patrolling together, looking for Nether or Hyperion or whoever the hell else we could find. He was still annoyed that I wouldn't set foot in the Nether, but I stuck to my guns, waiting just outside the tree line until he made an appearance.

"Really, Mollis, it's ridiculous," he said as soon as he came into view. "It's a place. Nothing more."

"Right. That's why you all gravitated to it like moths to a flame," I said.

He gave me an irritated scowl.

"And it's not the same, because Nether isn't there powering it," I added.

We rose into the air. "No, it's not the same," Hades said as we took off. "But it's close enough. It looks right. It even smells the same."

"And what are you doing about the souls?" Family business: people die, crows bring their souls to my dad, my dad passes judgment on how much and what type of punishment they need, then my mom and aunt make it happen. In the original Nether, the souls as well as anyone else my family had been punishing (usually demons) had resided in the Pit, and the worst of the worst had spent eternity in Tartarus. Both places had been powered by Nether (the being's) energy. Though from what Gaia had said, there was some sentient energy powering them too, which was why we had a new Nether. Life found a way.

"It's not perfect," he admitted. "West?" he asked and I nodded. We both tilted, turning that way. "Right now, we're using demons and the few Netherhounds I've managed to track down. I fear we've lost most of them, though."

"They stayed in the Nether, you mean?"

Hades nodded. "Right now it's working well enough. We'll have to figure out something eventually, but for now we're making our way through the backlog of souls that accumulated after Nyx destroyed the gateway."

"Do the souls generally give you much trouble? Do they try to escape and shit like that?" I asked.

He shrugged. "At first, they do. Once your mother and aunt start on them, they lose the will to even bother."

"Where are you guys staying? It's just forest, right?"

He gave me a look. "There is a palace. My presence there makes it so." I thought about that. I remembered his palace in the original Nether. He could change it at will, suiting his (and, usually, Persephone's) whims. "I am enjoying refining it, and your mother has excellent taste."

We flew in silence for a while, and I caught him watching me. "What?" I asked.

"You know you can always join the family business, Mollis. I know you feel at odds here."

"Mom has a big mouth," I muttered.

"And why do I have less right to know that than your mother does?" he asked, irritation tinging his emotions.

"You don't. She doesn't either. I didn't tell her that."

"So she felt it, which means it's true," he said. "And you really need to get over being annoyed that you're not the only one who can read emotions now. Why do you have to be so closed off to everyone all the time?"

"I don't know, Dad. Why do *you* have to be so closed off all the time?" I shot back, glaring at him.

He didn't answer, and we flew on in silence, both of us trying to sense for any indication that Hyperion or Nether was around.

"My reasons are likely different from yours," Hades finally said.

"Right. Remember that I'm one of the few who can read your emotions, Dad. And as much as I hate to admit it, I'm just as black and withered inside as you are."

"Not as much as me. Give yourself a few thousand years and then we'll talk."

I shook my head, turned to look at him again. "How does it work?"

"How does what work?"

"How do you do the judging thing?"

He took a breath. "You've worked by your mother's side as a Fury. What is it like for you?"

"Mom would tell me what the person had done, and any instructions you'd given. And then the soul would come into the room, and I'd break into its mind. After a little work, I could see what they'd done. And more importantly, I could see what they feared, and that was what I used to punish them with."

He nodded. "It took work to see their crimes, though."

"Yeah. I had to break into their minds," I said.

"For me, I can't not see those things. I look at someone – mortal, immortal, shifter, whatever – and I see, in an instant, every single sin they've ever committed. I see everything."

"Ugh," I said, and he gave a snort of a laugh. "I mean, I feel dirty seeing some of the things I see. I can't imagine having to see it all the time." And then a thought struck me. "Wait. So you knew what Brennan was hiding from me."

He gave me a dark look. "My abilities are for the dead.

I have no interest in interfering with the living."

"But you saw. That first day, when you showed up at the loft and bargained with me to have Asclepias save him... you knew that he was working for the government."

He shrugged.

I have never even considered lifting a hand in anger to my father (because that would be stupid, mostly) but I was seriously thinking about it then. "I'm your daughter. Do you know how much heartbreak you could have saved me?"

"Again, because you don't seem to get it: I have no interest in interfering in the day-to-day drama of the living, whether it's my child or not. I deal with enough dead assholes, I don't need to start poking my nose into the lives of the living. But in case it wasn't clear: I never especially cared for the shifter. Not for you, because he's not worthy. All right?"

I watched him. "So if I ask you if there's something Nain's hiding from me, or Brennan again, or E?"

He glared at me. "I will tell you what I've just told you twice already: I don't believe in affecting the lives of the living. I'm the Lord of the Dead. That's where my focus is."

"Yet here you are," I pointed out.

"Only because I like you, daughter."

I rolled my eyes, looked back down at the ground. This whole searching for Hyperion thing was starting to look like a lost cause. "Well, there's one way I'll never be like you, anyway," I said.

"Good," he answered. "The fact of the matter, Mollis, is that you'll always be lighter and better than me. I don't deny you take after me in more ways than I'd like. You are very much my daughter. But you have that streak of light that shines through everything else. Your mother has that. Don't lose it, because it's what makes you a hero and not a nightmare."

I didn't answer. I focused, sensed a power signature

nearby, to our right. Belle Isle. "Something big," I said to Hades, and he nodded. I gestured toward Belle Isle, banked in that direction, and he followed me. The nearer I got to the island, the more clearly I could feel him. Smug satisfaction was the predominant emotion, and I glanced at my dad.

"Um. This is probably a trap," I said. "He feels happy."

He shrugged. "I don't expect to lose to him today. Not when we're both there facing off against him."

I shook my head. He was somewhere in the more wooded area of the island. There were roads that led through the woods, and these were less well-travelled than the rest of the island. People usually preferred to drive along the edges so they'd get views of the Detroit River.

I was not a fan of this part of the island. I'd saved a girl who'd been held captive in the woods for weeks, when I first started out. It was one of my first cases. There were four girls I'd been too late for, and I'd found them in this area as well. That was what had convinced me to take my lost girl searches seriously. I'd gotten lucky a few times early on. Cocky. I'd let those four girls slip through my fingers, and by the time I'd made my way out to the woods, they'd been murdered. It was one of the things I'd never forgive myself for. It was the thing that had turned my searches into something I made the center of my life.

I thought their names as I came in for a landing.

Of course, there were good things about the island, too. The first time Nain really flirted with me, we'd been on the beach. Of course, that was also the same conversation in which he'd told me I was like the demonic equivalent of a vampire, a mindflayer. We had no idea until later that owning that particular power was my birthright, or that the other mindflayers there had been stories about had been none other than my mother and her sisters.

"So he's pretty armored up, from what Heph said," I said, forcing my mind to stop swirling. "Any tips?"

"Hit him hard," Hades said, and I shook my head.

"Be ready to dodge him. He probably wants to kill you more than he wants to fight with me," I told him.

"I don't need to 'dodge him,' Mollis," he muttered, and I ignored him as we landed in a small clearing in the woods. "Does the demon put up with that nonsense? With you telling him what to do?"

"Oddly enough, I never have to tell him what to do. My husband is smart enough to know better, and he doesn't have quite the amount of sexist bullshit going on that you do. He knows damn well I'm stronger than him, and it doesn't bother him in the least."

"Well, isn't he just all evolved and sensible," Hades sneered.

"Keep it up and I'm gonna leave you here for Hyperion to destroy," I told him. "Stop being such a prick."

"He's an Olympian. What else do you expect?" a deep, rich voice asked.

We watched as the Titan emerged from the trees in front of us.

He was... freaking huge. My dad is tall, and Hyperion towered over him. While the Olympians tend to look disgustingly perfect, from what I'd seen of the Titans, they were unique, not as human-looking. Hyperion was gold. Or, at least his skin shone with a metallic gold color, and his armor was gleaming gold as well. Huge shield that was about as tall as I was: gold. Same for the sword, which was not really all that long, but sported blades on both ends. Blazing yellow eyes glowed from a face that was actually quite handsome if you were able to get past the alien look of him. Straight nose, thin lips, strong chin.

"This is a good prize," he said, pacing a little, eyes on us. "The Lord of the Dead and his abomination."

"God, I am so sick of people calling me that," I muttered.

"Apollo's death will be avenged, Titan," my dad said, and Hyperion laughed.

"Ah, little gods. It took all of you, together, to capture

me. What hope do you have now? Pathetic pretenders. You've only seen the beginning of my plans for you." Then he laughed. "Of course, that's all the two of you will ever see. You forfeit your lives in coming here, your egos making you believe your minor powers stand a chance against the mighty Hyperion."

"God, I would have put him in Tartarus just for the fact that he never fucking stops talking," I said.

"Mollis, shut—" Hades began, just as Hyperion lunged at me and I barely got my sword arm up to block him.

Fuck, he was strong.

He drew back and struck again, and I tried to slice his shoulder, where there was just a small gap in his armor. He brought his shield up and blocked it easily, laughing.

I was aware of my dad circling around, getting ready to strike.

Hyperion noticed it, too, surprising both of us by lunging toward him, striking hard with his sword and catching Hades' thigh. My dad barely reacted, letting out a small grunt, then raising his hands and sending a blast of insane power at Hyperion, hitting him solidly in the chest. It knocked him back, but he sprung back up with a snarl and advanced on Hades again.

"Stay back," Hades growled at me. "He wants to fight, let's go." He gestured for Hyperion to come at him, and he laughed.

"You asked for this," Hyperion told him, and then he rushed at Hades, his sword moving so fast it was a blur, his shield clanging hard against Hades' head not once, but twice, and I winced, stood tense and ready, trying to decide how far to let Hades take this macho bullshit.

To his credit, he did hold his own against Hyperion. I realized I was used to just seeing my dad in his "lord of the dead" role. When he was in that role, he really didn't have to do more than look at someone in a certain way, whether the person was immortal or not, and he was obeyed.

Of course, I know better from experience. It takes a

whole lot of demonstrated punishment to get people to obey like that. I was just beginning to get that. And while it made me uncomfortable, it was preferable to having to kick ass all the time to get my way.

Yet here he was, fighting an obviously seasoned warrior, someone who could kill him, and he faced him with glee, ferocity in his face. He couldn't undo what Hyperion had done to my mother, but I could feel from him just how badly he wanted to give Hyperion some payback. And when he slashed out with the long black sword he'd drawn, and sliced across Hyperion's face, it took everything in me not to cheer. Hyperion howled in rage and the fight continued as blood dripped down his face and armor.

I stayed ready to jump, and soon enough, the moment came. Hades jumped back from a slash of Hyperion's blade, and he hit out with the shield. While Hades was ducking that, Hyperion stuck with the sword again, more quickly than seemed possible. I leapt at him, using all of my power to back me up, and knocked him back onto the ground. We rolled, shouting at one another. He had lost his shield in the impact, but he still held onto his sword. He grabbed my hair hard with one hand as we wrestled, and I bashed my head forward, heard that satisfying crunch of bone breaking.

I mean, it hurt me like hell, but still... I love that sound.

Hyperion shouted, cursed, tugged my hair harder, focused on drawing the sword up to my throat. I got my leg up and kicked his wrist, knocking the sword out of his grip.

"Ha!" I said, and he snarled, his face a mask of rage as he started shaking me, pulling my hair even harder. We rolled, wrestled further, and then he was springing up, surprising me with his speed again, and he leapt toward Hades, who had apparently been creeping up to get him off of me.

"Enough of the games, Olympian," Hyperion growled,

and his attacks against Hades came harder, more vicious. He had Hades down before I could even blink, and he was slashing toward him. I barreled into Hyperion again, and he swung wildly, missed me, then slashed out at me again.

He had one huge hand on my throat, squeezing hard. I tossed fire at him, and he roared in pain and squeezed harder.

Um. Okay. Someone having the upper hand when you're wrestling is never good. When that being is an enraged, humongous, fully-armored Titan, you start wondering if maybe getting into a fight wasn't one of your best ideas.

It was starting to get hard to breathe, and I was positive my throat was bruised. I bucked my body up, shot more fire, tried breaking into his mind.

Okay. Now where the fuck was my father?

I started feeling myself blacking out, tried rematerializing away.

"Oh, no you don't, Fury," Hyperion said, giving my neck another shake. "I am going to enjoy being able to tell all your sycophants that I took your life."

I wanted to laugh. Yeah, that's what I had. It would have been funnier if his face hadn't stated blurring in front of my eyes.

I feebly tried fire again. Apparently, no matter how supernatural you are, that whole "oxygen to the brain" thing is still important.

I tried twisting, trying to get a bit of relief from his grip on my throat. He was talking, snarling, and I couldn't make sense of any of it. No idea what language it was or if it was something that counted as a real language at all. I was able to turn my head just enough to see my father lying on the ground, knocked out cold.

Well, that was just perfect.

It felt like my eyes were going to explode. I clawed at his arm, but it was useless, my fingers just sliding off of the armor. Everything started going black.

At that moment, something knocked Hyperion off of me with such force that his fingers ended up ripping at the flesh of my throat, tearing deep gouges in the skin.

I didn't even care. I lay there, trying to suck in gulps of air, trying to get my head to stop spinning. My dad must have snapped out of it, I thought as I gulped for more air. I could feel the flesh of my throat knitting back together, but it was going slowly, since I was already weakened from having Hyperion choke the life out of me. I forced myself to sit up, and even that little motion had me feeling like I was going to puke my guts out. I gritted my teeth, swallowed hard, determined not to throw up on top of everything else. I glanced toward where my dad had been passed out. He was up now, but he was sitting, too.

So, clearly he hadn't knocked Hyperion off of me. I heard crashing and screaming in the sky above us.

I had to shake my head, close my eyes, sure my mind was messing with me.

Nether was fighting Hyperion in the sky, shooting that pure white energy she has, and her voice was clear, enraged.

"She is mine to kill, you Titan bastard!"

Well. Nice to be of value, I guess.

Hades stood up, made his way toward me, then pulled me up, not exactly gently. I gritted my teeth.

"Thanks. I didn't just almost have my head popped off by a Titan or anything," I said.

"You were supposed to be protecting me, I thought," he said, smirking, reminding me of my warnings before we'd started fighting Hyperion. We both looked up, watched the battle still raging above us.

"Should we, uh...do something?" I murmured.

Hades shrugged. "Maybe they'll kill each other and solve the problem for us."

"I kinda doubt it," I said.

It was mesmerizing. Hyperion (now wielding his sword again) slashing so fast it looked like he was on fast-forward, and Nether shooting those white blasts of energy at him, my flames. Hyperion's golden hair, which flowed down his back from beneath his helmet, was on fire, and it was enough of a distraction that Nether used it to her advantage, shot another force of energy at him, and Hyperion went tumbling through the sky above the treetops.

Nether was vicious. Holy shit.

She whipped Hyperion across the sky by his hair, threw more flames, keeping them concentrated on Hyperion's heavy armor.

Yeah. Fire plus metal. Not a great combination. Hyperion screamed in agony, and Nether kept tossing more flame at the armor, keeping a steady flame on the chest plate.

With a final scream of agony and rage, Hyperion disappeared with a "crack." Which meant he'd retreated to lick his wounds, but we'd be dealing with him again.

Nether landed in front of us, eyes on me. Her hair was still a mass of snarls, her clothing torn and filthy.

Hades went forward as if to confront her. Her gaze hardened, and I put my hand out, pulled Hades back.

I don't know why I did it. She was dangerous. She wanted to kill me. I knew that.

But I also knew that she wasn't right inside, and I wasn't interested in fighting with someone who had just saved my life.

Besides, I wasn't in any shape to fight. Not after the beating Hyperion had given me. And Nether had made Hyperion look like a lightweight.

"Thank you," I said softly, and Hades stared at me incredulously. "I know you only did it so you'll have your chance to kill me, but thank you."

Nether watched me, confusion written all over her face. "Another time, my Prison," she finally said. She gave me a short nod, confusion still flowing from her, and disappeared.

"Well, what the hell was that?" Hades demanded.

I took a deep breath and looked up at the sky. "I'm not strong enough to fight her right now," I tried to explain as we rose into the air. "Though I forget: you were knocked out cold while Hyperion was kicking my ass."

Embarrassment came from my father, then irritation. There was a shock. "I thought you said you had it," he said.

I didn't answer. I started flying toward the loft. My neck itched from healing. I wasn't bleeding anymore, and when I put a hand to my throat, the flesh there was no longer shredded. Of course, I had blood all down my shirt, but that was pretty much a daily occurrence. I just wasn't used to it being mine.

"You should have gone after her. You have this soft spot toward Nether, and I do not understand it, daughter." Hades was working himself up into a froth now. "Do you not remember her nearly killing your mother? How you had to give just about everything to save her? How that act led to Strife freeing her? How she used your body and powers…"

"All right," I snarled. "I remember all of that. All right? I remember. And considering that I was the one she was possessing, I don't think you have the right to be more pissed off than I am about it. Pull yourself together."

"You forget yourself far too often, Mollis. I am still the lord of the dead," he said.

I rolled my eyes. "Don't expect me to start kissing your ass anytime soon. You wouldn't expect it of my mother, so you sure as hell shouldn't expect it from me."

We flew in silence for several tense minutes. I was relieved when the neighborhood where we were renting came into sight.

"You're going soft on her, and I don't understand it," Hades said, making an effort, it seemed, to sound reasonable. "Like you said, she used you. Took control of you to hurt people you love. She's threatened you and everyone you have ever cared about. Yet whenever you have her in your sights, you don't go after her. It makes no sense."

"She's stronger than me," I said. "I need to plan something before I try to face her. On even ground, she'll wipe the floor with me."

I kept my gaze focused on the house. I couldn't wait to get there, away from crazy-ass immortals.

He wanted more of an answer, and I didn't have one to give him. He finally left with a "Good evening, then, Mollis," and blinked out of sight. I flew the rest of the way home in silence.

I couldn't give him the real reasons.

First: she was broken, and I don't hurt broken beings. It felt wrong.

Second: She was in no hurry to kill me. That much, I knew for sure.

And finally: I owed her my life. No matter what else she'd done afterwards, she'd saved my life when I was buried in the soil of the Nether. She'd given me enough power to free myself and get revenge on my enemies. And when I'd needed an extra jolt, she'd never held it back from me.

Despite all of the crazy, evil shit she'd done, I couldn't forget any of that.

I'd have to deal with her eventually. Just not right then. With a sigh of relief, I landed in the back yard of our rental house.

CHAPTER ELEVEN

For the next few days, life was fairly normal. It was the weekend before Thanksgiving, and, other than all of us being constantly tense, wondering when Hyperion or Nether would try to strike again, things weren't too bad. I spent a lot of time flying around looking for Hyperion. Nether seemed to have pulled a disappearing act. I checked for her at my old house twice after the Hyperion incident, and she wasn't there.

I didn't like it. I had hoped she'd stay put.

Nain and I got in late, both of us tired and annoyed after a fight against the final vampire cell that was opposing Rayna. Hopefully, this meant the vampires would be left alone for a while. I was looking forward to a hot shower, something to eat, and a warm bed with my husband in it.

The second we walked in the door, we were met with Brennan, pacing across the living room. It had been his babysitting shift, and a glance around showed both kids blissfully asleep.

He stopped pacing when he saw us. "Well, we heard from Hyperion," he said in greeting. "He said he's going to have a show for everyone during the Thanksgiving parade. He called it in to my personal line at work. And he called the DPD and the mayor, too."

I threw my hands up in irritation. "What the hell is even the point of that?" I asked.

"That's what I asked him. That guy is a major dickhead, by the way," he added.

"I noticed," I muttered.

"He said, and I quote, he has no reason to hide and is looking forward to spreading truth and making the mortals see the light."

"What an absolute asshole."

"He could be bluffing," Nain said. "Get everyone watching the parade, then attack somewhere else."

"Are we willing to risk that?" I asked, and he shook his head.

"Okay. I guess we're going to the parade, then," Brennan said.

"Ugh," I said in response. We spent the next couple of hours figuring out who to bring in for help and plotting our positions along the parade route. We talked to the local alphas of the shifter coalition. By the time we felt like we had a somewhat workable plan to protect all of the thousands of Normals at the parade, it was closing in on dawn.

I checked on Zoe one more time as Nain locked up behind Brennan, and then I pulled him into bed with me.

We spent the next few days coordinating with the feds and DPD, and working with the shifter coalition to plan our surveillance along the parade route. By the time Thanksgiving Day rolled around, we were all thoroughly sick of talking about it, and, from the emotions of my teammates, we were all significantly more freaked out about the whole thing. The big build-up, the planning, the wondering had us all more on edge. We were used to coming in and cleaning up. It was bizarre to have this much advance notice of possible trouble.

I had a sneaking suspicion that was part of Hyperion's game. That, and to get as many eyes as possible on the parade. There had been "leaks" to the media that a threat had been made for parade day, and it had been reported and debated almost nonstop on both local and national stations.

I spent the early part of Thanksgiving morning with Nain and Zoe, relaxing in our bed. An hour before parade time, we got up and dressed and dropped Zoe and Sean off with Gaia and Meaghan. Then Nain took my hand and we rematerialized on the corner of Woodward and Congress, which was where the parade route was supposed to end. We met the rest of the team there, and I immediately felt sorry for the mortal members of the group — it was freezing. I was relieved yet again that cold weather didn't seem to bother me. Brennan, Petersen, Jamie, and several of the shifters from the coalition stood with me, Nain, my parents, Megaera, Athena, Heph, and E. We were all there, except for Demeter, Persephone, and Gaia, who were with Meaghan, Zoe, and Sean. We weren't taking any chances with them.

"Okay. Eyes open. The Netherhounds are around, and they're acting as another couple sets of eyes," I said. "It's entirely possible this is a game, and he's going to attack elsewhere. We all know that. But I'm not willing to risk these people on that."

Petersen nodded. "Matthews, we're mobilized on this, right?"

Brennan nodded. "The entire division is out here today, patrolling the crowd. DPD has feet on the ground too, in uniform and plainclothes."

"If he shows, your job is to protect the Normals," I said. "Do not engage directly with him. Or Nether, if she shows. That's my job. If he ends up elsewhere, we have enough shifters watching out that we should get word soon. If that happens, immortals grab a mortal and rematerialize where we need to be."

I looked around, my daughter and friends at the forefront of my mind. I really hoped the bastard just showed up at the parade, despite the possibility of a bloodbath. "Okay. Let's do this," I said.

We split up, each team member heading toward the area of the parade route they'd been assigned to. Then I exchanged a look with Nain. "This is fucking terrifying," I said quietly.

"It'll be okay," he said, voice low, rough. I could sense the worry coming from him. Rage. Always rage. "Be careful, baby."

"You too," I said. "I love you."

He leaned down and kissed me, and for just a moment, I let myself revel in the sensation of his lips on mine, his tongue caressing mine, the feel of our power mingling.

"I love you, too," he said against my mouth.

Then he let me go, and, with a final glance, he stalked to the area he was supposed to be patrolling.

And that left me. I was kind of everywhere. I walked through the crowd, not bothering to try to hide from the excited looks of the Normals. I put up with the phones raised, taking pictures of me. I made myself ignore the way it felt like having my armor stripped from me every time someone captured my image. I maneuvered between people, keeping my eyes out for any sign of the gold that I now associated with Hyperion. Every once in a while, I'd catch sight of one of my teammates or my dogs. (Netherhounds. I still couldn't quite believe it.)

I started hearing the marching bands, and when I looked toward the parade route, I noted that the procession had started. The crowd started cheering. The first marching band was playing "Jingle Bells," and a float with a gingerbread house on it followed behind them. I kept walking, my mood very much not in alignment with the merriment around me.

Story of my life, really.

I didn't let my gaze rest on any one place for long, trying to see everything at once. It was some encouragement to know that my mom, aunt, and I could actually feel Hyperion as soon as he was near. He wouldn't take us totally by surprise. At least, that was what I was hoping.

I tried not to think about what would happen if he happened on one of my other team members first. Nain. If I let myself think about the danger he was in if Hyperion went after him, it was enough to make me nearly insane with fear.

The parade went on, bands and floats, giant balloons, dancers. Clowns. After an hour, I started hoping it had all been a ruse. He wasn't going to show. He was probably laughing his ass off, watching the parade on television.

The end of the parade was always Santa's sleigh. The nearest marching band started playing "Santa Claus is Coming To Town" and the crowd went nuts. I could see the sleigh coming along the parade route, hear the kids in the crowd shouting "Santa!" in excited voices.

Santa.

I felt something, turned toward the sleigh and the jolly man in the red suit. And then, Santa was being shoved out of the moving sleigh, and Hyperion was there, in his full armor.

The crowd started screaming, and I could hear Hyperion's laugh above the terror.

"Do you fear me, humans?" he roared, and it was met with more screams. The Santa was up and running away, and the crowd had started running away as well.

I guess they were finally starting to realize that sticking around when an insane being showed up was not the best idea. Better late than never.

As the people ran, it quickly turned into a situation that would result in people getting trampled. All those little kids in the crowd.

"Stop running, humans!" Hyperion thundered.

I rematerialized behind him as I noticed with irritation that many of them were stopping.

He turned, smirked, and then slammed me hard with his shield.

Well. There went my jaw. I could feel it hanging loosely as I tried to stand up. Screams erupted from the crowd again as I shot some of my fire at Hyperion, and he charged me, threw me into the nearest building.

"This. This is your champion. This pathetic, worthless being? Have you seen her past? Because I have, humans. How many has she murdered? How many has she tortured? How many of you, innocent humans, have had your minds, your memories tampered with by this monster?"

I pulled myself out of the crumbling brick of the office building he'd flung me into. I could feel blood trickling down my back. I was dizzy, but I tried to look strong.

"I am a true god, returned to Earth to save you from her and her kind."

I noted several of my team members urging the humans to leave, directing traffic away from the parade route. My dogs came and stood beside me.

"Netherhounds. How quaint. I remember you two," Hyperion roared. "You led them right to me, didn't you?"

Kurt snarled, and both dogs shed their mortal disguises, showing their boulder-like, plated black bodies, their glowing red eyes.

"Not now," I said, low. "Wait."

They stood, snarling, practically quivering with bloodlust.

He laughed, loud, full of good humor, and threw his sword at me. I ducked, and he laughed harder. I looked around to see where the sword had landed at the same instant I felt agony from Nain.

He'd been coming up behind me, and Hyperion had planned his sword throw so perfectly that when I ducked, it was at the perfect trajectory to hit Nain. It stuck out of his shoulder.

"I'm fine," he growled, eyes glowing. "Mess that fucker up, baby. I'll be right with you." He pulled the sword out of his shoulder with a growl, and agony flooded through our connection.

"Yes. Do mess me up, Mollis Eth-Hades. Hurt me in front of all of these witnesses and cameras. Show the world what a monster you truly are," Hyperion said. He grinned, produced another sword out of nowhere.

And threw it at Nain, who was bent over, healing his previous wound.

It struck his lower back, and I screamed as Hyperon laughed.

I'm fine, Nain said in my mind. *Go.*

I drew my flamesword, and the crowd, what was left of it, cheered.

I rose into the air, flew hard at Hyperion.

"I've never pretended to be anything other than a monster," I snarled, and I struck down, hard. He had another sword (What the fucking hell? Did he have a limitless supply of them?) and met my slash with one of his own. We fought, slashing, stabbing, and every once in a while I'd shoot flames to distract him. He hit me with his shield, and my still-healing jaw snapped loose again.

"There. That'll shut you up," he roared, laughing again.

I struck out harder, trying my best to ignore the pain in my jaw.

"Shall we get into it, then? Let us address your murders first," Hyperion said, voice booming over the crowd. "Clark Hanson was your first murder. You were seventeen. You set him on fire and walked away."

I tried not to be affected. I couldn't say anything in defense of myself anyway, couldn't speak around my swollen, broken jaw.

"And there were more, yes? Astaroth. Twenty-some men in a boarding house. A few dozen women elsewhere.

Gods. Did you know your champion, your hero, has murdered gods? What's to stop her from killing you?" he boomed, and I focused on trying to kill him, my rage overtaking everything else. I struck harder, landed one at the side of his neck, and he roared. It wasn't enough, but it sure as hell made me feel better.

"Do you see what she is? Murderous, vile. Bringer of death. Ares, Dionysus, Aphrodite, Hermes. Names you all know. Gods. She has murdered them all. She is the reason your city is the hellhole it is. She is the reason you can't sleep at night, wondering what monster will attack next. She is the monster, and she will destroy you all."

"Lies," I snarled, hitting him again. I used flames, tried to keep them in contact with his armor the way Nether had. He screamed, hit me harder, and I dodged so he couldn't get full contact with me. I moved into the center of the street, trying to draw him away from the Normals, who stood watching now, their fear and confusion surrounding me.

"Lies? That's rich coming from you, daughter of death," he said, his voice ridiculously amplified, bouncing off of the skyscrapers around us.

I glanced around. My parents, Heph, Nain, Athena, E, and my aunt Meg had approached and were surrounding us.

"Ask her how far into your government her taint extends. Ask how many of your lawmakers are her lapdogs. Sometimes literally," he smirked. "How does it feel to fuck an animal, daughter of death?"

"I don't know. Lemme ask your girlfriend," I managed, talking around the swelling in my jaw. Blood streamed down my arms from the multiple slashes he'd landed.

He laughed. "No need. You can just ask your mother how she liked it."

That did it. Every single one of the Olympians assembled sprung for him then, slashing, hitting. My father released a bestial roar and his scythe cut another deep furrow across Hyperion's face as the Titan fended off the rest of the Olympians.

"You see what they are, mortals of Detroit. Animals."

And then he was gone, all of us hitting at nothing, then trying hard not to hit one another with our swords and knives.

"Where did he go? I'll flay him alive and feed'"

"Hades, shush," my mom said, clamping a hand over Hades' mouth.

I turned away from the group, let my flamesword disappear. I went to my husband. Jamie was looking at his back.

"It's fine," he told her irritably. She saw me coming and backed away. He tried pulling his shirt back down over it and I shot him a glare and pushed it back up. There was a long, gaping cut across his lower back, blood still weeping from the wound.

"It's healing," he told me.

"I can help it along." He shook his head. "Not now. It's healing, and you need to stay as strong as you can."

"He knew. Take you out of the fight and he gets to me. And then I can't feed off you, can't focus, can't..." I broke off in irritation.

"He knew a whole lot of shit," Nain said as the rest of our team approached. The Normals were all standing still, watching us. Unsure. "How did he know that? Who fucking blabbed?" He glared around the circle. "Nobody knows about all that shit beyond a few people standing right here, and not even all of you knew everything. How'd he fucking know?"

"Any other secrets you've been keeping from Queenie, shifter?" Heph asked mildly.

"It wasn't him," I said quietly, hoping I was right. I kept my eye on my dad, who was studying Brennan closely. He turned his gaze to me, gave a short nod.

I felt a weight lift. "Thanks."

Hades nodded again, and even Brennan looked surprised that I stuck up for him.

"You never know. He might have bargained information about you for safety for his son," Heph pressed. "It wouldn't be the first time he's sold you out."

"Heph, I love you, but shut up. It wasn't him," I said. "There *is* someone who knows it all, including the name of the first guy I killed. I've only told that name to Nain."

Now everyone just looked confused.

"I told it to him when I was Nether's prison," I finished, hating it, but knowing that it was the only answer that made sense.

"I told you you should have…" my dad began.

"You know what, old man?" Nain roared, standing up and getting right in Hades' face. "You are not in her shoes. You don't fight the battles she fights. And maybe she knows Nether better than you do. Get off her back. Now."

Both Nain's and my father's eyes were glowing red as they faced off, nose-to-nose, neither one backing down.

"I am the god of death, demon. Do not even begin to assume that you can disrespect me," Hades said.

"Oh, for fuck's sake," I muttered.

"Hades," Tisiphone said, putting a hand on his arm.

"Fine. I'll be in the Netherwoods," Hades said, and then he disappeared.

Tisiphone gave me a hug, as did my aunt, and then they were gone, too.

"I need to get back to Meaghan," Heph said. "Unless you need me here." I shook my head, and Heph hugged me, then gave Brennan a sheepish apology, which Brennan waved off. And then, he was gone.

Athena, E, Brennan, Nain, Jamie, and I were all that were left. Well, us and several thousand Normals, who were watching us like they were worried we would sprout horns and then follow that up by eating their intestines or something. I looked around. The street was completely silent. Whatever else Hyperion was, he was a devious planner. He'd set out to make them fear me, constructed this spectacle on a day when millions of people would be watching. And it had worked. They were terrified. And not so much of him.

Of me.

And that fucking hurt. I couldn't pretend it didn't. I didn't blame them, because I'd be afraid in their shoes, too. Years of trying to protect them, of trying to earn their trust, erased with nothing more than a few words from Hyperion.

I took a deep breath and tried to calm myself. I noticed two women to my left step off the curb and start walking toward us. They were both older, and looked alike enough to be sisters, long white hair braided down their backs.

The taller one gave me a smile when they reached us, the corners of her warm brown eyes crinkling as she did.

"You're bleeding, Angel," she said, her voice loud enough that the nearest Normals could hear.

I wanted to cry. I wanted to scream, anything to release all of the emotions running through me. I bit my lip to keep the tears back, and she seemed to get it. She opened her arms, and I let her hug me, and hugged her back. Her sister joined in, and then I did cry.

It's hard to explain. I deal with so many assholes in my life, both mortal and immortal. When someone is genuinely kind and accepting, it never fails to throw me for a loop. When the two women released me, I noticed that they were both crying, too.

"We believe in you," the shorter sister said. "You've been here for us."

More Normals had joined the sisters. Many, many more had stayed back, still watching in concern. I was hugged by several other people, and I let it happen.

"You're our hero," a young woman said. "I don't care what some jerky gold freak says."

This was met with cheers and applause. I noticed the

other Normals, the more fearful ones, getting antsy, unsure how to handle what was happening.

"Thank you," I said "I'm sorry about what happened here. Thank you."

I met Nain's eyes, Athena's, E's. Then we each grabbed a team member and blinked out of sight, leaving the destruction and chaos behind us.

We ended up back at our rented house, where Heph, Meaghan, Demeter, and Persephone had agreed to meet us.

"Oh, jeez," Meaghan exclaimed when she saw us. She didn't seem to know whether to look at me or Nain. "What can I do, Molly?" she asked, and I shook my head.

"You've done more than enough. Thank you. I hope she wasn't too crazy," I said, leaning over the side of the crib and picking Zoe up. She was wide awake, her tiny fists clenched, red from crying. As soon as she was in my arms, she closed her eyes.

"She was all right. She cried a bit every now and then, but she seemed happier when she was near Sean, so we let them lay together in the playpen for a while, and that gave us a break," she said.

"Thank you." I cuddled Zoe close to me.

"We saw it all on the television," Persephone said. "What a mess."

I nodded. "Many people there seemed to take what he said to heart," I finally said.

"That was what we gathered from some of the interviews on the news," Persephone said, and E glared at her. "Well, it's true. And she should know that," Persephone shot at her.

I shook my head. "It's not a surprise. He knew that for the majority of the city, their trust in me is weak at best. Fear is high, and he capitalized on that. It was only a matter of time."

I looked down at Zoe, pressed my lips to her forehead. Nain came up behind me and rested his hands on my hips.

"Turn the TV on, please," I said to Heph.

"You don't need to watch that shit, Queenie," he argued.

"Please," I repeated.

He gave me a helpless look, then he turned it back on. The mayor of Detroit was on.

"The fact of the matter is that this has been a danger, a live bomb living among us for a long time. Look at all of the destruction we've had. That insanity in midtown a few weeks back. That fight near Grand Circus Park last week. All of those murders, and fires. As far as the accusations of the Angel having infiltrators in our local government, I am setting up an investigation now. We may not be able to control her, but we can sure the hell ensure that she is not running our city departments from behind the scenes."

"What would you like to say to the Angel?" the interviewer asked.

"I'd like to ask her to leave. I know she's done a lot of good. There is no denying that. But things are just getting worse, and I think it's clear that she's the reason. She has powerful enemies, and our city is paying the price."

"Fucking weasel," Nain growled.

I didn't answer, just kept watching. They ended the interview with the mayor, went back out to the scene of the attack on the parade. Debris from some of the floats still littered the area, and crowds were still milling around. The reporter was talking to people at the scene, and almost to a one, they seemed to be in agreement about one thing: I was a menace.

By the fifth person, I couldn't take it anymore. I sent a blast of power at the television. It sparked, and the screen blew out. The room went silent around us.

"It's okay. I didn't like that TV anyway, baby," Nain said.

"I need to be alone with Nain and Zoe for a while," I

told my friends. Everyone left, patting or hugging me on the way out. I heard Nain thank Meaghan for watching Zoe, and then, finally, it was just him and me, and our daughter.

Nain sat on the couch and held his arms out. I settled myself onto his lap, rested my head on his shoulder. I still held Zoe, who was blissfully sleeping, a tiny, sleepy smile on her face.

"Are you still hurt?" I asked Nain.

"I'm okay," he said, holding me tight. "How about you?"

"I'm healed," I told him. The dogs came into the room, settled themselves with groans onto the floor in front of the couch, and watched us with those too-knowing eyes. I took a deep breath, closed my eyes. "I'm so tired," I said.

"I know, baby."

"I gotta find Nether."

He didn't answer.

"My dad was right about that much. Me being so soft on her sure came back to bit me in the a— butt," I amended, remembering Zoe's presence.

"Not now, though. You need to get your strength back up," he said, and I nodded. "Just stay with me, Molls."

"Okay," I said sleepily. I forced myself to get up and set Zoe in her cradle. She was sleeping soundly.

"Watch over her," I told Kurt and Courtney, and I got a quiet whine of acceptance in response.

Nain took my hand and we went into our room, then stripped and stood under the hot water in the shower. I washed his body first, running a soapy washcloth lazily over his body, loving every single contour, every scar. I washed blood from his shoulder and back, laying kisses over his flesh as I cared for him. When I was finished, he did the same for me.

When we were clean, he carried me to our bed, where he reminded me yet again what it meant to truly be mated, bonded to someone. He laid me down and settled himself between my thighs, claiming my lips at the same moment he sheathed himself deep inside me, capturing my cries with his lips.

Feed, Molls. Take what you need, his voice, warm yet demanding, said in my mind.

Nain.

Do it, Molls. Let me do this for you.

And I did. I let myself take strength from my mate as our bodies writhed, as his demanding, hoarse whispers turned my mind to mush, as I gave him everything I could, just as he gave everything he could to me. When we were together like this, there was no holding back.

His hands were clasped with mine, pressing them into the mattress, his lips on mine, and when I cried out, I felt his release deep inside me, heard his satisfied groan. He just kept kissing me, holding me.

I love you. You're perfect, baby. I'm yours for the rest of my life and I swear to whatever's out there that I will give you everything I fucking can. If you need my strength, it's yours. If you need me to hold you, I'll do it happily. And if what you need is to fuck so hard you forget anything but me, you can have that too. I'm yours.

I kissed him harder, then let go of his hands so I could wrap my arms around him and run my hands over his muscled back.

"I'm yours. For the rest of my existence," I whispered to him. "It scared the hell out of me when you were hurt today." Then I let the tears come, able to really cry now that I'd let myself lose control with him. He held me, and nuzzled the side of my neck, and waited it out with me until I was able to get myself back together again.

"It takes more than that to kill me, baby," he murmured. "Nothing is gonna take me away from you. You know damn well I don't do anything I don't want to do."

I smiled a little, ran my hands up and down his back, and let his contented mood wash over me. It couldn't last, though. We had things that we had to talk about, no matter how much I wanted to ignore them.

"This is going to be a mess," I said, and he nodded, face still pressed into the side of my neck. His hands were in my hair, his body still joined with mine. "It's starting to fall apart."

"We'll figure it out," he said. "One thing at a time, Molls. We need to get rid of Hyperion's golden ass. Deal with Nether, get your imps back. We'll deal with the rest as it comes."

"I don't think it's gonna be long before the Normals start calling for my head."

"Well, they can't have it. Fuck them," Nain growled.

"And then there's Brennan and Jamie. They're obviously involved with me and everyone knows it. They're going to hear it all."

"So they can leave their jobs if they need to. They don't have to worry about money. We'll take care of them."

"I know."

"I'm gonna try to talk to Jamie tomorrow," I said. "And we need to make sure Meaghan is protected from all this shit."

"You put Gaia there. And Demeter and Persephone rarely leave her side. Meaghan is as protected as she can be," he said. "Stop thinking for a while."

I tried. I lay there beneath him and listened to his breathing slow as he fell asleep. I felt his entire body relax, and usually, it would have sent me right to sleep. Instead, my mind raced. Images of Nain getting hit with Hyperion's swords, the Normals running, as much from me as from Hyperion. The horror that had come from the crowd as he went through my past deeds. That was all for me.

My whole point in going public was to comfort them. It wasn't working anymore, and it wouldn't now that he'd said what so many of them most feared. Even if there was a way to disprove what Hyperion had said (and there wasn't, because every single thing he'd said was true, even if he had left out the reasons *why* those beings all had to die) — the fact was that the things they'd heard about me couldn't be unheard. And he'd gotten right to the crux of why I scared them: who could tell when I might turn all of my power on them, instead of using it to protect them?

I carefully slid out from under Nain's body and pulled on a pair of pajama pants and a t-shirt. I went out to the living room to check on Zoe. Kurt and Courtney were stationed right where we'd told them to be: next to Zoe's crib.

"Good demon dogs," I murmured, and they both thumped their tails on the floor a few times in response. Zoe was sleeping soundly, and the last thing I wanted to do was wake her up.

There was a light tap on our door, and I checked the peephole. E was standing on the other side, and I opened the door for her. She was dressed in pajamas as well, her normally sleek hair tousled as if she'd been trying to sleep.

"You can't sleep either, devil girl?" she asked quietly, and I nodded.

"I have hot chocolate," I said.

"Why do you think I came up here?" she asked with a smile.

I waved her into our apartment and we went to the kitchen, where I quietly made two cups of hot cocoa, E's with plenty of marshmallows, mine with none. I set the mugs on the kitchen table, and we both sat in silence for a few minutes, blowing on the cocoa and tentatively tasting it.

"It's always either too hot or too cool," I said.

"One of the trials of modern life," she said with a wry smile. "Have you heard from our vamp friend? How's Zero?"

I could have kissed E just then. The last thing I wanted to talk about was Hyperion and the parade, and she knew it. I grabbed a package of Oreo cookies from the counter, ripped them open and set them in the middle of the table. As I'd known she would, E snagged three immediately. "I called her yesterday in between baby crying fits," I said.

"Your crying fits, or theirs?" E asked with a smirk.

"Both, smartass," I answered, and she laughed. I joined her. "Anyway. She said he's adjusting really well, and I guess Rayna and Ronan are both impressed with how well he's controlling himself. She said they're mostly just kind of staying in their rooms while he adjusts to his new senses, but he's already itching to get out and hunt things at vampire strength."

E laughed. "He is perfect for her. Shanti has already done a lot toward securing Rayna's kingdom for her. With both of them at her side, I don't foresee many problems for our vampire queen."

I nodded. "Which is good for us. The fewer crazed vampires we have to deal with, the better."

"Don't worry. There will be some other nuisances who will rise and take their place. You'll never be bored," she added, and I got a sense from her, almost like longing. I studied my friend.

E was one of the people I was most grateful to have in my life. Not just because she was a huge help in every way, but because she was honest and straightforward, and she saw through my bullshit almost as well as Nain did. She'd seen me at my worst, and she'd never been fazed by it. She was the sister I'd never had.

And she was at odds with herself. I could feel that, every time she was around. Not about her role in our team and family. She enjoyed that. It was bigger than that.

"Have you been to the Netherwoods yet?" I asked her.

She nodded. "It's the same as the old one, and not. It's weaker than the old one. I'm guessing because the new Nether is missing Nether herself. There is no Tartarus, obviously. The place where they keep the souls for punishment is just called the Pit now. The souls and the demons who get captured for crimes all mingle there."

"How is it guarded?"

"Demons, mostly. And some of your mother's and

your aunt's power as well."

I nodded. We drank our cocoa for a bit.

"You fear it," E said, taking a bite of her last cookie.

"I know it's stupid. I still have nightmares about being trapped in the old Nether. Both in my grave and out of it. I just can't make myself go in and relive all that just now. I know my parents are there, and Zoe's there almost every day with them... I just don't want to face it right now."

"Fear definitely has nothing to do with logic, does it?" she asked with a small smile. "You do remember that it was Nether herself who was trying to keep you there, yes? And when she couldn't do that, she just gave up and transferred the rest of her energy into your soul."

"Logically, I know that," I said. "Like I said, I know it's stupid. Do you like it there?"

"It does comfort me, to be there. And in some ways, it makes me angry. But mostly, it reminds me of a time when I knew what my life was meant to look like." She was looking into her cup, swirling the last bits of marshmallow around in the chocolate.

"Would you be happier making your home there? You know my parents would be thrilled to have you in their household."

"Trying to get rid of me, my friend?" she asked with a smile.

I put my hand over hers. "Never, E. It doesn't take a genius to see that you're restless and frustrated here."

"It's just hitting me, I suppose. When my sisters betrayed your family, I was mostly angry. And then I was busy figuring out how to live in this world, and it was exciting being part of the team, having friends. Life is never monotonous with you, devil girl."

"I could take a bit of boring."

She let out a small laugh, like the tinkling of bells. "I'm with you there. But more than that, I suppose I am finally realizing that being the last of my kind, being obsolete... it wears on me. I feel at odds with myself and everything around me. As I've watched you grow into the woman you were obviously meant to be, it's left me wondering what this life has in store for me." Then she brightened. "Let's stop talking about that, though. I have discovered a television show about superheroes!"

And then she proceeded to tell me all about the old *Heroes* TV show, and I let myself relax and talk about things that were not about life and death for a little while.

CHAPTER TWELVE

I stood outside the Netherwoods, holding Zoe, waiting for my mom to come out and pick her up. I looked through the black branches, recalling my conversation with E the night before. All the logic in the world wasn't enough against the way my stomach twisted and the way my hands started sweating at even the thought of setting foot in there. The amethyst sky that I'd once found so beautiful haunted me now. Same for the black trees, let alone all that stone.

I bounced Zoe just a little, and I focused for a moment on the armband around my biceps. The stone in it was made of Nether stone, and I could still feel the angry souls imprisoned in it. I'd stopped wearing it for a while, but I was realizing once again that I'd need as much power as I could get to deal with Hyperion and Nether.

Nether. Had she really spilled everything to Hyperion? It was the only thing that made sense, yet I had a hard time picturing her sitting there gossiping happily with the golden asshole.

Zoe started getting fussy, so I rocked her in my arms, starting singing. I didn't really know any lullabies, so I ended up singing an old Smashing Pumpkins song. She didn't seem to mind the fact that I was utterly clueless.

I felt a presence nearby, and looked up to see my mom emerging from the Netherwoods, dressed as usual in the black uniform of the Furies.

"Are you working today?" I asked her, and she shook her head.

"I'm taking a break to give this little darling my undivided attention. Megaera has some rage issues to work off, so she's handling it today."

I nodded. My family is insane. This is where I get it from. We talk about punishing souls as if it's just another day at the office, because it is.

"Thanks for watching her so much. I hope things settle down soon," I said, placing Zoe in my mom's arms.

"You are needed. It is a pleasure to spend time with her. And she likes us!" she said, smiling. "So few are genuinely pleased to spend time around our kind."

I nodded.

She looked up at me, reached out and took my hand as she cradled Zoe in her other arm. "I am proud of you, Mollis. Don't let what happened yesterday get to you."

"Things are a mess."

"You can't control everything. This has been a danger since the moment you allowed the world to see what you are."

"Is Dad still pissed about Nether?" I shook my head. "What do you think of that whole thing? Do you still think I'm too soft?"

"I think Nether told him. I believe you were right about that. But I don't know that you could have done anything differently with Nether. We don't know how her mind works, Mollis." She'd mostly stopped with the "you're being weak about Nether" speeches, seeming to get that it wasn't helping. My dad was another story, and I didn't doubt that this had only affirmed what he'd been saying. And I didn't disagree with him about that.

173

"Don't you think it was weird that she didn't show up yesterday? I mean, she showed up when Hyperion attacked me and Dad before. Why not now?"

Tisiphone shrugged, a concerned look on her face. "Well. If they were working together, it's possible that they had it worked out so only he would be there. Hyperion has always craved attention."

"I'm going to kill him, mom. I promise."

She gave a small smile. "I don't doubt you, my love."

I nodded, then bent and kissed Zoe's forehead, then hugged my mom.

Next stop: check in with Heph and his family, then stop in and see Jamie.

When I arrived at Heph's house on the West Side, it looked almost unrecognizable. In the time he'd lived there alone, Heph's old brick bungalow had had a ramshackle, run-down look. It was ironic, really, that our repair genius had lived in the most run-down of all of our houses, but he'd always been too busy with his own projects and the team to put any time into the house and lots he'd claimed as his own. As I walked up the front walk, Meaghan's hand was evident. The shutters, which had once hung askew, or been missing entirely, were painted a deep green and now hung straight. The front door was a vibrant red, and the porch, which had been on the verge of collapse, was now fixed and sturdy. Two large planters with small boxwood topiaries flanked the front steps, and a bittersweet wreath adorned the door. Behind the house, I could see two large, almost commercial-sized, greenhouses. I smiled to myself. Heph had mentioned the greenhouses, how he'd wanted to ensure that Meaghan could grow her plants even in the dead of winter. And he'd gone on and on about solar-powered heaters and a worm composter he'd built and he'd eventually lost me.

But his joy in making things for the woman he'd fallen

hard for had been evident. Every time my friend talked about Meaghan, his face lit up and an irrepressible smile formed on his lips. And, to my delight, Meaghan was the same way about Heph.

My friends were disgustingly happy together, and I was determined to see them stay that way.

I knocked on the front door, and felt Gaia's power swirling nearby. A moment later, she pulled the front door open and ushered me inside.

"Meaghan just went to rest. Sick as a dog," she said, shaking her head.

"Can you do anything for her?"

"Asclepias was here. He brewed her one of his teas and sent her to bed. And her moron of a mate keeps hovering over her and she needs to rest," she finished.

"He's worried about her. Give Heph a break," I said, sitting on the sofa. The interior of the house, too, was a vast improvement. The walls were freshly painted, the wood floors gleamed, and the house was now furnished with comfortable furniture, both new pieces and items that looked a little worn and well-loved, which were probably from Meaghan's old house. There were still many of Heph's projects lying around, and the windowsills overflowed with lush plants, but now there was some order to the chaos.

"How are you liking it here?" I asked, hoping she would say everything was dandy so I wouldn't have to relocate her.

"Don't even think of moving me, Fury," she snapped. "I like it here just fine, and there's never been a girl alive who needed some mothering more than that one," she said, pointing up the stairs. "I'm staying right here, unless you want another irritated Titan on your hands."

I hid a grin. "If you insist," I said.

"I do. No upstart Olympian is going to separate me from my girls. Persephone and Demeter are here all the time. We spend almost all day in the greenhouses," she paused. "He's an idiot, but he did manage to make nice places to allow for the Earth-witch to garden."

I nodded, not wanting to point out that Heph was far from an idiot. It seemed like he'd ended up with the mother-in-law figure from hell. I'd have to apologize. Sensing for the Titan, though, it became clear that despite her words, she actually liked and respected Hephaestus.

Well, she had good taste. And she was devoted to protecting Meaghan and her child. All points in her favor. I took a breath, feeling some of the tension leave my body.

"Hyperion has always been one for dramatics," she said, watching me. "I should have seen something like that coming. He seems to know a lot about you, Fury."

I nodded. "He does."

"How?"

"I have my suspicions," I answered.

She was watching me, those bright blue eyes not missing a thing. "Nether."

"I think so. She's the only one who knew a lot of the things he said. That, or I have another enemy out there."

"I doubt it. You've killed just about everyone who has been a danger to you."

I sensed for her. She was calm, but tense. "And what do you think of that?" I asked quietly, not even knowing why I cared what she thought. She didn't know me.

"I think some don't deserve the life Nyx gave them," she said slowly. "You are doing what your line does. I'm not a fan of Hades, necessarily, and I could never live the way he and your mother and aunt do, but I recognize that they serve an important role. I am not sitting in judgment of you, Fury."

I smiled. "Well, you'd be the first, Gaia."

She let out a soft chuckle. "I am too old to care. One thing I know is that none of us truly knows the mind or heart of another. We can fool ourselves, let ourselves believe that we know better. The truth of the matter is that none of us, barring maybe your father, knows what is in another's heart. It would be so easy to believe you a power-hungry menace. And maybe you are," she shrugged. "But you have given me no reason to believe that. I have no issue with you, Mollis," she said. "Unless you decide to try to move me out of Meaghan's home. Then we may have a problem."

"Understood," I said. "As long as she and Heph still want you here."

"Of course they do. My presence is a blessing and protection all its own. A gift, truly."

"I need some of your self-confidence, Gaia," I said, standing up.

"Live a few thousand more years. You'll get there," she said sweetly. I shook my head and opened the front door, told her I'd check in on Meaghan another time. I focused on the building downtown where the federal office for supernatural affairs was located. Time to go see Jamie.

I'd been in Brennan's office once or twice, so it was easy to rematerialize there. Jamie was his assistant, so she actually spent more time in the office than Bren did. He was usually out on calls or in meetings. When I rematerialized, Jamie was sitting in the chair behind the desk, dressed in the typical dark suit everyone in the department wore. She jumped a little, but relaxed when she saw it was me.

"Hey. Sorry I startled you. I didn't want anyone else to see me," I said.

"No problem," she said, smiling and gesturing to one of the other chairs. "Take a load off. What can I do for you?"

I sat, then took a look around Brennan's office. There were framed photos of Sean on the desk, amid all the other papers and folders.

"His desk is almost as messy as mine," I said.

"Messy desk is the sign of an active mind. At least, my

dad always said so," she said, smiling a little.

"Your dad was a smart man," I said, and she nodded in agreement.

"I miss him."

"I don't doubt it. I'm sorry."

"You have nothing to apologize for," she said. I bowed my head. Jamie was one of those people who, for whatever reason, had a really high opinion of me. I didn't understand why, and I fully expected it to turn to hatred after her father was killed fighting assholes from my home realm.

"Being affiliated with me is not exactly being regarded kindly these days," I said slowly.

She was silent for a moment. "No. But it never was, really. I mean, my dad allied himself with you, but he knew that it could come back to bite him in the ass. The thing was, he really didn't care. He believed in what you were doing."

"And you?" I asked, meeting her eyes.

She leaned forward, resting her chin on her hand. "I believe in you even more than he did. I'm not going anywhere. And if people get pissed at me for being one of yours, they can fuck right off. I have family members alive today because of you."

"You have family members dead, too," I said.

"No. I have family members dead because of murderous gods who didn't have the guts or honor to fight my father face to face. You avenged him, and I will never, ever forget that."

I nodded, touched by her words. My eyes settled on the desk, and there was a manila file with my name on the tab. Or, not my name. "The Angel."

"Is that my file?" I asked.

She glanced at it. "Yeah."

"The one Brennan was keeping on me?" I asked, and she nodded again.

"If you want to look at it, go ahead. It's about you,

after all," she said, closing the document she'd been working on. "Just don't tell anyone I let you do that shit."

"Thanks," I murmured.

I picked up the thin file and steeled myself, expecting to find everything from what color underwear I wore to my favorite sex positions, since he knew many of them. I flipped it open. The top piece of paper was a color photograph of me. Old-time me, before the glowing eyes. It was probably from around the time Nain brought me into the team. Below the photograph, written in Brennan's handwriting, were my vitals. My age (approximate, he'd noted), height, weight, eye color, hair color. In the section labelled "powers" he'd written "telepathy, super strength, fire." Name: Molly; surname, unknown.

I wrinkled my forehead. He knew damn well more than that. I flipped to the next document, which was several pages of reports about people I'd saved, including eyewitness accounts of my actions. Things everyone could have seen. The next thing was a memo from Ross, filing an official complaint about Brennan's lack of forthcoming when it came to sharing information about me, especially since it was noted by several people that he and I were romantically involved. The next thing was a memo from Brennan, indicating that while he very well might be sharing my bed, I was no more forthcoming with him than anyone else, that I was insanely private and kept him and everyone else at arm's distance. He also noted that he had asked if anyone else wanted to take over his duties, and no one had volunteered.

The next thing was his report indicating that he'd outed himself to me, and my response. To sum it up: I was not happy. He also indicated that he was fine continuing in his role watching me as the person in the department closest to me.

I flipped it over. "Where's the rest of it?" I asked Jamie.

"That's it," she said, stapling the pages she'd printed out.

"Oh, come on. There's nothing in here about me and the immortals, or about me resurrecting, or self-healing, or any of that. None of the big stuff is in there. He knew what my childhood was like, and he left that part blank."

She just gave me a look. "Well, duh."

"What do you mean?"

"What do you think?" She lowered her voice. "He left shit out, obviously. Don't you know he has this job as much to protect you as anything else? That the only thing that allows him to put up with Ross's bullshit day in and day out is the knowledge that he's the only thing standing between you and some overzealous asshole who wants to know every single secret you've ever had?" She looked around on her desk. "You see your file, right? Here's Esmerelda the witch's file." She plunked a thick file down on the desktop. "You can't look in there, though."

"Okay. Uh. Esmerelda doesn't do anything," I said.

"I know. Her case worker is very, very thorough. Everyone other than Ross just pretty much accepted that you keep to yourself and everyone's afraid enough of you to know better than to push it. Nain's file is about five times as thick as Esmeralda's, mostly because until the time when Brennan came in, he had other case workers gathering info on him. There was a file on Ada and Stone. Those have mysteriously disappeared, and no one seems to know that Shanti exists. I wonder why that is," she finished, raising an eyebrow at me.

I just looked at the thin file in my hand. "Why isn't this on the computer?" I asked dumbly, trying to work it all out.

She laughed. "The idea of some asshole hacking us and finding all of this out and scaring the hell out of everyone is too big of a risk. So paper files, and we lock them up. Brennan has access, and since I'm his assistant, I have access. Other than him, there are five other people with access to the files in this department."

"This is really all he reported?" I asked quietly.

"Of course." It seemed to hit her, and her voice took on a tone of disbelief. "You really thought he was telling them everything." I gave a short nod in response. "He said he told you he didn't."

"I didn't believe him. He hasn't exactly been honest with me about things," I said defensively.

"He protects his friends, Molly. He's reported the bare minimum on everyone on the team as long as he's had this detail. Just enough to be able to keep his job, not enough to make a damn bit of difference. As far as anyone knows, my father and I are nothing more than Normals."

I didn't know how to respond. "Why wasn't he straight with me, if this was all he was doing?"

"Maybe he expected you to believe in him enough to trust him," she said. "And if he wanted to keep his job, and do what he was doing, he couldn't exactly blab about how he was handling his business, right? You had to look clueless or people would have suspected he'd told you. He was supposed to be undercover," she reminded me. "He was walking a fine line, I think."

I tossed the file back onto Brennan's desk. "He shouldn't have lied to me," I said to no one in particular.

"Would it have changed anything?" a voice I knew all too well said behind me. I'd been so absorbed in taking it all in that I hadn't felt Brennan's presence nearby. "Can you excuse us, Jamie?" he asked, and Jamie nodded and waved at me. Brennan sat on the edge of his desk, facing me. "Would it?" he asked again. I glanced up, then averted my gaze. It still hurt, sometimes, just to look at him. To see those eyes that had taken my breath away. To smell him. I had everything I wanted. Nain was my one and only, and there was no conflict in my heart about that. But it didn't change the fact, that, once upon a time, I'd loved this man and planned for a future with him. It didn't change the fact that I could still remember what it had felt like in his arms. That when he spoke, sometimes, I was reminded of promises whispered against my lips.

Loving Nain didn't erase Brennan from my memories. Sometimes, I wished it did. And times like this, when he was close to me, when we were alone and he was studying me in that way that made me feel like he was taking in every single detail... times like this just made me remember things that were best left in the past.

We'd burned too many bridges, and neither one of us were the same.

"You lied," I finally said.

"I was doing my job. And I was protecting you and everyone else I care about." He was silent for a bit, and I could feel his gaze on me, that sad longing that, though weaker, was still there when he looked at me. "When I left to do my training for this job, I did it thinking there had to be something more to life than just beating up vampires and werewolves all the time. I thought this would give me that. And it did, but not until I realized that the best use of my time was protecting those who protect everyone else. When you came into my life, it became even more important." He took a deep breath, raked his fingers through his hair. "I wanted to tell you, Molly. We've been over this."

"I know." I took a breath. "Why didn't you tell me you could only bond once?"

He didn't answer right away, but I could feel his gaze on me. "Who told you that?" he finally asked.

"Artemis."

"It doesn't matter. It's done now, and it was the right thing to do."

"You should have told me."

"Would it have changed anything?" he repeated.

I didn't answer. It still hurt, remembering Artemis's words, her anger when she told me he'd never have the life he should have had, that loving me had cost him that. As angry as I was with him, I wanted him to be happy.

After a few long, awkward seconds of silence, he spoke up. "To answer my own question, it wouldn't have changed anything between us, because I am not Nain."

I glanced at the folder again. "Is what happened on Thanksgiving causing trouble for you here?"

He shrugged. "Nice change of subject. Not really. I'm getting a lot of sidelong glances from some of the lower-rung agents, but everyone I've been working with since I've been here, other than Ross, has been cool about it. Agents aren't inclined to believe the words of some asshole in a gold suit who shows up out of nowhere and starts talking shit about someone they've seen in action for years."

"You guys weren't really his audience. He wanted to scare the Normals. And he did it."

He grimaced.

"Right?" I pressed.

He nodded. "Yeah. We're getting a lot of calls from angry, scared Normals."

"Do they want me hunted down?" I asked with a smile.

"That wouldn't end well," he said, giving me a small grin in return. "Mostly, they don't know what they want. They mostly seem to want to tell us they're scared and they're pissed off about being scared." He shrugged. "Honestly, it's mostly bitching."

"Ross must love that," I said, and Brennan rolled his eyes.

"It's taking every bit of discipline I have not to knock him out," he said. "Petersen gave the order, by the way. I'm director now, officially. I've been trying to get hold of Petersen to ask if I can transfer Ross's ass out of the department, but I haven't seen him since then, and his secretary says he hasn't checked in. He could be out on a mission or something, though. Wouldn't be the first time."

"Well, congrats. You're going to be a lot better at it than he was. And as far as the complaints, I'm…"

"If you apologize to me, I'm going to be pissed," he warned, though the trace of a smile on his face belied his words. "They can complain all they want."

"Fine."

"Fine," he said back, and I laughed.

"All right. Any other secrets you want to spill?"

His expression tensed, for just a second, and then he shook his head.

"Okay. See you at home. It's your turn to babysit tonight, by the way," I added.

"Great," he grumbled, and I focused on rematerializing.

I spent the afternoon both trying to avoid the Normals, not wanting a confrontation, and trying to find Nether. And hoping I ran across Hyperion.

I wanted to hurt him so bad I could taste it. When I saw him again, I would destroy him, I promised myself. I would find a way.

Shortly after sunset, I gave up and headed toward home, looking forward to my husband, my daughter, and several cups of hot coffee.

Most of my time over the next week or so was spent looking for Hyperion. Nether was keeping a low profile, which wasn't something I wanted to think about too much. When I wasn't working, I was with Nain. And I was trying, really really hard, to figure out the whole parenting thing with Zoe.

I flew toward home after another day of fruitlessly searching for my enemies, and I let my thoughts wander, which, lately, wasn't really such a good thing.

As much as I adored Zoe, she was a pain in the ass.

And I'm probably shit, because parents aren't even supposed to think that sort of thing about their kids. Right? Nain agreed that she was a pain in the ass, and then said that Brennan and Stone and every kid he'd ever taken in was a pain in the ass, too.

But this is Nain we're talking about. Sweet and warm are not his forte, unless he's in the right mood and he's alone with me. And even though he was against it, even though demons don't really do "sweet," it was obvious to everyone that he absolutely doted on Zoe. He was turning more often to Brennan, asking him about baby stuff since Bren had experience with Sean, and that seemed to be smoothing out the weirdness that had lingered between the two of them. Watching an enormous, three-hundred-year-old demon and an alpha shifter discussing diaper brands is one of those things I never thought I'd see.

Lately, Nain, E, Brennan, and my parents were spending more time with Zoe than I did.

It felt like I should have been able to handle more of it myself. Especially on those days when my searches for Hyperion went nowhere, and the most I managed was beating up the errant vampire or two. The days I managed to find lost girls were a highlight, though, to be honest, Shanti and the vampires had slipped into that role seamlessly. I spent most of the time when I was out trying not to be noticed, not wanting to deal with either my fans or my detractors. There were many, many of the latter. I was hoping that keeping a low profile would calm them all down eventually.

I felt... weird. Just weird. I was happy with my family, still madly in love with Nain. But I felt wrong, somehow. Restless. And it was starting to feel, more and more, like I didn't quite fit in anywhere.

Which was kind of hilarious, since the world had gone insane mostly because of me and what I am. But the fact of the matter was that I felt like an asshole beating on vamps and shifters. It was like a professional boxer challenging a two-year-old to a fight. I didn't even get any satisfaction out of it anymore. I mean, I liked that I hurt beings who deserved it. But I was overkill, and thanks to the way we'd managed to organize not just our team, but also the vamps and the shifters, I'd kind of ended up making myself unnecessary for most things. That should have been an awesome thing, and I should have been looking forward to grabbing Nain and Zoe and all of us going on a long vacation after this Nether mess was over, but that's not me. I need to be of use.

I shook my head, forced my thoughts away from the somewhat depressing path they were heading down. Instead, I focused on the city, on the way the streetlights and porch lights in the neighborhoods below sparkled in the night. I looked forward to falling into bed with my mate. When the house we were renting came into sight, I was relieved. It wasn't as nice as coming home to the loft, but all of my favorite people were there, and that was all that really mattered.

When I landed in the backyard, I could feel an array of power signatures nearby. My family. Nain. Shanti. Brennan. Heph and Meaghan. E.

My stomach dropped in dread. If they were all here, something was seriously wrong. I picked up my pace and pulled the back door open, then raced up the stairs to our apartment. I could have rematerialized, sure. But if something was really, really wrong, I almost didn't want to know.

"Please, nobody else be dead," I muttered as I pulled the door open.

"Surprise!"

My ears echoed with the shouts, and then laughs as the assembled supernaturals in my living room took in my response. I looked around. Balloons, streamers. Cyndi Lauper was playing on the stereo.

"What the hell are you all doing?"

"Happy birthday, devil girl," E said, smiling at me.

"Uh. It's not my birthday, though. My birthday isn't until January."

"Wrong," my dad said, crossing his arms. "That's what the state had on your paperwork. Your mother knows better."

I transferred my gaze to my mother, who was standing there smiling at me. I looked around again and shook my head a little, a lump rising in my throat.

"You are such a bunch of assholes," I said, trying to talk around the fact that I was about to start weeping like an idiot. They laughed, and I walked toward E and took Zoe (who was screaming like a little banshee) out of her arms. "Shh. Shh, munchkin," I soothed, bouncing her just a little. Awkward. That was me in every single way, but she didn't seem to mind my awkwardness too much. After a few moments, she quieted, and I smiled down at her.

Nain came up to us, put his hand on my lower back, and I warmed at his touch.

"Happy birthday, Molly," he murmured close to my ear. He held a box out, and my mom took Zoe out of my arms so I could open it.

I tore the ribbon off and opened the black velvet box. It was the kind jewelry comes in, and this one held, other than my wedding band, the most precious piece of jewelry I'd ever seen. I could feel power in it. I peered up at Nain, then back down at the ring.

It was made of silver, inlaid with a second band that was decorated with thorns and vines set in a deep gemstone, which I realized after a moment was hematite, like our wedding bands. I could see Heph's craftsmanship in it, the fine detail, the precision no human hand or machine could ever master.

"It's... wow," I said softly.

Nain picked it up out of the box and took my right hand in his. He placed the ring on my ring finger. "It's not just decorative," he said.

"I can feel power," I said, and he nodded.

"Twist the ring," he told me. Then he looked at Heph. "If this doesn't work, I want my money back."

"You didn't pay me anything, demon," Heph reminded him. "I did it out of the goodness of my heart, and of course it'll work."

Meaghan laughed a little and leaned her head on Heph's bicep. I could feel his happiness, and it made me smile. If anyone deserved that much happiness, it was him.

I looked up at Nain, then spun the upper band of the ring as he'd instructed.

And, as if a switch had been flipped, I could no longer see my hand. I looked at my body. Couldn't see that either. My friends and family cheered.

"No. Way," I breathed.

"Same idea as Hades' helmet," Heph said, obviously pleased with himself. "Just less obnoxious and attention-seeking,"

"Watch it, blacksmith," my dad muttered, and the group laughed.

"Turn it again, and it'll reverse," Heph instructed, and I did it, watching my hand blink back into sight.

"This was your idea?" I asked Nain, and he nodded.

"I know the press bullshit, and now, even more, the way the Normals are, drives you nuts. All the assholes with their phones. Maybe this'll help."

I stood on tiptoe and pressed a kiss to his lips. "Thank you so much, husband," I said softly against his mouth.

He kissed me back, then wrapped me in his arms, where I stood happily for as long as I could before I had to turn my attention to someone else. I opened gifts from everyone. Heph and Meaghan had brought me a bunch of Meaghan's handmade candles and Heph had crafted a new knife for me.

"Gorgeous," I murmured.

"Give her a weapon, she's happy," Shanti joked and I laughed. Shanti (and Zero, who was still adjusting to his turning and had stayed home with the vampires) had given me a bunch of comic-book-related t-shirts and trade paperbacks of comics I'd missed. E gave me a pretty blue vintage McCoy planter, and seemed nervous, then pleased that I liked it so much. Brennan gave me a vintage Wonder Woman lunch box, and I thanked him. It was his thing, with me. Wonder Woman. I swallowed a little, gave him a quick hug in thanks.

The final gift came from my parents. My dad handed me another small box that contained a delicate black metal chain. I wasn't sure what it was made from, but guessed it was something from the Nether. On the chain hung a tiny, delicate pair of black wings that looked a lot like mine. I glanced at Heph, again recognizing his work.

"They all kept you busy, huh?" I asked.

"It was a pleasure, Queenie," he said, obviously pleased that I had recognized his craftsmanship.

I looked up at my mom questioningly.

"I know how you despise your wings," she said. "How you wish you didn't have them."

I didn't deny it. They were a pain in the ass. I wished on an almost daily basis that I didn't have them. The only benefit to them was that they made travel convenient. That, and my husband is turned on by them and knows how to touch them in just the right way when he wants to drive me insane.

"No one in existence has wings like that, other than your family, my love. Remember, even though it took us forever to find you, that you are eternally, and always have been, one of us. That you are loved beyond reckoning. That, if we could have, we would have moved Earth and the heavens themselves to protect you."

I ran my fingertip over the delicate work, the black metal. "Thanks, Mom and Dad," I said, stupidly on the verge of bawling again. I hugged my mom, then kissed my dad on the cheek. I held the box out to Nain, and he fastened the thread-like chain around my neck. The charm fell just to the hollow of my throat.

Oh. He liked the way it looked. I glanced at my husband, my body instantly aware of how he was looking at me. *You get turned on by the weirdest things*, I thought at him.

Nope. Just you, he thought back, and I felt my entire body warm.

Just then, Hephaestus boomed, "Cake. Now!"

They sang an absolutely horrid rendition of the

birthday song to me, and we demolished the chocolate cake in minutes. We sat and laughed and talked and it was the most relaxed I'd felt in forever. Slowly but surely, our company started trickling away, leaving my parents, Heph and Meghan, E, Nain and me. At some point, Nain had taken Zoe out of my arms, and he was walking back and forth across the kitchen with her. My mom and dad were sitting at the kitchen table with E, and I headed back in there after I saw Shanti out.

My mom set a plainly-wrapped package down on the table and held her hands out for Zoe. Nain handed her over, and it made me ache, how tender he was, how careful he was when he was with her.

Something must have flowed through our connection, because he met my eyes at that instant. *Okay. You were right. She's worth saving, and we'll do whatever it takes to keep our baby girl sane*, he said in my mind, and I smiled.

I'm always right, I thought back at him, and he shook his head, but not before I detected a tiny smile on his lips.

"Look at you, you gorgeous angel," Tisiphone was cooing at Zoe. "We are going to teach you how to swing a sword and disembowel your enemies and…"

"Mom," I said.

"What?"

"She's six weeks old. No disemboweling of enemies until she's in kindergarten."

"Fine," my mom said, turning back to Zoe. "And you will learn every song Cyndi Lauper ever recorded and when you're old enough, I will share with you the glory that is Richard Marx."

Nain made a gagging sound as my mom sat down at the kitchen table, cradling Zoe in her arms. She nodded toward the box, then looked at Nain.

"It occurred to me that I never properly welcomed you to the family, demon," she said. "That's for you."

Nain and I exchanged a glance, and Nain stepped over to the table and lifted the lid off the box. I was beside him, peering around his body to see what it was.

There was an ax in the box. Long handle, wicked crescent-shaped blade. The whole thing was about the size of a steak knife.

"Uh. Thanks." Nain said. "It'll... look nice in our living room." It was cute, watching him trying to be polite to my mom.

"Pick it up, you jackass," Heph said, and Nain flipped him the bird. He reached into the box and picked it up. Nothing happened.

"Okay," Nain said, hefting it.

"Focus, demon," my mom said. "This is your weapon, made only for you by the most talented craftsperson in this age or any other. Think of it as your weapon, and it will become all it was meant to be."

Nain looked at me again, then down at his hand. He closed his eyes, and, as I watched, the ax changed, from something that was small enough to be a toy, to an ax with a handle almost as tall as Nain, a razor edge to the rounded blade. The carvings I'd seen on the head were easier to see now. It was the crest of the Furies, the scales of justice ringed in flame.

"Wow," I breathed. "It's gorgeous, Heph."

"Thanks, Queenie. It'll look a lot prettier stained with the blood of our enemies."

"Boys," my mom muttered.

Nain had opened his eyes gain, and his gaze traveled the weapon. "I've never used one of these before," he said, still studying it.

"This is similar to the flamesword the Furies have," Heph explained. "It's instinctive. Molly had never held a sword until the day her flamesword appeared, right?" he said, this last directed at me.

I nodded, unable to take my eyes off of my husband and his great big... ax.

Nain looked down, a little a smirk forming on his lips. *Such impure emotions, baby*, he said in my mind.

As soon as Zoe's asleep, I'm showing you just how impure, I thought at him.

"So I'll be able to use it right away," Nain said to Heph after clearing his throat.

"Gods, the hormones flowing through this place," my mother crooned at Zoe. "Like rabid sprites, these two."

"Mom!"

"Rabid sprites in heat," Heph corrected.

"Oh, Christ," I said, plopping down into one of the other chairs.

"Okay, so now that we've got that settled..." Nain said.

"Yeah, you can use it right away. It should do a little something extra, if our theory is correct," Heph said.

"Theory?" I asked.

"Just hold it like you're about to take a swing at something," Heph said to Nain.

Frowning a little, Nain took the ax in both hands and moved, swinging the ax in a close arc.

As soon as he moved, black flames, like the ones on my flamesword, began to dance along the edges of his blade.

"Black flames, of course," my mom said. "It would be."

"Just like Queenie's," Heph agreed.

Nain was staring at his ax with an almost reverent look on his face. "I don't get it," he said after a moment, still watching the flames dance.

"All of that lovely blood you've exchanged with my daughter," my mom explained. "She already told me you have healing abilities now. We can safely assume your lifespan is much, much longer than is natural for your kind, thanks, again, to her blood and power flowing through you. This is just another sign of how your powers have joined with hers. Our powers are usually passed on to our children. I've never even imagined it would happen via mating before," she finished.

"He's worthy of it," Heph said.

"Yes, he'd better be," my mom said mildly. Then she handed Zoe to me and stood up.

"Thank you, Tisiphone," Nain said, bowing his head to her.

"You're very welcome. Now, here is the rest of my welcome to you. If you hurt my daughter, ever, in any way, I will rip your testicles off and make you watch as I feed them to Cerberus. Understand?"

Nain cleared his throat. "Perfectly. What is it with you Fury women threatening my balls?"

"We're experts at effective torture methods," my mom said with a smile.

"Right," Nain said. "You know I'm never going to hurt her."

"Keep it that way, demon," she said. Then she came over to me, kissed my cheek, and bent down and pressed a series of kisses to Zoe's head. "I need to get back to Megaera."

"Bye, Mom," I said, then I hugged my dad, and they winked out of sight. After a hug for me and a handshake for Nain, Heph and Meaghan followed suit.

Nain and I looked at the ax still flaming in his hand. "I think your mom likes me," he said finally.

"Of course. She has excellent taste," I replied.

He lowered the ax, and it stopped flaming. He seemed to focus, and it shrank back to the size of a knife.

"Handy," I said.

"Very," he agreed.

CHAPTER THIRTEEN

I was heading in for my semi-regular press conference, which, to my surprise, no one had cancelled in light of that mess on Thanksgiving. I had asked Bren multiple times if he was sure it hadn't been cancelled, and he said that as far as he knew, it was still on. He still hadn't managed to get Petersen on the phone but he hadn't heard otherwise. I left Nain and Zoe, and drove (like a normal person) to downtown Detroit.

Sitting in the driver's seat of my Barracuda felt like being home. I'd nearly forgotten how much I liked to drive; the scent of leather and exhaust, the feel of the engine rumbling. Being out and about among regular people doing regular things was soothing. I needed to give myself time to drive more often. Flying and rematerializing were convenient, but they weren't nearly as comforting.

Of course, getting from the street to the office I needed to be in was another matter. Rematerializing was the lazy girl's way to deal with that, so I did, focusing on appearing at the Fisher Building.

When I appeared in my usual place, I was surrounded by guns.

I stared. A ring of men in black uniforms surrounded me, guns raised, aimed at my head.

My heart pounded. I wasn't afraid. Not really. It hurt like hell to get shot, and I wasn't looking forward to it. It was more rage than anything else. I tried to tamp it down.

I raised my hands, palms out. "Where's Director Matthews?" I asked.

"Matthews never should have been put in charge," one of the gun-toting men said. I recognized him. He was one of the guys who'd been in the SUV with Ross the day the supernatural affairs division had approached me at my house.

"I'll ask again, then," I said. "Where is Matthews?"

"Here," Brennan said. I looked toward the exterior door of the office I had rematerialized in, and Brennan was there, a gun at his head as well, held by none other than former Director Ross.

I laughed. I couldn't help it.

"What are you laughing at?" Ross shouted. He kept his gun trained on Brennan. "I swear I'll kill him, you crazy bitch. I lost everything because the two of you showed me up."

"You pathetic little excuse for a man," I said, aware of the snarl, the slight hiss in my voice. The fear level in the room rose significantly. "Of all the shit I'm dealing with right now, you are about the least terrifying. And you're fucking stupid to boot."

I focused, and, half a second later, I rematerialized behind Brennan, and pulled him to just outside the office.

"Are we leaving this alone or kicking ass, Director?" I asked.

He was already stripping, getting ready to shift. Shouting erupted from the other side of the door, angry voices.

Brennan shifted, tall, blond man to humongous black panther with the same blue eyes.

"Ready?" I asked quietly, and the panther gave an almost-human nod.

"Should I be scary?"

I felt humor from Brennan, and I grinned and released a blast of energy. One of the men screamed, and then the gunfire started. I brought out my flamesword, started slicing out at our attackers, rage and instinct guiding me. I could hear Brennan snarling, and caught the sight of him with his jaws around Ross's throat. We'd done this dozens of times: he'd hold the one who knew the most for me to question while I took out my aggressions on the others.

In this case, it was mostly about crowd control. I used the sword to knock the guns out of their hands. It wasn't hard. Without their guns, eventually every one of the men surrendered, sinking to their knees and raising their hands. It took some time, but I broke into their minds and made them forget everything about what they'd been involved in with Ross. I may have also made them piss themselves, but considering that they'd just had their guns pointed at my head, I thought I was being pretty merciful. I watched them leave, all looking confused and kind of lost.

Then I turned to Brennan, who was still holding Ross down, huge teeth clamped around the man's throat. I grabbed the pile of clothing Brennan had shed in the hallway and closed the door, which was hanging crookedly on its hinges after the way I'd blasted it in.

Oops.

"Okay, let him up," I said. Brennan did, with a final growl, then shifted back. Ross lay on the floor, shaking, glaring at Brennan. I tossed Brennan his clothes.

"You're lucky I didn't bite down," Brennan told Ross as he started pulling on his pants. "Move, just a little. Give me an excuse to rip your throat out. Please," he added.

"Where's Petersen, Ross?" I asked.

Ross just glared at me. Brennan and I exchanged a look, and he stepped over to where he'd knocked Ross's gun out of his hand, picked it up and hefted it in his hand.

"It's been a long time since I've shot anybody," he said conversationally.

"I bet. You usually go for the ripping and slashing," I said.

"Something satisfying about blowing off kneecaps, though," Brennan mused. "And considering you set up one of my best friends just now — stupidly, by the way. Did you even pay attention to all the times she *hasn't* been taken down by gunfire? — I'll be more than happy to hobble you permanently."

It really was heartwarming, when my friends threatened to maim someone on my behalf.

"So let's try again," I said. "Where's Petersen?"

"There are shallow graves all over this city, Angel," Ross said with a sneer. "You know about at least a few of those, don't you?"

"Why?" I asked. "Why go after him?"

Ross just smirked at us... and Brennan lost his patience. He shot Ross in the foot, a shot that barely grazed the side of his big toe, but scared him enough that he screamed like a little girl.

"That was a warning shot," Bren said, aiming again. "Answer her question."

"She's so big and bad, why doesn't she take care of me? Why does she need you?"

"Oh, she doesn't need me. I've just been looking forward to making you bleed," Brennan said.

I had to turn away then. As insane as this was, I had to try not to laugh. I could feel how much Brennan was enjoying this. He was enraged, sure, but I could tell this had been a long time coming.

"But if you really piss me off, I'll step aside and let her do her thing. Believe me, you'll wish you'd been shot. Answer her question."

For a minute, Ross just cradled his wounded foot. Then he muttered, "He was working on smoothing things over with the city, reassuring the mayor and the police department that you're not nearly the menace that gold guy claimed you were. And he was getting through."

Now it made sense. Fewer articles and news reports lately about what a menace I was. That was thanks to Petersen.

And now I was really pissed at Ross.

"And because he demoted you," I said.

Ross clamped his mouth shut.

"We can't kill him now," I said to Bren. "He has crimes to answer for, and Petersen's family deserves to know what happened."

Bren nodded and took his phone out of his pocket. I could tell from his end of the conversation that he was talking to someone in the DPD's supernatural division.

He hung up, still keeping the gun on Ross. "DPD's on the way," he said.

"I'm sorry about Petersen. I know you liked him," I told him.

His voice was subdued as he said, "He was a good guy. He got it. He saw the big picture. And he understood that we should all be kissing your feet instead of making your life harder."

I grimaced. "Ew, feet," I said, and he let out a short laugh.

"This is so disgusting," Ross said.

Neither of us looked at him. Bren squeezed the trigger again, grazing the side of Ross's other foot, and I shot just a teensy bit of flame. Just enough to singe his eyebrows and eyelashes. He shouted a bunch of profanity at us, and Bren rolled his eyes.

"If you need me to make a statement or whatever, let me know," I said, and Brennan nodded his thanks.

DPD showed up a little bit later, four officers altogether. They cuffed Ross, greeted me. There was no weirdness, no fear, and for that I was grateful.

Brennan and I followed them out and watched them load Ross into one of the cars.

"I should have known something was up when I couldn't get Petersen," Brennan said finally. "I'm sorry, Molly."

"Actually, that was kind of satisfying."

His gaze landed on my car. "You mean you actually drove?" he asked, and I nodded. We walked to my car, and he ran his hand over the hood, then looked back at me. "You're changing."

"Nothing stays the same," I replied. "Hopefully once this current mess is finished, I'll have some time to figure it all out."

I glanced around, noting that, unfortunately, I was being recognized. Passersby had their phones raised, and the emotions coming from them were mostly fear and uncertainty.

"You should try not to be seen with me too much," I said.

"Am I supposed to be ashamed to be your friend?"

"It might complicate things with your job."

"Molly, my job is watching you, remember?"

I opened my car door. "Believe me, I'm trying to forget. Do you need a ride?"

He shook his head and pointed a few cars down, where his SUV was parked.

"Okay. Um. Is it weird to say that was kind of fun?"

He chuckled softly. "I'm glad it's not just me."

He started walking away, and I shook my head again and got into my car. I made sure he got into his and drove away without any issues, and then I left as well, heading toward the Netherwoods to pick up Zoe and Sean.

CHAPTER FOURTEEN

I was on my way to Delray and the Netherwoods when my phone rang. I dug it out of my pocket, glanced at it. Nain's number.

"Hey," I said.

"Where are you?" he sounded stressed. Pissed.

"On my way to pick up Zoe and Sean. I'll be there in about ten minutes. Why?"

"You need to get there now," he said, and my stomach twisted.

"What's going on?"

"Hyperion's attacking. The whole fucking thing is burning."

I pulled over to the curb and slammed the Barracuda into park. I focused, rematerializing just outside of the Netherwoods, where I usually dropped Zoe off with my parents. Nain was there.

The Netherwoods were on fire.

I ran toward the woods, and Nain caught up with me and grabbed my arm.

"Wait," he said, and I struggled, trying to get in, trying to get to our daughter.

"Zoe," I said, pulling harder.

"You know this is a fucking trap. You know it. Everyone else is coming. Just wait a second."

I stopped struggling, staring at the woods. Nain was tense, worried. Angrier than he'd been in a long time.

"She's in there, Nain," I said.

There was a loud series of "crack" sounds behind us.

"Then let's go get her, Queenie," Heph said, striding forward with Athena, Asclepias, E, Hestia, Persephone, and Gaia.

I nodded, started walking forward.

"Babe," Nain said, reaching out and pulling me back to him again.

"What? We have to do this now," I said, looking at the woods, the flames leaping from some of the trees.

"I know. Listen to me. If you need it, you take what you need from me. Feed, absorb, whatever you need. Okay?"

I pulled my arm out of his grip. "You're not a walking battery, Nain. I'm not going to weaken you."

He tossed his ax to the ground and wrapped his hands around my biceps, then pulled me close to him. He looked into my face, his eyes locked on mine.

"I am your husband. I am your mate. I am your fucking happily ever after. I will be whatever you need me to be, because you're the most important thing in my life. So if you need to use me as a walking, ax-swinging battery, you do it so we can wake up together tomorrow morning. So we can spoil our daughter rotten and do all that parent shit we're clueless about. Okay?"

My breath caught in my throat. This man. What in the hell had I ever done to deserve having someone like this in my life? I leaned forward and pressed my lips to his as tears escaped my eyes. I sniffed, and he kissed me again, then kissed my eyes, banishing my tears with his lips.

"It's not just me. I can't lose you," I said.

"You won't. I'm depending on you saving my ass if I

ever need it. Don't forget that," he said.

"I love you, Bael," I whispered.

"And I love you, Mollis Eth-Hades," he murmured. "Promise me you'll use me if you have to, baby."

I nodded and kissed him again. "I promise."

"Okay. Let's go find our baby girl."

We walked into the Netherwoods together, all of us, and the second I was inside the outer line of trees, I could feel the familiar, yet different, energy of the Nether. The amethyst sky was clouded with smoke, and, several hundred feet away, trees were burning.

We ran, charging as one toward the fires, and the closer we got, the more clearly we could hear sounds of battle. My father's booming voice, throwing insults, my aunt occasionally calling out instructions to Hades.

In the middle of it all was Hyperion, dressed head to toe in gold, as always, his golden face sporting a pair of long, jagged scars from my father's scythe and sword from the last times they'd faced off.

Without a word, we charged him. E and I took to the air, and the rest stayed on the ground. Hades and Hyperion were fighting, and Hyperion laughed when he saw us.

"How convenient," he shouted. "I should have done this a long time ago!"

With a roar, Nain, in his full demon form, charged forward, swinging his ax, the black flames hissing as the blade sliced through the air. Hyperion ducked it easily, but that was the plan; Heph stood to Hyperion's unprotected side, whipped a length of heavy chain (which was glowing red as if it had just been taken out of the fires), and it wrapped around Hyperion's throat.

Hyperion screamed in agony, and Heph tugged.

My turn. I soared over Hyperion and brought my flamesword down toward his throat. At the last second, just before I made contact, he reached out almost impossibly quickly, and grabbed my ankle, pulling me down, which saved his neck from my blade. He threw me hard to the ground, and my wing crunched under me painfully.

I ignored it. I charged him again just as he got free of Heph's chain. Nain was swinging at him again, and he was swinging his golden sword back at Nain.

I charged him, barely recognizing the enraged shriek that escaped me at the sight of this golden asshole slicing at my mate.

On impact, I hit him so hard my teeth rattled. It was like hitting a concrete wall, but it was enough to get him off of my husband. He got ready to strike me, and Hades appeared to his left, slicing out with the black-bladed sword he uses sometimes.

He caught the edge of Hyperion's armor, and Hyperion sneered and shoved him back.

"You," he roared, glaring at me with those freaky gold eyes. "You have gotten in my way too many times, abomination. All I wanted was to come here and kill your father for these scars he gave me. For the insults and squalor he forced me to live with all those centuries. Maybe to eradicate those children everyone is so intent on protecting. And you have to come and stick your nose in it. You have continually gotten in my way. I thought keeping you busy with hordes of fearful humans would work until I was ready to deal with you. They are even more idiotic than I realized."

"Sorry your witch hunt plan didn't work," I said. "Nice try, though. Asshole," I added, swinging out.

He moved to block my strike, which was just what I wanted. Nain stood behind him, ax poised, and he brought it down hard. He was aiming for the neck, of course, but Hyperion moved just before he struck, and Nain's blade mostly hit armor, though it did cut nicely into the flesh below Hyperion's ear. The gaping wound there streamed blood, and Hyperion roared in rage.

"Now," I shouted, and all of the immortals attacked at

once, Heph swinging a giant, deadly-looking hammer, Nain with his ax, my aunt with her flamesword, E with her daggers, Hestia and Athena with bows and arrows. Asclepias stood back, ready to jump in and heal any of us who needed it. Hades snarled and swung his sword.

Hyperion just laughed, and then he started turning kind of an orangey color.

"Take cover!" Asclepias shouted. As quickly as they could, the immortals dove behind trees and boulders. Nain shoved me behind an outcropping of black stone, then covered my body with his.

I heard Hyperion laughing, and then there was a gigantic "boom," like the sound of something exploding. Heat washed over me.

It passed, and I shoved at Nain. He got up, pulling me up with him. He had his ax at the ready.

"Holy fuck," I muttered.

For several feet all the way around Hyperion, the world was burning. Flames licked along the ground, and everything was scorched. My father had been the last to try to take cover, and his robes were on fire.

Yet he and Hyperion lunged at one another, my father snarling.

Hyperion was obviously weakened from his insane blast attack, yet he met my father's attack and struck back. Their swords clanged, and the immortals slowly but surely started converging on Hyperion again.

Hades stumbled.

"Fuck," I said, my stomach sinking. I focused, rematerializing behind my dad so I could pull him away.

It took a fraction of a second.

By the time I got there, his head was falling to the ground. Hyperion was laughing.

"Enough for today, godling," he said, giving me a sarcastic salute. And then he was gone.

I could barely hear him. Not over the anguished scream that came from my parents' castle behind us. I couldn't hear or feel anything over the agony coming from that direction.

From my mother.

I crumpled to the ground, her agony and anguish flooding me. I screamed, and heard my aunt doing the same.

It was bad enough on its own.

But worse, feeling my mother's devastation over the loss of her mate, over the snapping of that bond, brought me right back to that night in the Packard plant, right back to the instant I'd felt Nain die. I relived it all over again: the pain, the emptiness, the overwhelming sense of loss so strong, so complete that the last thing in the world I wanted to do was contemplate living another moment.

My mother was going through it. And she'd had thousands and thousands of years of loving my father, of wanting him from afar.

God, I could feel it. Such immense loss I swore it would swallow the whole world.

I was peripherally aware of Nain holding me, of his strong arms around me, yet all I could do was wail both in commiseration with what my mother was feeling, as well as with my own loss.

It hit me: I'd lost my father. I could barely contain my emotions, and a high-pitched shriek that barely seemed to belong to me escaped me. I was crying so hard I could barely move, and my own sense of loss was only compounded by my mother's lingering anguish and the mourning of all the immortals around me.

I sat up slowly. Nain pulled me close to him, put his hands in my hair.

"Don't look, baby. You don't need to look," he said, his voice full of emotion. I'd forgotten how my grief would hit him now, how this was making him re-live his own grief over the breaking of our bond. His heart was pounding, his hands shaking under the effects of what he'd felt from me.

"I can't fucking feel that again," he said, voice low and hoarse. I cried, holding him tight, grasping the fabric of his shirt in my hands as I clung to him. I kept my face buried against his neck.

From the palace, I could still hear my mother's wails.

I started standing up. "I need to go to her," I said. "And Zoe." Nain nodded, holding me tight against him as we walked toward the castle, Nain using his body to shield my father's body from my sight.

I heard Asclepias saying he would stand watch over the body. He sounded hollow.

My aunt Meg was kneeling on the ground, sobbing, and when we reached her, I held out my hand and she took it. We walked into my parents' home that way, hands clasped, both of us trembling. Aunt Meg knew where my mother had been staying, guarding the babies, and she led us through the corridors to an interior room. Inside, my Netherhounds were standing guard beside the crib the babies were in, eyes glowing, ears back. Kurt raised his head and gave a mournful howl, and Courtney joined him. I looked around, and saw that my mother was crumpled in a corner, tears streaming down her face. She was ripping at her hair as if she had lost her mind.

And she had. I've been there. The insanity that comes from feeling that bond break is the worst thing I've ever felt. Feeling it secondhand, through her, was enough to make me want to lose my mind right alongside her. I went to my mom, knelt beside her, and gathered her into my arms.

She was shaking, keening. Aunt Meg gently took her hands away from her hair and held them firmly in her own so my mom wouldn't hurt herself.

I watched Nain lean over and pick up a crying Zoe out of the playpen, then lift Sean in his other arm. He looked helpless, and clueless, but he did it nonetheless.

For some reason, that only made me cry harder.

I don't know how long we stayed that way. I know that,

eventually, E and Hestia came in and took the kids. There was a lot of talking, immortals and demons coming in and out of the room as arrangements were made. No one dared disturb my mother in her grief. Meg and I sat there with her, holding her, and her tears seemed endless.

Nain came in and quietly told me they were taking Zoe and Sean home, and asked if there was anything I needed. I reached out for him, and he took my hand, crouched on his heels. His eyes met mine, and I could see that his were red-rimmed, as if he'd been crying.

Nain pressed his lips to my fingers, lingered there.

"You've been everything I need," I said in answer to his question. "I love you."

"I love you. Take all the time you need. I've got everything else under control, all right?"

I nodded, and he kissed my fingertips.

"I am sorry for your loss, Tisiphone," he said to my mother, bowing his head to her.

"You made her feel this," she said in a hoarse whisper.

"Mom," I said softly.

"I want to kill you for that. I had no idea it did this. But I understand now why she forgave you. If I had another chance with Hades, I'd take it in a heartbeat. I won't get it. I won't get it," she repeated, and then she was incomprehensible again. Nain looked at me helplessly, sorrow and guilt flowing from him.

I love you. I'll be home soon, I thought at him.

Love you more, he answered. Then he rose and walked out of the room.

We sat there for hours, and I started noticing things. Feeling things.

Something was different.

Not just our mourning. Not just the overwhelming sense of loss that seemed, just then, to envelop all of existence.

Something else.

I opened my eyes and looked at my mother, who was

still crying, rocking back and forth in my aunt's arms. And I saw so much more than I usually did.

I saw... everything.

Her best moments. Her happiest.

Her worst.

I saw her sins. The things she felt most guilty about. The things she wanted no one else to see.

Chief among them, the moment she left me in the mortal realm. It was as if that instance, that scene of her life, that moment she left a screaming, raven-haired baby on the front stoop of a Detroit church, was front and center, her shame. There were others. There were many things I didn't want to see about my mother. About how she had sex with Cithaerus, her former lover, trying to pretend he was Hades. How she'd held such deep hatred for Persephone. There was guilt over the fact that her sister Alecto had betrayed me, and she'd never seen it coming. Thousands of sins, from the almost ridiculously meaningless to the big ones; I saw them all.

I heard myself gasp. I closed my eyes again, trying not to see it. And when I opened them and looked away, I ended up looking at my aunt Meg, and it happened all over again, an instantaneous cataloguing of her sins.

I let go of my mom and grabbed my head.

"What's wrong, Mollis?" my aunt asked worriedly.

I was freaked out so much that the emotions coming from me were enough to snap my mother out of the haze of grief she was in. She took my shoulders. "Mollis?" she said.

I shook my head.

"Mollis!" she said, louder.

"Mom," I said. "I don't want it."

"Don't want what?"

I opened my mind. And I let her see.

The next thing I felt from her was grief for me, mingling with her grief for her mate.

"No. No, no, no," she murmured, holding me closer.

"My baby. I don't want you to live the way he did. Oh, gods," she cried.

I disentangled myself from my mother and aunt, and stood up.

I couldn't take it anymore.

"Where are you going?" my mom asked, struggling to her feet as my aunt took her hand.

I felt my rage rising.

"I'm going to go hurt a fucker. I am going to avenge Apollo. And most of all, I am going to avenge my father."

"Mollis…" my aunt began, but my mom put a hand on her arm and silenced her.

She took me into her arms. "Do what you need to do. Cause some pain for me while you're at it."

"I will," I promised her.

"Are you stupid?" Aunt Meg cut in, unable to hold herself back anymore. "Did you see him? Did you see where there was an entire group of immortals attacking him, and he walked away?"

"I saw," I said, keeping my eyes on my mom. "He won't walk away again. I'll do whatever it takes."

I turned and walked out.

Hyperion would pay. But first, I'd find Nether. And I'd do what needed to be done.

CHAPTER FIFTEEN

I made my way out of the palace, studiously ignoring the demons who dropped to a knee and bowed as I passed.

Did they know? Did they know I had all of my father's abilities? Did they know that every time I looked at them, I could see every dark, twisted, disgusting moment of their lives?

Did they know how strong my father had truly been? Along with his ability to effortlessly see into the souls of every being I passed, I'd inherited the power of the god of death.

I felt it surging within me. It didn't add to my power, necessarily. It was hard to explain. It felt like my existing power was focused. A razor blade instead of a bludgeon.

As if it would take no effort at all for me to hurt whoever I was looking at in the worst way possible.

This, I wanted.

This, I would use for all it was worth.

I stalked through the courtyard. My father's body had been removed. I wasn't sure what came next. I couldn't think about it right then, anyway.

I left the Netherwoods, taking a deep breath of relief when it let me go. I'd been half expecting to be trapped there, just like before. I never wanted to go back. I would, because I had to.

I could feel panic setting in, shoved it aside. Not now. I'd think about that another time. I tried to think. Tried to remember all of the places I'd seen Nether.

The freeway.

Downtown.

Belle Isle.

My house.

I'd try there first.

I rematerialized back in my old neighborhood, the empty lot where my house had once been. The last place I'd seen her.

I remembered her parting words to me: "Hatred makes me strong." At the moment, I could understand them, even if I didn't agree. Because while I hated Hyperion, without a single doubt, it was my love for my parents, my love for my husband and child, that made me determined to hunt him down and make him pay.

He would not take another person from me. I would give my mother her vengeance.

I looked around. It was dark. It had snowed, just a little, and that made the world brighter than it should have been.

She was there. I could feel her.

I drew my flamesword, the black flames giving the area around me an eerie glow.

I walked across my former lot, toward the back where the huge lilac hedge still stood, branches bare now with the onset of winter.

I numbly realized that it was only a week before Christmas. It's crazy, the shit that comes to you at times like that.

I could feel her. She was full of rage and hatred.

She was afraid. Terrified.

And she felt guilty.

As my gaze landed on Nether, all I felt was pity.

She was so broken. Her white hair was still snarled, bits of twigs and leaves and who knew what all else ensnared in the strands. Her clothing was practically falling off of her, it was so torn, disintegrating with filth.

In addition to the normal filth, there was blood. So much blood. She stank of it, and she sat there rocking, her empty gaze locked on me.

I put the sword away. "Nether," I said, settling myself beside her.

She just kept rocking, though her gaze followed me. She was uncertain. Confused. When I looked at her, I saw everything.

Uppermost on her list of sins was injuring Aether. And she'd been forced to do it because he'd been attacking her just as insanely as she'd been attacking him. She had just been the one to finally land a lucky blow.

There weren't many others. How much can you really do when you've been in a prison, serving as a prison, for most of your existence? Ironic, isn't it, that the embodiment of evil had fewer sins to her name than anyone else I knew?

The other sin I saw explained all of the blood.

And it explained how, exactly, Hyperion had known so much about my deeds. I could see it there, an instant of knowing, of seeing and feeling what she'd felt. Hyperion had found her. Approached her. Tried to reason with her. And when she'd refused to help him, he'd gone away and come back later, doing what Hyperion does, apparently.

He took what he wanted, through force. He caught her by surprise and tortured an already-broken being until he got what he wanted and left her bleeding after she finally gave in. The sneak attack had been the key. He never would have been able to defeat her fairly. It enraged me.

I wondered why the imps hadn't protected her.

"Nether, where are the imps?" I asked her.

She shook her head. "I didn't want them. I told them to go to the demon's loft and stay there."

"Nether, they could have helped you," I said.

"They were yours. Mine by rights, but yours in their hearts. I hated them."

We sat in silence, the night quiet around us except for the distant sounds of traffic. The sky was overcast above us, a full moon trying to shine through the clouds. Nearby, I could see my Netherhounds watching, patrolling.

"Freedom is a nightmare," Nether finally said in her flat voice, and it made my heart ache.

"Not always," I said softly. "I'm sorry he did that to you, Nether. He's a monster."

She nodded, eyes still glassy, staring. "I tried not to tell him. You are mine."

"Yours to kill, right?" I asked with a tiny smile.

"Maybe not. Just mine, my Prison," she said. "I have been in your soul. I've told you before that you are as black and broken as I am."

"I remember."

"You are a warrior. You never stop. It confuses me."

"I don't know how to stop, I think," I said, and she nodded.

"That is true. That is part of why he was so determined to destroy you in as many ways as he could. Hyperion knew that if you were still able to fight, you would always be in his way."

"He's strong," I said. "He killed my father."

"The Lord of the Dead is gone?"

I nodded.

"But not entirely. Lady of the Dead," she said.

I hesitated. "I don't want it."

She was watching me, still rocking, still afraid and full of rage. "We rarely get to choose our fate, my Prison," she answered.

"But we can choose how to handle it," I said.

"I never was very good at that part."

"I can't defeat him on my own. You should have seen it, Nether. Every immortal on my team was attacking him, and he did this crazy explosive blast, then killed my father and walked way."

"You need me," she said, and I sensed something from her. Relief? Happiness? It was hard to tell, mixed in with all of her rage and confusion.

"I need you," I agreed. "I won't force you. I won't take what isn't mine. But you keep telling me freedom is a nightmare." I stopped. I couldn't believe what I was saying, what I was offering her. I also knew it was the only way to avenge my father and keep my family, my world, safe from Hyperion.

"You would be my Prison again," she said softly.

"Or your sanctuary, depending on how you look at it," I answered.

"You know what I am. You know how I am. There is no good in me, my Prison. I would betray you."

I shrugged. "You might. But, as you say, I'm yours. Would you really betray something you've claimed?"

"I would eventually want my freedom. I would forget what a nightmare it is to be free. I would forget the noise and the oppressive sense of space around me. I would forget it all and rage against you for my freedom."

"And if that happened, would you want me to free you again? Or would you want me to fight to keep you contained?"

She was silent for a moment. Then she said quietly, "I am lost here, my Prison. I don't know how to exist. Once upon a time, I knew. I knew what it was to be free, to love, to know the ecstasy that comes with letting myself feel. It's been too long, and I don't know how to be anything other than a prison. A power source. And I'm tired. So tired. All I want to do is sleep, my Prison."

"I know," I answered. Oh, I could definitely relate.

"You will hurt him," she said.

"Badly," I answered.

She watched me for a few moments, and I was afraid to hear her response, either way. Whether she said yes or no, in some ways I was completely screwed.

Like I said. I'd do whatever it takes.

"You are the only Prison worthy of me, Lady of the Dead," she said. Then she held out her hands, and I held mine out, and she settled her small, cold hands in my palms. "Give me my rest, my Prison," she said.

I bit my lip, trying to fight back tears. I was getting what I wanted. I was getting Nether contained, and getting a power boost so I could kick Hyperion's ass.

I also knew I was setting myself up for a lifelong struggle to keep her contained. Because she would forget.

I would have to stay strong. I would have to be a worthy prison.

"You're sure?" I asked softly, and she nodded and closed her eyes. I studied her for a moment, determined to remember this broken being, with her white hair and black eyes, so that when she did rail against me, I wouldn't hate her. She'd felt enough hatred in her lifetime.

I blinked back tears. "Nether, as the goddess of death, the ultimate judge of souls and their punishment," I began, saying words similar to those I'd heard my father use many, many times, power beginning to swirl like a hurricane around us, "I sentence you to eternity served in a prison created entirely of the Nether, a being created entirely of the Nether." I paused, taking a breath as tears rolled down my cheeks. "It will be so," I finished.

I felt my power snap, and the embodiment of Nether started to dissolve, transforming before my eyes to a black mist. When it came toward me, I stayed still and absorbed every bit of it.

I felt Nether settle herself into that empty place in my soul, the one she'd inhabited before.

"Thank you, my Prison," she whispered in my mind.

And she slept.

I sat there for a moment, letting her feel my gratitude. I hoped it came across. Then I stood up, and the dogs came to me.

And, from the shadows, my imps.

"Mistress," Dahael and Bash said, each thumping a fist to their chest, dropping to a knee. Tears were streaming down Dahael's face, and Bash was blinking hard.

"My friends," I said, putting a fist to my chest as well, and bowing my head to them. Then I pulled Dahael into a hug, and she hugged me back with a small, crackly laugh.

"Missed you, Mistress," she said, patting my shoulder.

"I missed you, too. Life was weird without you guys around."

"We are useful," Bash said.

"You're part of my crazy, bizarre family. I missed you."

I felt a bit of embarrassed happiness from the imps as I looked over the small group with their toothy grins and wrinkled faces. And, standing to the right of them, my Netherhounds, who had been my companions before anyone else.

"Well. Shall we hunt? I have a father to avenge."

The imps smiled their sharp little grins, and the Netherhounds howled, and that was all the affirmation I needed. I rose into the air, knowing my imps and hounds would catch up with me.

As I flew, I noticed a shape to my left, and felt Eunomia's presence.

"Devil girl," she said in greeting.

"E," I said.

She took my hand. "I only wish there was a soul I could have the honor of escorting to your mother, my lady," she said, and I squeezed her hand. "But seeing him die will be satisfying, and I will bear witness."

We flew, E's bat-like wings and my feathered wings propelling us through the freezing night air quickly. I was focused. We circled over the city, making our circles smaller, working our way in.

"He's near," I said after a couple of hours. The sky was starting to get lighter in the East. E nodded and followed me in as I started soaring down to the Earth's surface. The familiar landscape of the city centered me, and I realized where I was.

The fucking jerk.

The Packard plant.

"He really needs to die a painful death, Mollis," E said as we landed just outside the part of the factory where the gateway had once existed.

The part where Nain had died.

"He will," I said.

E and I stalked into the dark factory, the scent of decay and urine greeting us. It was nearly pitch black inside. I could make out the vague shapes of concrete pillars. Further down, exactly where I knew the bastard would be, I could see the flickers of a fire. I nodded my head in that direction, and E followed me. I drew my flamesword.

It was bigger now. That did not surprise me in the least.

"Size matters," E murmured.

"Always," I agreed, and she let out a short laugh. I was really glad she had come with me. "I do the fighting," I told her.

"Of course."

My imps and my hounds had found us, and they travelled in the shadows of the factory, watching.

"He will try to escape," E said under her breath.

I glanced at the Netherhounds. "He won't manage it."

As we approached, it was to see Hyperion sitting on what looked like the discarded seat from a car. A fire was burning in a steel barrel nearby. At the left was the place where the gateway had once existed.

He leered at me. "This is where it happened, isn't it?" he asked.

I didn't need to look at the spot he was gesturing to. That patch of pitted, blackened concrete was etched into my memory for the rest of my long existence.

"Did it destroy you, Fury? Did you curl up in a ball and cry? It must have been something, that moment when you realized you'd killed your own mate. Wish I could have seen that."

His sins were a running montage in my psyche. He had much to atone for, not the least of which was murdering my father, raping my mother, and torturing the most lost girl I'd ever known.

I raised my sword in front of me. "It will be cleansed with your blood," I said, and I barely recognized my own voice.

In an instant I was on him, slashing, listening to the comforting sizzle of the flames from my sword as it hissed through the air.

I'd forgotten what it felt like to have Nether's power infusing me. As I slashed and stabbed at Hyperion, I remembered that day in my father's throne room in the original Nether, the way I threw Ares and Dionysus across it and into the wall. The way it had taken nothing more than a wave of my hand to end immortal life.

I soared with it. Full. My arms didn't tire, my body didn't ache. My sword soon started to rend his golden armor, flaying it wide open. I didn't slow down, and soon his confidence turned to confusion.

And then, my favorite of enemy emotions: fear.

I fed, and I slashed, and eventually, his armor hung in tatters.

He backed away, trying to get out of my reach.

And then I felt his power change, as he prepared to try to rematerialize. And that's when Kurt and Courtney charged in. Each of them grabbed a hold of one of his ankles, their huge, sharp teeth puncturing the armor there.

"No!" he shouted, trying to kick the hounds away. They just snarled, eyes glowing up at him, preventing him from taking the coward's way out yet again.

"Ridiculous Titan. There is no escape from death," I hissed.

That was when terror began to roll through him, and it was delicious.

"This is for Apollo," I said, slashing at his now-exposed stomach, and he howled. My sword hissed as blood met flame. The hounds let go, but stayed close, watching ever move Hyperion made. This was their role. Hunters, trappers. Dogs that had once served my father, assisted my mother and aunts in their work. There was no escape when a Netherhound decided to trap you. Finally, I understood.

I advanced on Hyperion again.

"This is for my mother," I said, hefting the sword high and bringing it down, stabbing him through the chest, and he screamed.

"For Nether," I said, and slashed across his throat and watched his blood flow over my blade and down his destroyed armor.

I exchanged a glance with E, and she gave me a somber nod.

"And this is for my father." I said. "In the immortal words of my husband, checkmate, motherfucker."

Then I released it. I let Nether's insane power flow through me. I let it blast into him, and he screamed, and soon there was nothing left.

E, the imps, my hounds, and I stood in silence for a long while.

E walked over to me and wrapped me in her thin, strong arms, and I hugged her back.

"I have served as a witness to Hyperion's downfall. I will report what has happened here to your mother, my friend."

"Thank you, E."

She gave me a tiny bow. "Go home to your family."

I nodded and watched her leave.

And then I flew toward home, trying to give myself enough time to calm down. Adrenaline was still flowing through me. Rage. Mine and Nether's.

There was relief, too. It was done. I'd figure everything else out later.

When I got home, I unlocked the door to our apartment, realizing we could finally go home to the loft now. The thought made me smile.

I closed the door behind me and tiptoed over to Zoe's bassinet. I glanced down at myself. I guessed I wouldn't be picking her up. My black clothing was still soaked in blood, crusted over with blood older than that. Instead, I leaned over and looked at her.

"My beautiful girl," I whispered, drinking in the sight of her soft baby cheeks, her long black eyelashes and her mass of shining curls. "I love you, my munchkin."

Look what you helped me protect, Nether, I thought, and felt a contentment deep in my soul. I smiled and turned around when I felt Nain's presence.

He was standing in the doorway to our bedroom, dressed in a pair of low-slung sweatpants.

He held his hand out to me.

I went to him.

And he made me feel sane again.

After saying so many things without the need for words, Nain and I lay in our bed wrapped in each other's arms, and I told him everything. About how I had inherited Hades' mantle as ruler of the dead. About Nether, which he wasn't happy about because he knew better than anyone what it had taken for me to try to keep her under control before. I told him about Hyperion's end, and felt his anger, as well as his satisfaction at my victory.

"I should have been there," he said.

I shook my head. "I needed to know you and Zoe were safe. Which meant away from him. You were exactly where I needed you to be."

He held me tighter as I told him what it was like to have Hades' ability. The nice thing about being with my mate was that I'd already seen all of his sins. He had many. So many, from the time before he reformed, and many since. There were no surprises in that regard, and for that I was grateful. It was a relief to find that there wasn't anything he'd been hiding from me.

Honestly, I didn't think I could take any more revelations. Not from him, anyway.

We talked about more. Mostly, we talked about what would come next. And by the time Zoe woke crying for her morning bottle, we'd come to an agreement about what our lives would look like now that we didn't have any more insane immortals to deal with.

Nain got up with Zoe, and I ended up falling back to sleep. When I got up it was late afternoon, and I could feel the power signatures of my closest friends nearby.

I got dressed, and it hit me again that my father wouldn't be sitting out there. He wouldn't be holding Zoe or looking at my mother with that adoring look on his face. He wouldn't be there giving Nain his pointed insults or threatening to kill Brennan just out of spite.

I brushed my hair, remembering the night my father had sat with me when I was terrified I'd lose Shanti. How he'd helped me search through dumpsters for someone he didn't know, because she mattered to me.

I made myself stop thinking, because I was in that weird place between sadness and rage, and I didn't know how to deal with it just then.

I looked at the closed bedroom door.

The last thing I wanted to do was go through that door and see all of my friends' sins. Their worst moments. I felt like I'd already seen too much. I understood now, at least a little, why my dad had been such a prick sometimes. Seeing the worst in every person you look at, not by choice, but because you can't *not* see it, is a really strange way to live.

I took a deep breath and opened the door that led into the living room.

Nain was there, holding Zoe on his lap, talking to Heph and Meaghan. Brennan was sitting on the couch, talking to E. Sean was playing with wooden blocks on the living room floor. To my surprise, Artemis was there as well.

I avoided looking at Brennan, focusing instead on Artemis. I couldn't look at him. I didn't want to know what else he'd kept from me. Because there were things. I knew there were. Artemis came to me, and I tried to ignore the images that played in my mind as her sins were catalogued. She pulled me into a fierce hug, and I hugged her back.

"You avenged him," she said, and I nodded.

"I am sorry about your father, Mollis," she said. "He was an ass, but he was decent, too."

I nodded again.

And then my gaze settled on Brennan. The images began to flash across my mind.

I was aware of Nain watching me closely, tense.

Brennan was watching me too, nervousness rolling off of him. Guilt. Anger. Sadness.

I shared what I was seeing with Nain. He stood up. "You two should go outside or something," he said. "Talk, kick his ass, whatever. But this shit ends now. There are no more secrets. Not anymore." Nodding, Bren stood, and Nain clapped him on the shoulder. "Go," he said, meeting my eyes.

I gave him a small smile and nodded toward the door. Brennan followed me.

We walked out the back door and into the yard. We'd had a small storm earlier in the day, and the grass was coated in a blanket of fresh snow. I noticed some of my imps in the trees nearby, and it made me happy. I looked up at Brennan, who was studying me closely, arms crossed over his chest.

"Nain told you about what happened with Hades?" I asked, trying to keep myself from getting teary over my father. "What I can see now?"

He nodded.

We stood in silence for a moment. And then I just said it.

"She spelled you. And you lied to me. I want to know why," I said softly, and then I couldn't keep the tears back anymore. "You let me think you didn't care enough about me to stay loyal to me. You let me and everyone else believe you were a complete and total asshole. You hurt me, and you let it keep hurting, and it was based on a lie. Why?" I asked, the images I'd seen, of the witch approaching Brennan, of him waking up naked and confused in a strange bed, of him telling me he'd messed around on me, playing over and over in my mind.

He started pacing.

"Brennan," I said.

He stopped pacing. He looked at me, met my gaze with those slate-blue eyes I knew so well. "You can sense emotions, Molly. Have you ever felt something you wished you hadn't?"

"Of course. All the time," I said.

He gave a small nod. "Okay. I can't do that, but when I was bonded to you, I could feel your physical reactions to things, right? Even over a distance, even when I wasn't even sure where you were, I could feel you." He took a breath, but kept his eyes on mine. "When you were with him, I could feel how you responded to him. How your heart rate spiked, how your stomach twisted, how your body heated up. How there was this ache inside you. It was

223

a physical thing," he said, shaking his head. "And that day in the Nether, when E was dragging me to safety and Nain went to find you, right after we realized he wasn't actually dead, I could feel the second you felt him. Your whole system went haywire, and there was that ache, that breathlessness. You never, ever felt that with me," he said, gently, sadly. I bit my lip, swiped at the tears falling from my eyes. "I could feel it. You loved him. You needed him. He was yours. And I still wanted you."

He paused again. "That happened with the witch. Then Sean happened. And then you were back. I loved you even more than I had before, and even though I knew the right thing to do was let you go, I didn't want to. I took the easy way out. I told you I'd cheated on you, because telling you to walk away wasn't a possibility. I figured you'd break it off with me, and you'd have what you wanted, what you should have had. But I was incapable of breaking up with you, even knowing I wasn't what you needed. So I lied, because when it came to you, I was a complete idiot, and you were still determined to stay, even after that. I convinced myself that we'd make it work. That over time, you'd feel for me what you felt for him. That you wouldn't love him forever."

It took him a moment to go on. "And then you left, not because of the witch or Sean, but because you thought you were putting me in danger. You stayed away, and I missed you. I made so many mistakes when it came to you, Molly. You were the one thing in my entire life I never planned or trained for. I didn't know it was possible to feel the way I felt with you."

He paused, stood watching me, and as fucked up as this whole thing was, I felt relief from him.

"It comes down to, I was weak and stupid. I wanted you even though I knew you wanted Nain. I wanted two impossible things: I wanted you with me, and I wanted you to have everything you wanted. And the two weren't the same thing. I didn't know how to handle that, and I lied, repeatedly, to the one person I should have been honest with, no matter what."

I didn't know what to say. We stood in awkward silence.

"What I realized, during that time away from you after you got back from the Nether, was that eventually, even if you'd wanted to stay with me, I still would have lost you because no matter what else I am, I'm not him. He's what you want. And I would have resented him for that. I would have lost both of you eventually. The thought of you not being in my life... You're one of the most amazing people I've ever known. And I can say that now not just as someone who was in love with you, but as someone who's fought by your side, who's seen the dark and light sides of who you are. I want you in my life. I want Nain in my life. What I knew I didn't want was to lose the woman who's come to be my best friend, and the man who's practically a brother to me. I've come close to losing that so many times. And there are no secrets left between us now."

I stood there processing it all. I took a deep breath. Love turned people into complete idiots. All you had to do was look at me, at that moment my parents had defied a gloom-and-doom prophecy and loved each other anyway. At Persephone's love for my father, even though she knew better. At how messed up loving Nain, and then Brennan, and now Nain again, had made me.

It was still worth it, though, I realized.

"You could have told me after Nain and I were back together. It wouldn't have changed anything, other than maybe not making me think you were such an uncaring asshole for so long," I said, but there was no anger in it.

He shrugged. "I could have. I didn't really think there was much point. You were good and pissed at me, and I deserved it for how I handled things. You've had more than enough to think about without that... and I didn't realize it made you feel that way, which was stupid."

He came up to me and took my hands gently in his. His

hands were warm, just as they always had been. "I'm sorry, Molly. It's not an excuse, but everything I did, I did trying to either protect you or give you the life I knew you wanted. I made a royal mess of it. But I hope you can believe that hurting you was the last thing I ever wanted."

I sensed for him, and there was relief there. Sadness, too. It would take time to get past that, for both of us.

"I believe you," I said. And then I smiled. "That's the only good thing about Hades' ability. I know damn well you're not lying to me now."

He laughed, and he stepped forward and hugged me. I hugged him back, hard.

"You're a good man, Brennan," I said near his ear. "You just forget how to act like it sometimes."

"Major character flaw," he said with a laugh.

"Well. You're related to an immortal. It runs in the family," I said. "I want you in my life, too. Nain wants you in our lives. Okay?"

He nodded and hugged me again, and when we released one another, it felt like a weight had lifted from my shoulders.

"I'm sorry about your dad," he said as we headed back into the house, and I nodded. "Even if he did want to kill me," he added, and I had to smile.

When we got back inside, I sat next to Nain on the couch and took Zoe's tiny hand in mine.

"Okay?" Nain asked, and I nodded.

We had a busy few days ahead of us. Plans to make, things to organize. But when it was over, I swore to myself that Nain and Zoe and I would have some time to just relax and be together.

CHAPTER SIXTEEN

Eventually, just about everyone ended up in our tiny apartment. Athena, Heph, Meaghan, Demeter, Gaia, Hestia, Asclepias, Shanti and Zero, Rayna, Ronan. All of them gave their condolences on the loss of my father.

The immortals each gave me a bow, acknowledging my new status, which I did not want.

My mother and aunt were still in the Netherwoods. I knew, because I'd been there, that my mother probably just wanted to die.

I was aware that Persephone wasn't there, and I approached Demeter, who was standing in the kitchen talking to Meaghan. She acknowledged me with a nod.

"Hey. Is Persephone all right?" I asked quietly.

"She mourns. Not the way your mother does, but as a woman who loved him and spent millennia at his side."

I felt tears spring to my eyes again for what felt like the thousandth time in the last day. "She shouldn't be alone," I said.

"She is not. She mourns with Tisiphone. They are preparing his body together."

I stared at her in surprise, and she gave a small smile. "I

thank your mother for sharing that with her. It was Tisiphone's right to do alone, and it was gracious and generous of her to let my daughter have that final closure."

I nodded. "So what happens now?"

"There will be a remembrance service in the Netherwoods tomorrow night," she explained. "The widow and family usually spend two full days preparing and mourning in private. You should go to your mother soon," she added, and I nodded. "And then, tomorrow night, there will be a remembrance ceremony to honor him. I suspect that, for that, the Nether will allow immortals to bring mortals in, if you want that. People will speak. As the being highest in power, Gaia will preside." I didn't say anything, and she smiled. "Classy, my lady, not to point out that you're actually the strongest now. I know what resides within you."

I just gave a small nod.

"But she is the oldest and traditionally she would be the strongest," she continued. "She will speak, and any others who want to will speak. At the time of his death, his funeral pyre will be lit, and we will remain and honor him."

I thanked her, and then I went over to where the vampires and Brennan were sitting. Shanti was holding Zoe. Zero was standing against the wall nearby, Ronan close at hand.

I studied the new vampire. I'd been right. He was even more gorgeous. And he looked stressed out.

There were sins on his soul, too. None that bothered me too much. If and when he died, I realized, it would be my job to place judgment on his soul.

Damn, that was weird.

"I can't believe how well you're holding up, considering all the immortals you're surrounded by right now," I said to him.

He gave a pained smile. "We needed to be here. And Ronan is here to keep me from doing anything stupid, like trying to feed from a god. They brought a lot of blood for me."

I glanced down at Shanti, who was looking up at him adoringly.

"Zero's a strong bastard. I can't believe how disciplined he is. I was a raving lunatic when I was first turned," Ronan said. I already knew that. I had seen it the moment I looked at the huge vampire.

"I'm impressed," I said. "But please know that I won't be offended if it becomes too much. It means a lot to me that you're going through this to be here."

"Shanti loves you, and you saved Shanti. So I guess I kinda love you by extension," he said, and Shanti laughed. I smiled and shook my head.

Then I said to Rayna, "We have things to discuss."

She sobered. "Things are not the same," she said softly, understanding. I nodded. I sat down beside her, and Nain sat beside me. Brennan was in the chair opposite me. Ronan leaned in, still standing next to Zero, to hear.

"I can't be as central to everything anymore. After what happened on Thanksgiving, I'm not a comfort to the Normals. We all know that," I said when Brennan and Shanti started to protest. "Pretending otherwise is pointless. Yes, some of the Normals and supernaturals still believe I'm a hero. Some fear me, but recognize that I've always fought to protect them. But for the most part, they just want me gone. You've seen the interviews and articles. And remember that I can hear their thoughts." I paused. "It was necessary for me to be visible when it came out that supernaturals exist. When they were getting used to the idea of all of us living side by side with them. They know now. We have a Detroit Police unit that's specifically devoted to supernatural crimes, and we have Brennan in charge of the federal supernatural investigation and affairs unit here. I did what I was supposed to do. I bridged the gap until they got used to the idea. Now it's time to move on."

I paused. They were all watching me.

"I am not going anywhere," I said. "I have duties I need to attend to in my father's place, and I'll do it, but I'm gonna do it my way." I already had ideas for how things would change as I started my work as Lady of the Dead. "When I'm not doing that, I'll be here. I'll be fighting by your side when you need me. I'll protect this realm from any big bads who decide to cause trouble. But I can't be the face of this particular super-team anymore."

I met Rayna's eyes. "Your family has been integral in keeping peace on the streets. You've almost completely taken over my lost girl searches and there aren't words enough to express my gratitude for that. I felt like I was failing them, and it means a lot to me that you guys stepped up. I'm happy to say that you're even better at it than I am, for the most part."

Rayna smiled. "That's mostly Shanti and Zero's doing. We police the vampire population, and Shanti and Zero punish our worst and also find your lost girls. We're pleased to help. You know that."

I nodded, then turned to Shanti. "I want to make good on that offer of imps to help you, now that I have them back." I'd offered them to her once, to guard Zero, but then Strife had happened and we'd never gotten around to it. "They can help you search. They're amazing at that."

"I'd love their help. I know how good they are at surveillance," she said.

I beckoned to three of my imps, Brazien, Flalog, and Murlog, and they came over, bowing their heads. "My friends," I said. "I would like you to work alongside these vampires and help them find lost girls. This is the best way you can help me."

"It would be an honor to do so, mistress," Murlog said, bowing his head and putting a fist to his chest. The others followed suit.

"Thank you," I told them.

I transferred my gaze to Brennan. "So I'm guessing I

can count on the shifter coalition to continue working with the vampires and Nain's team."

"Of course," he said.

"You can consider this my resignation from your department's PR team, Director," I said with a smile.

"Good. I was going to fire you anyway," he said with a wink, and I laughed. "You don't have to do this, but I'm hoping you'll give one last press conference, maybe to reassure everyone that you're resigning your government-related role."

I nodded. And I knew it was nothing personal. We both knew his job would be easier without all of the rumors of my involvement in the department. I mean, the rumors were true, but the general public didn't need to know that. If it made them feel better to believe that their government wasn't tainted by my particular brand of crazy, then that's what we'd give them.

"So I'll still be here, like I said before. But I'm going back to a background role. I've always been happiest in the shadows. I don't know how to stop fighting, so I'm not going to. But I'm not a politician and I sure the hell am not a figurehead. I'm going to do my best not to be seen much, which will make your jobs easier and ease some of the tension caused by Hyperion. And it will help me keep my sanity," I added, and Nain squeezed my hand.

"And what about the immortals?" Rayna asked.

"For the most part, they're settled. The ones who remain are peaceful, and I consider them friends and family. I don't think we'll have any trouble, but if we do, that's what I'm here for."

She nodded. We talked some more, and then it was time to go see my mother. I left after kissing Nain and checking in on Zoe.

"We'll be there for the memorial thing tomorrow," he said, and I kissed him again, then headed to the Netherwoods.

When I got to the Netherwoods, it didn't frighten me. I

felt at home, almost as much so as I did in Detroit. As I walked through the newly-constructed stone walkways toward the castle, I was greeted with bows and salutes from the demons I passed. Murmurs of "my lady" clanged around in my brain, not seeming real.

I walked into the castle, two burly demons opening the main doors at my approach. I nodded to them and hurried through.

I sensed for my mother's power signature, felt her somewhere off to the right. I travelled through the black stone corridors, watching the light from the sconces on the walls flicker. The walls seemed to sparkle with it.

I entered a room and realized it was my parents' bedroom. My father's body was laid out on a large black stone table along one wall, my mother and Persephone's work evident. He'd been wrapped in rich black fabric, only his face visible. I relived images of watching his head fall to the ground, and I closed my eyes and willed them away. I looked again and noticed his two loves' additions to his funeral wrappings. Tucked into the fabric were multitudes of dried and fresh flowers, Persephone's touch. And my mother's addition, his black sword woven into the fabric over his chest, obsidian blade shining. There was a long rope of her raven hair wrapped around the blade.

I tore my eyes away from it and looked toward my mother.

God, I'd been there. I felt it all again through her.

She lay on their bed, her head on one pillow and another in her arms. I knew it was my father's pillow she held.

The scent. It was the only thing left to hang onto. I understood all too well. I started crying, overwhelmed by my mother's grief and my own, as well as the very real knowledge of what my mother was going through.

"Mollis," she said, her voice hoarse from crying. I looked up, and she gestured me over. She placed my father's pillow under her head, and held her arms out to me, and I climbed into bed with her. She held me, and I cried in my mother's arms in a way a child would.

"He was so proud of you," she said, her voice shaky. She ran her hands over my hair. "He loved you as much as he ever loved anything or anyone."

"I miss him," I said. "Everyone was at the apartment today, and it hit me that he wouldn't..." I trailed off, unable to talk anymore, and she held me tighter, humming a soothing, haunting melody.

"I miss him, too," she finally said. "I feel like my heart is gone."

"I know."

"I don't want to even consider having to face another day without him. This is hell. This is my Tartarus. This is worse than any torture I've ever administered. Everything in me is shredded and it feels like my soul is bleeding," she said.

I just nodded.

"How do I do this?" she whispered, so quietly I could barely hear her.

"However you need to, Mom. I didn't talk for months afterward. I didn't eat. I mostly just lay in his bed holding his pillow, and then I went out and hurt people because I knew that was what he would have wanted me to do. He always did like it when I beat assholes up."

She stayed silent.

"No one gets to tell you how to grieve him. And if anyone tries, so help me I will kick their ass. You do what you have to do to make it through, and it takes as long as it takes."

"I am so grateful we made you," she said softly.

I didn't say the words I was thinking.

"You can't control the things that happened after I gave birth to you, Mollis," she said, reading my thoughts. "Neither of us would take it back. Even now, with him gone..." Her voice broke, and she took a moment to calm herself. "Even now, I wouldn't trade the time I've had with you, the time he had with you, for anything. We love you. And the woman you've become honors us. He loved that his daughter was so feared."

I laughed a little.

"And I've always loved that my daughter is respected," she added. "Sleep now. Tomorrow will be long and terrible."

I spent the day with my mom and Persephone, mostly in silence. Persephone looked just as lost as my mother, and they mostly sat holding each other's hands and staring off into nothingness.

It made me want my husband by my side.

As it got closer to time for the funeral, there was more activity in the castle. Demons started preparing the large hall, setting out food and wine. I asked Persephone where it all came from, expecting something magical, and she said, "Grocery stores." I just let it go, because really, what more could you say about that?

I left my mother and Persephone and went into a separate room. Demons had set out a fresh set of clothing, the typical uniform of the Furies. I knew I'd be wearing it a lot more often. I would judge the dead, and sometimes I'd punish them, too.

But I would use Hades' ability in my own way, as well.

I pulled on the form-fitting black pants, the knee-high black leather boots, the long-sleeved tunic with its built-in corset. I grimaced as I tightened the laces. The corset was more than a fashion statement (though I did have to admit it looked kind of amazing). It was reinforced with metallic black chainmail, protecting the gut, since that was one of our more vulnerable areas. Really, I wished I'd been wearing something like it the several times I'd been shot or stabbed in the stomach over the years. Self-healing is great, but if you can prevent the injury in the first place, even better.

I braided my hair in a long rope over my shoulder, the same way my aunt and mother always did. I straightened any errant wing feathers.

I looked at the dresser, where whoever had set out my clothing had placed the black circlet my father had worn when he was working in his throne room. It was simple, all black stone that dipped down into a point in the center of the forehead. I picked it up with a deep sigh and placed it on my head.

It was heavier than it looked.

I stared down at my hands, which were still shaking a little. Too much emotion since Hades had fallen. And too much time away from my mate, when I needed the comfort he could give me. The hematite band on my left hand gleamed, as did the silver and hematite invisibility ring on the other hand. The wing necklace my parents had given me hung at my throat, and I ran my fingertips over it, remembering the surprise birthday party they'd helped put together.

A knock sounded at the door.

"My lady?" a demon asked.

"Yes?"

"It is time."

I closed my eyes, took a deep breath, and headed out, nodding to the demon as I did. I could feel the presence of many, many beings. Immortals and mortals. I walked out into the courtyard where my father had died. Rows of chairs were set up there, inhabited by my friends and family. The stars in the amethyst sky seemed almost obscenely bright, and my father's body on its stone slab was situated at the front. My mother and aunt and Persephone sat in the front row. I saw Nain and Zoe sitting with Brennan and Sean and E, and I went to them. Nain handed Zoe to E, stood up, and I went into his arms. He held me tight.

"Missed you," I managed, because fuck it all, I'd started crying again.

"Same," he said. "I love you." He leaned down, still holding me tight, and nuzzled the side of my neck.

"Love you more."

"You keep saying that. It isn't possible to love someone more than I love you," he said, standing up straight and meeting my eyes.

"I'm so grateful we got a second chance, Bael," I said, thinking of my mother's grief, and how she wouldn't get one.

He took my chin in his hand, his fingers gently caressing my jawline. So gentle, only for me. "We're going to make good use of it," he promised me, and I nodded. He leaned down and kissed me again, then released me reluctantly. I took Zoe from E, kissed her forehead and nuzzled her soft skin. She'd been fussy for E and Nain, and she settled in my arms.

"How the hell do you do that?" Nain asked, and I smiled down at Zoe. She seemed more peaceful than she normally did, even in my arms. I looked up at the sky, then sensed for Zoe again. She felt safe and relaxed. Calm.

Interesting.

"I'll hold her. I need to try to hold it together here, and she helps," I told Nain, and he nodded, then ran his hand up and down my back. I nodded to Brennan and Artemis, then headed toward the front of the assembly. I was about to sit next to my mother, but she shook her head. I looked at her dumbly.

She gestured to the left, at the front of the seats, off to the side of where my father's body was.

I looked that way and saw a dais there with a simple ebony stone throne upon it.

I shook my head fervently, and she gave me a steely glare.

Do this, Mollis. You are the Lady of the Dead. Honor your father by taking your place.

I gritted my teeth. For today, I'd do this. Thrones are not my thing. Never have been, never will be.

I took Zoe up to the dais, ignoring all of the bowing. I settled myself onto the cold, hard seat, and nestled Zoe close to me.

Once I was seated, it began. Gaia rose, and she talked. Mostly, she ran through a series of Hades' deeds: battles he'd won, opponents he'd defeated. She included my birth in his list of great achievements, and I wanted to disappear. She recounted the high points of his long existence, and ended with her own thoughts on Hades.

"He was a phenomenal blowhard, but I respected him," she said, and then she sat down to muffled laughter from many of the assembled immortals.

Others got up to speak. Hephaestus talked mostly about how Hades' existence had not been an easy one, that what he'd done was mostly a thankless, but entirely necessary, job.

His dark gaze flitted to me. "He did the thing none of us were able to. He judged the dead, and ensured, along with his wife and her sister, and, later, his daughter, that those who had harmed others would pay in full for their crimes. He gave no escape to evil. If he was cold, if he was impatient, I understand now, better than ever, why that was. And now, his daughter, one of my best friends, shoulders that burden." He broke his gaze with me, let it settle on various members of the audience. "I appreciate what she gives up to take up her father's mantle. She deserves the respect, fealty, and assistance of everyone gathered here, whether you consider yourself Aether or Nether or mortal or whatever. I don't care. And it no longer matters, does it? Here we are, all jumbled together. I know I'd like to see us all continue to work together under Mollis Eth-Hades' leadership." He paused. "It's what he would have wanted." He glanced at me again, then stepped down.

Others spoke. Megaera, on behalf of the Furies, since my mother could not be expected to speak. Asclepias, Athena, and Poseidon, who, to my shock, had left his oceans to attend Hades' funeral. He had only good words for Hades, and was genuinely sad over his death.

Gaia got up and gestured to me, and I was about to shake my head, but then I stopped.

I stood up, trying not to freak out over all of the beings watching me.

"I don't have a lot to say right now. My heart is broken over the loss of a father I feel like I barely had a chance to know. In the time I had with him, he was coarse, rude, bossy, and irritating." I smiled, happy to see my mom give a little laugh. "He was also so much stronger than I realized. Physically imposing, with power that dwarfed nearly everything around him. But emotionally strong, too. I live now with his abilities, and I am awed that he lived with it for thousands of years without ending up completely mad. If he was coarse and irritating, I understand why. And yet, when I needed my father to be understanding, when I needed him to be supportive, he tried to be. He was able to set aside the constant barrage of vileness that comes with being Lord of the Dead, and he found it in himself to focus on me. On my mother. On my daughter, who he named," I said, looking down at Zoe. "I think it's easy to believe someone is all one thing or another. Hades was all bastard or all benevolent. In reality, he was a benevolent bastard," I said, and the assembled immortals laughed, even though many had tears in their eyes. "There is light in darkness, and darkness in light, and that's what makes existence interesting."

I paused. "I mourn, alongside the two women he loved most in his life, my mother and Persephone," I heard a sob then, from Persephone, and I had to fight back the emotions rising in me. "He is missed. But he would expect us to go on. He would expect me and my family to continue his work. And it will be done," I said. "To Hades," I finished, and it was met with a chorus of "to Hades" from the assembled supernaturals.

When I finished talking, a gong sounded, and Gaia

approached with a torch. I went to my mother and aunt and Persephone then, and took my mother's hand in mine.

We watched as Gaia slowly lowered the flames to his wrappings.

We sat in silence as my father's body was reduced to nothing.

And when it was done, we sat in silence, each with our own memories of the god we'd known as Hades.

As the crowd started dispersing, finally, E came up to me and pulled me aside.

"How are you holding up, my friend?"

"I'm okay. He would have wanted me to be," I said, and she smiled.

"I'm proud of you. I'm so glad we became friends, that I didn't stay as aloof as my sisters. I'm glad I trusted my gut and got to know you. It has been a pleasure, devil girl."

I studied E, my heart sinking. "Why does this feel like goodbye?" I asked her, and she shook her head.

"It's not goodbye. Not forever. You have found your place, Mollis, and it is time for me to find mine."

"Where will you go?"

She shrugged and gave me one of her small smiles. "I am not sure. All I know is that without my former role, without my sisters to assist me, I don't know what to do with myself. Helping you has eased that, for a time, but I need to figure this out for myself now, and we've reached a point at which you no longer need me."

"I'll always need you, E," I said, and she smiled. "But I understand."

She nodded. "I don't know who I am anymore, or what my purpose is. I've never had a reason to learn it. I can become lost, or I can go out and find myself somewhere out there. I am just sorry to do it now, with everything else that has happened."

I held back tears. She'd seen me through the worst times of my life. I knew she needed this. To say that the past few years of E's existence had been tumultuous would be an understatement.

"I'll miss you so much, E," I said, hugging her.

She hugged me back, hard. "And I will miss you, my friend, my sister, my lady. If you need me, I will be here. Know that."

I nodded, and we stood hugging each other for a few moments longer. When I released her, I didn't want to.

She smiled and bowed her head, just a little, to me.

And then she rose into the air and I watched her until I couldn't see her anymore.

CHAPTER SEVENTEEN

I stood in the press room at the Fisher Building for the last time, looking out at the rows of reporters and cameras. Brennan was behind me, and Nain was at the back of the crowd, watching and waiting for me. Once this was done, we'd finish moving back into the loft.

Seeing my husband hanging Wonder Woman curtains in Zoe's new nursery had been the highlight of the morning, and I couldn't wait to settle in again.

I got the signal, and I focused, looking into the cameras.

"Thank you," I began. "As you've undoubtedly heard, there was quite the mess here on Thanksgiving Day, caused by a being who was after me and my family. He said things about me that made many of you wonder whose side I'm really on. I'm on the same side I've always been on. Yours. I lived much of my life in the shadows, protecting you in secret, because I'm more comfortable there."

"The things he said are..." I smiled, shook my head. "Well. They're *unbelievable*, right? But one thing he may have been right about is the fact that I bring additional strife to this city. Maybe I am a beacon for troublemakers." I shrugged. "It's possible. We can't really know that. What I do know, however, is that I agreed to let my life become more public because supernaturals were no longer hidden. You were faced with the fact that beings with crazy powers lived alongside you, and had for a very long time. It was terrifying, and believe me, I understand that. But I have to say that I'm proud of this city, and the rest of the nation as well, for how well you've adapted to this. Have there been issues? Of course. But our government, our local authorities, now have the tools they need to keep you safe and ensure that human and supernatural relations continue to develop in a positive way."

I paused. "I'm no longer necessary. I've organized and talked myself out of a job here."

Several of the reporters laughed, and I gave them a small smile. "I've never been comfortable in this position, or in the spotlight at all. So I'm here for the last time today to announce my official resignation from any involvement in the supernatural law enforcement community. I'm here to resign my position as a spokesperson for our government, because they don't need me. They've got this, and you're no longer shocked by craziness. You're pros at crazy by now."

Another round of laughter, accompanied by the flashes of cameras.

"So I'm done. I'm retired from this role, and it's a relief for me, and, I know, for many of you. If you're wondering whether I'll be here if you need me, don't worry. This city made me. This city is my home. If there's trouble, I will protect it. Just watch the shadows, because that's where I'm happiest. Thank you."

There was a mad flash of cameras, and a barrage of questions, which I just shook my head at. I turned to Brennan, and he gave me a small smile and gestured toward Nain.

Meet you downstairs, Nain thought at me.

I'll beat you there, I bet.

Showoff, he answered, and then he headed toward the elevators. I went into the nearest office and I focused on rematerializing downstairs, after spinning my invisibility ring so I wouldn't be seen. When Nain walked off of the elevator, I knew he could sense me. I touched his arm, and we walked out toward the street. He opened the driver's side door of his truck and I climbed in, scooted across the seat, and he followed, slamming the door behind him.

"Let me see you," he said, and I turned the ring again. "Better," he said, leaning over and claiming my lips. I sighed happily against him as he kissed me and tangled my fingers in his hair. When he pulled back, I was breathless. He nipped my lower lip, then smiled at me. "Ready to go home, Molls?"

I nodded, leaned forward and pressed another kiss to his lips. He settled his big hand on my thigh and pulled out of the parking space, and we drove home, where the rest of our crazy family was waiting for us.

When we got to the loft, the Supremes were blasting from the kitchen radio and Heph and Asclepias were arguing over where the best place for the new big screen television would be. Artemis was holding a panther stuffed animal up and then lowering it, tickling Zoe's nose gently with it as Sean ran and shouted through the mostly-empty loft, reveling in the echoes he was making. Demeter, Meaghan, and Gaia were putting dishes in the kitchen cabinets and talking about greenhouses. Meaghan's baby bump was just starting to show, and she was radiant. Bash and Dahael and my dogs patrolled, and every once in a while, I'd see them on the ledge outside the windows. Stone and Ada had just gotten back, and Ada already had her sewing machine up, making a quilt for Zoe. She'd nearly died of happiness to discover a baby girl in the house when they'd arrived at home.

Brennan came home a while later, and my team, my family, spent the rest of the day moving back into the only place many of them felt at home.

By nightfall, we were fully moved back in. I came out of my bedroom, still pulling at the ties on my Fury uniform. The television was on, and Nain, Brennan, and Stone were sitting on the couches and chairs in the living room. Zoe was snuggled into the crook of Nain's arm, and Sean was finally asleep, sprawled on the couch beside Brennan.

No one had the energy or desire to move him.

I glanced at the television, where the evening news was on. I was there, telling everyone I was retiring. The debate seemed to be, had I really meant that I would be there to protect them, or was I just saying it to make everyone feel better?

Most people seemed to believe I'd left for good, that the government or whoever had forced me out, and they were pretty evenly split between being happy and sad over the thought. The camera cut to a young woman who was shaking her head.

"I don't believe for a minute that she's gone. I can't believe it. I don't think we'll see her again. I don't think she wants us to. But do I believe she's still out there, protecting us, being the Angel we need so badly? Yeah, I do. Do I believe she cares about us enough to keep her word? Yeah. She gave a lot of us something to believe in when we had nothing else. I can't imagine this city without her in it, and I don't think we need to."

Nain had turned his head, and was watching me. I met his gaze.

"Time to go to work," I said.

He stood up, careful to avoid jostling Zoe. "Kick ass, baby," he rumbled, leaning in to kiss me.

"You know I will."

"It's what you do," he agreed.

I looked at my husband and daughter, and I nodded. I gave Nain a small smile, and then I headed up the stairs to the roof.

I flew through the cold December air toward the Netherwoods, the lights of my city sparkling below. There, I'd judge and punish the dead.

And then I would come back, and use Hades' ability to protect the living. It was amazing how much good you could do when you could see every single sin in a person's soul. Unlike my father, I had no compunction about using my powers in the world of the living. I smiled to myself. The Detroit Police Department was about to have an unprecedented number of criminals coming in to confess, and then plead guilty, to their crimes.

With a little bit of persuasion from me, of course.

Punish the dead; protect the living.

Live my life and love my family.

I'd find a way to make it all work.

It's what I do.

EPILOGUE

One year later...

"Now, you can't just hack at it like that, you buffoon. Give me that before you hurt somebody."

Gaia waved Heph away and took the butcher knife from him. Then she went to work, carving the gigantic turkey Ada had roasted. My mother and aunt tried to keep Zoe focused and busy, while she seemed intent to use her newly-achieved ability to run and dodge to grab at all of the breakable stuff on the long dining room table. Sean threw a football across the living room, and Brennan told him for at least the fifth time that we don't throw stuff in the house. Meaghan sat on the couch, where she held her and Heph's son, Michael, on her lap. He had his father's dark hair and eyes and Meaghan's mellow personality.

Shanti, Zero, and the other vampires gathered around the television, shouting as the Lions fumbled yet again. Stone waved at the television in disgust and walked away. The game had technically been on earlier in the day, but we'd recorded it so the vampires could watch it with everyone else. I kind of regretted that decision now.

On the brick wall behind them, there were dozens of framed photographs, and I smiled every time I looked at them.

Me, Nain, and Zoe on a beach in Hawaii.

Nain, Heph, Meaghan, Brennan, Zoe, and Sean sitting around a campfire at one of the wooded cabin hideaways Nain had attained over the years.

Zoe, dressed as a tiger for her first Halloween.

We'd done our best to try to actually live, to make our family work alongside our roles as protectors. Sometimes, we managed all right. And when we didn't, Nain and I still had each other's arms to find comfort in.

Every day with Zoe was an adventure. We'd discovered that not only did the presence of other creatures of the Nether soothe her, but being in the Nether itself did as well. She spent a lot of time with me there when I worked. I just hoped that, as she got older, it would be enough to keep her sane.

Nether still slept, still granted me every one of her powers, and I tried to make sure I let her know how grateful I was. It was another of the many things I hoped held together.

I shook myself out of my thoughts and turned back toward the kitchen, where my family and friends were beginning to plate up food for the huge Thanksgiving dinner we'd prepared.

Nain and I helped Ada, Demeter, Asclepias, and Persephone load the table with so many side dishes and platters that I wondered how the hell we'd eat it all.

And then I remembered how much Heph and Nain can eat, and wondered if we'd have enough.

I kept checking my phone for any updates about trouble.

"We've got people out patrolling," Nain reminded me in a low voice as he passed me carrying yet another platter of something.

"I know," I said.

"Relax."

"Make me."

He came up behind me and wrapped his arms around my shoulders from behind. "Later, I definitely will, woman."

"Horny demon," I muttered, even though I couldn't hide the smile stretching across my face.

"That's how we got into this mess to begin with, isn't it?" he rumbled in my ear, and I could hear the smile in his voice. He lowered his hands, settling them over my stomach, gently rubbing the barely visible bump there. Happiness mixed with that ever-present demonic rage alongside his need for me. It turns out that, given enough time and effort, I'd managed the same thing as my mother: life grew within me, and it was another thing to be grateful for.

I gently bumped back against Nain, and he groaned.

"All right, either get a room or cut the fondling shit so we can eat," Heph bellowed, and the rest of the team laughed and started walking toward the dining room.

I turned in Nain's arms, and he pulled me close.

"Can we please, please kick their asses out now?" he asked, bending down to kiss me.

"Ugh, holidays," I said, grinning, and he nodded.

He leaned down and grabbed Zoe as she tried to run past, and swung her into the air, and she shrieked happily. "Papa!" she giggled. Nain turned her upside down and she laughed harder.

"Happy Thanksgiving, baby," he said, leaning down and kissing me.

"You too, Bael."

THE END

A LETTER FROM THE AUTHOR

So, we've reached the end! This has been a long, crazy journey, and I have many people to thank. I am very blessed to have so many supportive people in my life.

Thanks and hugs and kisses to my wonderful family. To my kids for forcing me to get out of my own head and for making me laugh on a daily basis. I love you guys. Thank you to my mother-in-law, Peggy, for being wonderfully supportive and badass and talking my books up to everyone she knows. Thank you to my brother-in-law, Will, for proofreading and childcare help. And thanks, especially, to my amazing husband, Roger, for being everything and anything I've needed him to be, from therapist to tech help to layout and design guru. I love you so much, and all of this was possible because of you.

Hugs and thanks to the phenomenal Elizabeth Hunter for encouragement and advice and for fangirling over the Avengers with me.

Thank you to my amazing beta readers for being both encouraging and honest. These books are stronger because of you, and you have all been tremendous fun to work with. Hugs to Susan Cambra, Shawna Cerda, Jennifer G., Amber Hegarty, Sarah Leenart, Kathie Littlemore, Jayna Longstreet, Katherine Helen Peters, Rachel Scott, and Sarah Wicks.

Thank you to my lovely editor, Carol Davis, for her amazing attention to detail and her attempts to get me to stop falling back on certain phrases.

And, finally: thanks to everyone who has taken a chance on the *Hidden* series. It has been a crazy, amazing experience. Thank you for loving Molly. Thank you for caring about her story. Thank you for the emails, tweets, Facebook updates, and reviews. Thank you for letting this story into your lives. There are no words to express how much that has meant to me.

If you're wondering what's next, you'll find an excerpt from the first book in my *Copper Falls* paranormal romance series in the next section of this book. I'll also be giving the vampires from *Hidden* their own series in 2015! There will be superhero romance, too.

And... what about Molly? This part of her story is done. She may well show up in other books, and, who knows? Maybe someday I'll tell the next part of her story, because her life as a hero is far from over. If you'd like updates about my upcoming releases, please sign up for my newsletter at colleenvanderlinden.com

Thank you again.

Colleen Vanderlinden
Detroit
November 24, 2014

Keep reading for a sneak peek
at the first book in the *Copper Falls* series
Coming Spring 2015

COPPER FALLS: CHAPTER ONE

Sophie unlocked her front door with a sigh of relief. Long day. A busy day, which was always good, but she was more than ready to take a cup of tea out to her garden and lose track of everything other than the perfume of herbs and the trilling melodies of the birds in the woods that bordered her cottage.

As she turned and grabbed her mail out of the box, she noticed a rumbling motorcycle turn into the driveway down the road. The farm had been empty for nearly a year. She grimaced. The idea of hearing a motorcycle all the time wasn't exactly appealing. She shook her head and went into the house.

The second she walked in, everything just felt right. She breathed in the clean, natural scents of the herbs drying from the beams above, beeswax. The soaps she'd made the day before were curing on wooden racks in the next room, and they perfumed the entire house. She flipped on the radio, started bobbing her head immediately as Rihanna wafted from the speakers.

She shrugged out of the white button-down top she wore to work, shimmied out of the crisp khakis. She pulled on a pair of well-worn jeans and a faded Detroit Red Wings t-shirt.

She was in the kitchen, debating over whether she wanted a salad or scrambled eggs for dinner, when there was a knock at the door. She glanced in that direction, then at the clock. She never got visitors out here. That was the entire reason she'd been so thrilled to have inherited this in the first place.

She sighed and glanced out the round window in the door. There was a man standing on her porch, clad in denim and a t-shirt. He was facing away from her, looking across the road. Longish, wavy, dark blond hair. Very, very broad shoulders.

Sophie opened the door a little, kept it braced with her leg. "Yes?"

The man turned around, and Sophie's mouth went dry.

His hair was a little unruly, and he had a short, neat beard. Long black lashes. Icy blue eyes.

Eyes she'd dreamed, not knowing what it meant. Visions that spoke of danger and heartbreak, and always, those eyes. Sophie tried to force herself to remember to breathe.

"Hi," he said, and his voice was deep. Low. Almost a growl. "I just moved in across the road. There's a goat in my yard. Wondering if it's yours."

She blushed. "Oh, shit. That would be Merlin. Sorry." Sophie slid her feet into the sandals she kept by the door and stepped out onto the porch. Beside him, she felt tiny. He was easily over six feet tall, and her five-five put her roughly at chest level.

And what a chest it was, she thought to herself. Holy broad-and-muscled, Batman.

"I'll get him. I'm so sorry about that. I just got off work and haven't even checked on them yet." Stop babbling, she told herself, and clamped her mouth shut.

"It's not a problem."

"It will be if you plan on having livestock. I've been

putting off reinforcing the fencing. I'll have to get on that."

"Not planning on any livestock," he said as he followed her across the road.

"No? You've got over sixty acres, right?" she asked.

"Yeah. Mostly, I just wanted somewhere quiet and where I could spread out a little. No neighbors on top of me."

She smiled to herself. He sounded like her. "And your first day in, you have a neighbor's goat in your yard."

"Well, goats I don't mind so much," he answered, and she could hear the smile in his voice.

They crossed the two-lane road side by side, and it occurred to her that she was walking away from her home, her sanctuary, her safe haven, with a man she'd (maybe?) seen in frightening visions.

If she was one of those witches who could summon fire or wind or something, she'd have less to worry about it.

She cursed her stupidity, but walked with him nonetheless. It was entirely possible this was not the man from her dreams. And, anyway, she was new at this witch stuff. What the hell did she know about visions?

She followed him around the side of the house, up a long gravel driveway, and there was Merlin, standing there, calmly chewing at some grass near one of the fence posts.

"Merlin, you devil," Sophie muttered under her breath. She clicked her tongue at him, and he raised his chocolate-brown head and studied her. She walked toward him calmly, nonchalantly. As if she had no intention whatsoever of grabbing the blue nylon collar he was wearing and leading him home. She was aware of tall, muscled, and gorgeous watching her, and felt even stupider for the ploy she was making.

Sophie sprung at the goat and he tried to buck away, but she grabbed his collar and held tight when he tried to fight his way away. He pulled, and tried to pivot, and she planted her heels in the soft soil and tried to hold him fast. After a few attempts of breaking free, he just gave her a bored look and bent to chew at the grass near their feet.

That settled, Sophie chanced a glance toward her new neighbor. He was watching her, an unreadable expression in his eyes.

Sophie gathered as much dignity as she could and led Merlin back toward the driveway.

"Sorry about that," she muttered, well aware that her face was burning with embarrassment.

"No problem," he answered. "Does he get out a lot?"

She was walking down the driveway, and the fact that he joined her only made her nervous. "Yes. I'll fix the fencing. I just need to get the replacement fence." And the money to pay for it, she thought to herself. "Goats are a major pain. Wish I'd known that before I bought them," she said aloud.

"Why do you have them, then?" he asked, putting his hands in his jeans pockets as they crossed the street again.

"For their milk. I make soaps," she said, shrugging. "Made more sense to have them around for that. I was stupid to accept a male, though, since I could just borrow a male when I need one for the girls. I felt sorry for him," she finished, feeling like a babbling idiot.

She glanced toward him, noticed a blank expression on his face.

"Anyway. It won't happen again," she said, looking with hope toward her door. Something in her told her to run from him, to get away and stay away. She'd be setting wards tonight, she thought. Weak as hers were, they were better than nothing.

"If it does, at least I know who he belongs to," he answered. "I'm Calder, by the way."

"Sophie," she said, glancing toward him again, feeling relief once they stepped into her yard. She could feel the energies of her own magic, that of her ancestors, there. It was the only place she felt safe.

"Well, Sophie'" Calder began, when a delivery van pulled up. The driver jumped out and passed a clipboard to Sophie. She knew what it was already, tried not to show her panic. She signed, and the driver handed her the thin brown envelope, departed without another word. She looked down at it, hating that her hands were shaking.

She'd failed.

She took a breath. "Sorry again about the goat. Welcome to the neighborhood," she said absentmindedly. "Excuse me."

READ MORE IN
THE COPPER FALLS SERIES
COMING FEBRUARY 2015

Visit http://www.colleenvanderlinden.com/hidden
for news, updates, and more

Never Miss an Update!

Sign up for the Hidden Newsletter.
http://bit.ly/hiddennewsletter

For backstory material, news, and upcoming events be sure to check out
http://www.colleenvanderlinden.com/hidden

ABOUT THE AUTHOR

Colleen Vanderlinden is the author and publisher of the *Hidden* series, which currently includes *Lost Girl*, *Broken*, *Home, Strife, and Nether*. She lives in the Detroit area with her husband, children, and two lazy cats. She enjoys reading, obsessing over comic book characters, gardening, and playing World of Warcraft.

Website: http://www.colleenvanderlinden.com
Facebook: facebook.com/colleenvanderlinden
Twitter: @C_Vanderlinden

The Hidden Series

Book One: Lost Girl
Book Two: Broken
Book Three: Home
Book 3.5: Forever Night
Book Four: Strife
Book Five: Nether

Hidden Novellas

Forever Night
Earth Bound